WITCHING
WHISPERS

THE WITCHES OF HOLLOW COVE
BOOK SEVEN

KIM RICHARDSON

FABLEPRINT

FablePrint

Witching Whispers, The Witches of Hollow Cove, Book Seven
Copyright © 2021 by Kim Richardson
Cover by Kim Richardson
Printed in the United States of America

ISBN-13: 9798750047987
[1. Supernatural—Fiction. 2. Demonology—Fiction. 3. Magic—Fiction].

WITCHING
WHISPERS

THE WITCHES OF HOLLOW COVE
BOOK SEVEN

KIM RICHARDSON

CHAPTER

1

I ran my hand over the pillow next to me, my fingers tracing the impression where Marcus's head had been all night. He'd left early this morning to drive his mother to the airport but not before waking me up for another round of panty-melting horizontal boogie. Who am I to say no?

A smile curled my lips as I let out a long sigh. I couldn't be happier. And I wasn't talking about just the sex—though still mind blowing and probably illegal in some parts of the world—I was talking about my life in general.

Beverly was safe and had been cleared from Nathaniel Vandenberg's murder charge. Ruth and Hildo, her true magical aide, had bonded as witch and familiar companions. Dolores? Well, Dolores was happy to have her life back to normal so that she could be herself—sergeant major of the Davenport household. And last, but not least, Marcus and I had made up, and Vorkan—aka infamous demon hit man—didn't want to kill me anymore.

Life was good.

My father had snuck away two nights ago, though, and I still had a list of questions for him. Specifically, why exactly had Vorkan just up and left me after he'd sliced my arm with his death blade and then told me the contract on my life was voided? I had my suspicions. But I was afraid the possibility was still open for other demons in favor of my death. I had no idea how things worked in the Netherworld, which was another question for my daddy dearest.

A string of excited shrills and half-hysterical laughter came from downstairs followed by the sound of some enthusiastic clapping. The walls and floors shook and quivered under the weight of bodies jumping.

They couldn't be throwing another party this early in the morning. Could they? Of course they could. They were Davenport witches. It was *never* too early to throw a party.

A smile quirked my lips. "Ahh... ladies. Looks like you skipped on the coffee in your Baileys again this morning." I laughed. Whatever had my aunts in such a state was worth me getting my ass out of bed to find out. I wouldn't lie. The thought of a little Baileys in my coffee sounded pretty good.

Hauling myself out of bed, I checked my phone on my nightstand. The clock read eleven forty-three.

Crap. I'd slept the morning away. I'd planned to work on a website for a client this morning, but it wasn't too late. I could still manage a few hours of work.

After a quick shower, I got dressed and went downstairs in search of all the commotion. And found it.

"I'll need a new wardrobe, of course," Beverly was saying, staring at her reflection in her compact mirror. She tucked a strand of perfectly styled, blonde hair behind her ear and checked her makeup. "And a complete makeover." She snapped her compact shut, her face blossoming into a radiant smile. "What am I saying? I don't need a makeover. Only plain women need makeovers." She looked down at herself. "With breasts like these, no one will be looking at my face." With a hand on her hip, she asked, "Girls, be honest. Do I look like a slut or a respectable woman in this outfit?"

Dolores looked up from her newspaper. "Like a ten-dollar hooker."

Beverly's green eyes flashed and she cocked her hip. "I always knew I was a ten."

3

"Oh! I'm so excited I could burst!" exclaimed Ruth. Flour spotted her face and was smeared over her apron down to her black ankle-length skirt. The white bun piled on top of her head bounced as she began to jump on the spot and clap, sending clouds of flour in the air while Hildo circled her legs like a dog chasing his tail. If he started barking, then, yeah, I'd be worried.

Nothing wrong with a little crazy from time to time. Especially when the crazy was the fun kind.

I laughed as I reached the coffee machine, grabbed an empty mug, and poured myself a cup. Deliciously bitter and wonderful-smelling steam rose to my nose as I took a sip. "Hey, where's the Baileys? I'm in for a little crazy this morning too. You can't be the only ones having fun."

Dolores looked up at me from the table. Her long gray hair was tied into a braid down the middle of her back. Her usual scowl was replaced by an expression of humble gratitude like someone had just complimented her. She put her reading glasses down and said, "We haven't put any Baileys in our coffee."

Beverly scoffed. "Speak for yourself."

I leaned my back against the counter so I could see them all at once. "So, why all this excitement?" I cocked a brow. "Are you guys still drunk from last night? You naughty witches," I teased. The fact was, I had no idea how long the celebrations continued last night since I went to bed early with a certain sexy wereape.

Dolores stared at me, her dark eyes gleaming with contented fervor. "The Sisters of the Circle are here in Hollow Cove."

I took another sip of coffee. "The who?"

"Sisters of the Circle," snapped Dolores, her customary frown coming back to say hello. "Have you never heard of them? How is that possible? They're famous in our paranormal circles. Every witch knows of the Sisters of the Circle."

I hooked a thumb at myself. "Um, still coming to terms with everything witch." I shrugged and then confirmed, "Never heard of them."

Dolores leaned forward in her chair, her eyes sparkling. "It's a coven of female witches," she began importantly. "A small elite group for the upper crust of witch society. They are extremely picky about who they let in."

It sounded like a snobby country club. Not my cup of tea. "Why are they here?"

"Isn't it obvious?" asked Dolores, looking smug. "They want *me* to join."

"You mean *us*," added Ruth, the lines at the corners of her blue eyes deepening with her glower. "All of us. Not just you."

Dolores smiled but said nothing. She just sat there with a contented grin on her face. It was creepy.

"That's right," agreed Beverly, her red lips pressed into a thin line. "We're just as accomplished as you in magic, Dolores. Anyway, we'll know soon enough. They always throw a party when visiting a new paranormal town. We should be getting our invitations shortly. They'll want to seek out *all* the witches in Hollow Cove first." She arched her back and inclined her hip. "They'll recognize a clear winner when they see one," she added with a smile.

Dolores gave her a skeptical look. "You mean you? The Sisters of the Circle will be looking for witches with exceptional *magical* abilities, not the ability to sleep with the entire town's male population."

Uh-oh.

To my surprise, Beverly's smile widened. "If that's not an *exceptional* ability, I don't know what is." She looked at me, her eyebrows high like I was supposed to congratulate her or something. "Maybe that's exactly what they need," she added, looking back at Dolores. "A woman with *worldly* experience."

"More like mattress experience," mumbled Ruth, staring down at Hildo who was now curled around her feet, warming her toes.

"Did any of you see Iris this morning?" I asked, hoping to change the subject. "I wanted to thank her and Ronin for helping me out with Silas." If it hadn't been for her and Ronin, I wouldn't have known about what Silas had done to Marcus, how he'd beaten and tortured him, especially with that amulet that kept him from healing. A flicker of fear stirred inside me. I didn't want to think about what could have happened if I hadn't reached him in time.

"Ugh. Don't ruin the day by mentioning that dreadful witch," spat Beverly, grabbing the chair opposite Dolores and sitting. "I hope to never see that horrid man ever again."

I frowned down at my coffee cup. "That makes two of us." Though I wouldn't mind seeing him just once more to have a real go at him. Maybe just to peel the skin off his body.

"Iris had breakfast and then left to meet Ronin." Ruth moved to the sink and began to wash the flour from her hands. "She had Dana with her too. Something about fish scales or rat tails? I can't remember which."

I snorted. "Knowing Iris, probably both." Was this for another one of her hexes on Allison? Just thinking about it brought a stupid smile to my face. That wereape had to go.

Beverly sighed and leaped to her feet. She started to fan herself with her hand, her legs shifting like she needed to use the bathroom.

Dolores frowned at her. "What's the matter with you? Will you stop that? All that jerking around is giving me a headache."

"Oh. Is it a yeast infection again?" Ruth wiped her hands on her apron. "Told you not to put all those bombs and oils in your bath. It's important to keep your vagina healthy."

Yeah. Maybe I should have stayed in bed.

Beverly rolled her eyes dramatically. "I don't have a yeast infection, you white-haired hobbit. This is what happens when I haven't had sex in days. I get these hot flashes."

Dolores chortled. "It's called menopause."

"It's not *menopause*," whined Beverly. "It's more like hives."

"Hives?" Dolores folded her hands on the table, eyeing her sister like a professor scolding her student for cheating on a test. "You're trying to make us believe you break into hives when you're… abstinent?"

"I'm cursed."

Dolores raised a brow. "You're… cursed?"

Beverly sighed dramatically. "Cursed by the goddess herself by making me so devastatingly beautiful. I've known about it since I was sixteen."

"When you discovered you were a slut," commented Dolores.

Beverly continued to fan herself. "Being incarcerated does things to your sex life." She eyed Dolores. "Not that you would know. You

8

haven't gotten laid since the eighties. Nothing but cobwebs down there."

Dolores's cheeks reddened, but she kept her mouth shut as she grabbed her newspaper and pretended to read it.

Ruth scoffed. "I'd hate to see what happens after a month." She laughed. And then she and Hildo said together, "Shingles."

Ok-a-a-a-y.

The sound of the front door opening and closing reached me. A moment later, Iris popped into the kitchen.

Her gaze swept across the room, her large brown eyes accentuating her sharp features and pretty heart-shaped face. She smiled and said, "You'll never guess who I saw."

Ruth clapped her hands once and blurted, "A nutcracker!"

Coffee flew out of Beverly's mouth.

Okay. It was going to be *that* kind of day.

"Uh… no," answered Iris with a quizzical brow. She brushed back a strand of her silky, straight black hair that fell just past her jawline. "The Sisters of the Circle."

The kitchen erupted in a chorus of oohs and aahs as Ruth let out a little peal of laughter and clapped her hands again. Dolores pushed back her chair and stood. Then the three sisters all began to hug one another, like they hadn't seen each other in years, totally out of character.

Now I *really* wanted to meet this coven of witches.

I looked over at Iris. "You knew about these Ring Sisters?"

"*Sisters* of the *Circle*," growled Dolores, her sergeant-major persona snapping back into place.

I was never really good with names.

Iris gave me a strange look. "Of course. Every witch knows about them. You didn't?"

"No." I felt a tinge of regret that I had missed out on so much of the paranormal world, growing up. Still, this coven of witches wasn't something I'd want to be a part of.

Beverly broke away from the awkward hug Dolores was giving her and focused on Iris. "Tell me. Did you meet them? What did they look like? Were they stylish? Chic? Oh, I bet they were... just dripping with jewels and sophistication."

Iris looked a little embarrassed. "Uh... they looked normal, I guess? Ordinary?"

Apparently, that was not the thing to say, if my aunts' frowns were any indication.

Iris looked over at me and I shrugged. Like hell if I knew why they were acting like fangirls.

The Dark witch cleared her throat. "They asked me to give you this." She pulled out a shimmering gold card with *Sisters of the Circle* written in elegant red letters, which Dolores snatched up before I had a chance to blink.

Dolores's lips curved into a smile as she turned the card over. "It's an invitation."

"What does it say?" Beverly asked, stepping forward to get a better look at the card.

Dolores cleared her throat. "With great pleasure, the Sisters of the Circle cordially invite all the witches residing at Davenport House to Cocks and Broomsticks—"

I choked on my coffee.

"Please join us at 1240 Mystic Road at 7 p.m."

I coughed, trying not to laugh. "Wait a minute…" I coughed some more. "Did you just say… *cocks*?"

Iris put a hand to her mouth, her face taking on a darker shade of red.

Dolores dismissed me with a brush of her hand. "You're overreacting."

"Cocks?" I repeated.

"Just a minor spelling mistake. Cock*tails* and Broomsticks," said Dolores, though she looked a little rattled.

I didn't buy that. I found it strange that this so-called classy coven would make that kind of mistake. Mind you, it had my imagination running wild.

"We're all invited," said Iris, looking excited at the prospect, too, for the first time. "You too, Tessa."

I wanted to tell them I wasn't interested, that these kinds of social gatherings weren't my forte. But since it seemed so important to my aunts, I knew they'd be upset if I refused to go. Keeping up with appearances and all that.

A dreamy look came over Dolores as she clasped the card to her chest. "We're *in*."

I let out a small snort, causing Dolores to shoot a glare in my direction. "Coffee up my nose."

Iris grabbed my arm and pulled me around to face her, saving me from Dolores's wrath. "Forgot to tell you something. I saw Allison on my way to Ronin's this morning."

"Yeah, did she join the petting zoo?"

Ruth burst out laughing, though Hildo gave me a strange look.

"No." Iris took a breath and said, "I saw her get in the back of Marcus's Jeep with his mother."

Hot anger swept through me, born of outrage—some primal instinct of wanting to hold on to what was mine with a bit of insecurity.

And then something odd happened.

A string of black energy blasted out of my fingers, shot past Ruth within an inch of her ear, and hit the kitchen window. The window shattered with a jarring boom.

I jerked back, surprised, as my coffee cup slipped from my fingers and crashed onto the hard floor. The sound mixed with the echoing of shattered glass.

Damn. Did *I* do that?

I was numb for a few seconds. Cold January air seeped in from the broken window as I tried to make sense of what just happened. My heart hammering, I stared at my hand as I turned it over, not sure what I was looking for.

What the hell just happened?

"House, if you please," called Dolores.

A sudden ripple of energy washed through me, causing my skin to tingle. The shards of glass from the floor rose in the air, coalesced into a perfect sheet of square glass, and snapped back into place as though it had never been broken.

"Tessa?" questioned Dolores, her tone hard. "Is there something you need to tell us?"

I looked up from my hand to find everyone staring at me, mirroring my shocked expression with a touch of fear. Ruth reached up slowly and touched her ear like she was making sure it was still there.

Iris's mouth hung slightly open, a haunted look on her face, and the anxiety in her eyes verged on panic.

A gut-twisting thought spun through my mind, one I'd stuffed away, hoping I was wrong.

I knew what *it* was. I just didn't want to say it. I'd seen it before, just yesterday, only it was aimed *at* me, not the other way around. Fear grabbed my throat and squeezed until it was choking me, making me light headed.

I swallowed, pushing down the panic, and said, "That… was demonic magic."

CHAPTER

2

Of all the things I wished I'd inherited from my father, demonic magic wasn't one of them. Not because it wasn't cool because, let's be honest, it was. But because it pegged me as a demon, or rather, *others* would peg me as a demon.

Demons weren't exactly welcomed with open arms in my paranormal community. Granted, I was a half-breed, but I didn't think it mattered.

Over the last few months, my overall opinion and outlook on demons had changed and evolved as I came to realize and understand that though their world might be a little darker, we all had a lot of similarities. Just like there were bad and good witches, some demons were also decent—like my father—while some were pretty nasty, like Vorkan, not to mention a plethora of other vile and evil creatures.

Still, being a half-breed wasn't something I wished to make known to the witch community, at least not yet. Just like Ronin, as a half-vampire, was shunned by most vampires, I knew the same would likely happen for me. I just wasn't ready to deal with that. I needed to deal with myself first. I needed to figure out what this meant and if it would last.

Would these powers diminish eventually? Or was I stuck with them for the rest of my life?

These questions really needed answering, and the only one who could tell me was my father. I needed to speak with Obiryn.

But first, I had to tell Marcus. I'd made a promise to myself that I wouldn't keep things from him anymore. Especially not after what happened between us. I wouldn't risk it. Not again. I trusted him, and it was time for me to show him I did.

I grabbed my phone and texted him.

Me: *I need to talk to you. Call me when you have a moment.*

"You ready?"

I looked up to see Iris standing in my doorway wearing a beautiful black cocktail dress that fit her tiny frame perfectly.

"You look amazing," I told her. Her brown eyes were lined perfectly with black in a cat eye, making them pop. "I've never seen you with your hair up like that. You look beautiful." She really did.

Iris's cheeks reddened. "Thanks. I wish I could say the same to you." Her face screwed up in a frown. "Why aren't you dressed yet?" She marched into my bedroom and picked up the black halter dress I'd tossed on my bed. "We're leaving in, like, five minutes. Your aunts are going to freak."

"I took a shower *and* shaved my legs," I said as though that was reason enough for not putting myself together. I let out a breath. "Why are we going to this thing anyway? It sounds like a bunch of stuffy rich witches. I have nothing in common with the rich. They have money. I don't."

It wasn't a total lie, but the real reason was because of my earlier window-shattering experience. These new powers had me freaked a little. I didn't know how to control them. What would happen if one of those snotty witches insulted me and I accidentally unleashed my inner demon? It wouldn't go so well for me or my aunts.

"Because it's important to your aunts." Iris held up my dress. "Strip. Let's go."

"Fine." I yanked off my lounge pants and top before pulling on the silky halter dress that hit just below my ankles. I wish I could have seen the need to admire its beauty, but I really wasn't feeling up to it.

Iris's frown reappeared as she stepped back. "Your hair is still wet, and we don't have time to blow-dry it." She let out an exasperated breath. "A chignon, it is. Sit," she ordered and pointed at one of my empty chairs.

I did as I was told and sat. While letting Iris pull my hair into a fancy low bun, I quickly applied some taupe-colored eye shadow, penciled in my eyebrows lightly, coated my eyelashes with some mascara, and finally added some colored lip balm.

"Done. Let's go." Iris stepped back as I stood. "I know you're upset about the… demon magic thing."

"Ya think?" I moved to my walk-in closet and grabbed some black kitten heels. No way was I wearing anything higher.

"It doesn't make you bad, if that's what you're thinking," said Iris. Her gaze moved to my hands. "I'd kill for that kind of skill. I mean… think of what you can do with it. You don't need to rely on demons for their magic. You have your own. No more exchanging souls. No more summoning."

I searched the Dark witch's face. I knew she was telling the truth. Dark witches had to depend on summoning demons to borrow their magic.

"I guess. I wished I knew how to control it, though. I had no idea it was in me until…"

"Until I spoke the word Allison, and you nearly took off Ruth's ear." Iris smiled. "We now know it was somehow channeled or awakened by your anger."

"What if it comes back and I can't control it?"

"Try not to get angry," offered Iris.

"Are you trying to give me an ulcer!" Dolores's loud voice came from downstairs. "Tessa Davenport, if you're not down here in one minute, we are leaving without you!"

Iris rolled her eyes and laughed. "You'll be fine. I'll be with you the whole time, so if I feel something is amiss with you, I'll just curse you with an immobilization curse so you can't do any damage."

"If I can't breathe, I guess I can't do much, now, can I?" I laughed.

Iris took my hand. "Let's go before Dolores decides to leave us behind."

"If only."

When we hit the bottom of the stairs, a honk from the Volvo greeted us.

"You better hurry," said Hildo, lying comfortably on the side table next to the entrance. "Dolores is about to have a stroke if you're not in that car in twenty seconds."

With our coats and winter boots on and our heels hooked around our fingers, we hurried out and clambered into the waiting and hot car.

We sped down Stardust Drive, Dolores not bothering to stop at the intersection, and then took a hard left on Mystic Road before zooming through the wet, snow-covered street.

A buzz sounded from my phone, and I yanked it out of my coat pocket. The screen lit up with a text message from Marcus.

Marcus: *Are you okay? I'm stuck in a meeting with Grace. Budgets. Very boring. You want me to come with you to the lady party?*

I laughed, remembering that's what he'd called it when I talked to him earlier in the day to tell him of my plans with my aunts. I texted him back.

Me: *It's fine. I'll call you when I get back from the lady party.*

Marcus: *Miss you.*

My heart did a little dance at his last text. What? I couldn't help it. The wereape did that to me.

At that moment, we hit a bump and were all suspended in midair for about two seconds before we came down hard, my phone flying out of my hand.

"I'm driving next time," I growled, my head down next to my thighs as I rummaged in the dark to find it.

Dolores gave a mock laugh. "In your dreams. Aha! Here we are, ladies."

I found my phone and glanced up as we pulled up into a circular driveway in front of a massive Victorian home. It was a tad smaller than Davenport House but still impressive, and it was a thing of beauty.

The green and red trim architectural masterpiece rose as high as perhaps a three-story building to look massive in comparison to the neighboring smaller homes that surrounded it. A sign illuminated in garish blue and green letters read STIFFS' FUNERAL HOME above the front door.

I laughed. "Are the dead invited too?" That would make for a better party in my opinion.

Dolores whirled around in her seat and glared at me. "The Stiffs let it out for important soirées. It's a charming building. You just wait."

"It always smells like formaldehyde in there, which gives me the heebie-jeebies," commented Ruth, her wide eyes on the sign. She reached up on her shoulder as though to touch Hildo for comfort.

"Don't be ridiculous," scolded Beverly, snapping her compact shut. "Shh. Someone's coming. Ooh, it's a man. And a handsome one too."

A young man in a black wool coat, who I hadn't even noticed, walked over to Dolores's side and opened the door for her. "Good evening. I'll park your car for you, ma'am," he said after helping her out.

Wow. These witches had valet parking? They were loaded.

We all clambered out of the car and stood watching while the young man drove the Volvo around the lavish house to some parking lot behind it. I took a slow look at my surroundings. We were on the other edge of town, more toward the east end. Hollow Cove wasn't a huge town, but I'd never visited this part before.

"Ladies." Dolores led the way up the driveway, and we all joined her on the front porch.

When we reached the door, I halted.

Runes and sigils burned with a golden radiance, covering every inch of the door's frame in an intricate lattice artwork. Their energy hummed in the cold air and ran through my skin like tiny electric currents, reminding me of the wards Silas had put below the gurney that supported the dead Nathaniel.

But these were different. More powerful. More… invasive.

"It's warded?" My body tightened like I was being wrapped in barbed wire, which gave me a queasy feeling like if I stepped through, I'd be trapped in. "Why the hell is it warded?"

"As it should be," answered Dolores. "This is a *private* party. Witches only. It's a solid magical defense. If you don't possess any magical ability, you can't come in. It's genius."

"It's psychotic," I mumbled for only Iris to hear.

Again, I didn't like the prejudice nuances I got from this coven. What if I wanted Marcus to join me? He wouldn't be allowed in? Or if he stepped through, he'd be harmed?

It took every bit of effort not to turn around and walk back home. I had to keep reminding myself I was doing this for my aunts. Obviously, this was important to them. I'd just have to suck it up for a few hours.

Iris gave me a wide-eyed look, sensing my hesitation.

And then it hit me.

Witches only.

What if *I* couldn't walk through? What if the recent change in me triggered an alarm of some kind?

Guess I was about to find out.

Dolores grabbed the door handle and pushed open the door.

I was hit with another wash of energy, and a gush of warm air followed by the sound of happy chatter.

A woman with the palest skin I'd ever seen watched me from down a long hallway, with the intense look of a hungry animal glimmering in her dark eyes. Yeah, not awkward at all. Now I had an audience.

If I couldn't pass through that door, everyone would know something was off with me. Not that I really cared. Something had always been off with me. But I was thinking of my aunts. The last thing I wanted was to embarrass them or bring unwanted attention to them. This was their night, and I didn't want to mess it up.

My pulse racing, my body shook with adrenaline as I watched my aunts step through the warded door, one by one, followed by Iris. They'd all made it through without a problem.

My turn.

Giddyup.

I took a breath, gritted my teeth, and stepped through.

CHAPTER

3

Have you ever been on a roller-coaster ride? The really, really tall one that takes you up the steepest hill and then plunges suddenly, where your stomach ends up in your throat?

Well, that's exactly how it felt to walk through that doorway.

Nausea hit, and a feeling of dizziness swept through me so suddenly and violently that I strained in an effort not to collapse.

Next came the pain.

A searing kind of pain throbbed in my head, like my worst migraine times a hundred. I felt like my eyes were about to pop out of their sockets.

Shit. I wasn't going to make it through.

I halted. A wild impulse to flee—a combination of the fear of pain and the unknown—hit me. Clamping my jaw tighter, I forced myself to take another step. Then another. It could have been twenty minutes or just a few seconds. I had no idea. All I knew was the overwhelming pain and sickness.

My heart throbbed as I tried to quash the panic from my thoughts. I closed my eyes and focused—on the pain, the fear, and the reason I was doing this.

Over the past few months, I'd grown some serious lady balls. (Yes, I know how that sounds.) I could do this.

Concentrating on the pain in my head gave me a concrete, though unpleasant, foundation. I fixated on it until the nausea subsided a little.

It was good enough.

With a last burst of will, I took another step and passed through the threshold.

As soon as my boot made contact with the wood floor, the pain and the sickness vanished.

"Damn," I said, taking in a deep breath. "Phew. That was *interesting*. I'm sweating like a mother f—"

"Tessa," hissed Dolores. She gave me her *wide eyes*, which I assumed was her way of telling me to shut the hell up.

A young man dressed in all black took our coats while we put on our shoes. He was stupidly handsome, just like the valet. With his chiseled face and slicked-back blond hair, if he'd added a tux, he'd have looked like James Bond Junior. He didn't give off any witch vibes. In fact, he didn't give off any sort of paranormal vibes. Human perhaps?

The pale witch I'd spotted watching me joined us. "Welcome, welcome," she said, her voice smooth and sounding rehearsed.

Though parts of her face could be considered attractive, her pale skin was pulled and stretched tightly over her features, making her more terrifying than beautiful, like she'd had way too many unnecessary face-lifts. She wore an Audrey Hepburn-type red dress that was fitted on top with a flared skirt, completed by matching red shoes and red lips. Her hair, which was a dark blonde and looked like it had been box dyed recently, was annoyingly perfect, styled in a 1950s' sort of fashion around a string of pearls and studs in her ears.

As she neared, the scent of pine needles and wet earth emanated from her along with something else... something bitter I couldn't decipher. Her dark eyes shone with a calculated coldness, and they were still fixed on me.

Not one to shy away from a stranger staring, I stared right back until she finally pulled her gaze away from me.

While Ruth looked nervous and kept fidgeting like she needed to pee, Beverly eyed the witch with much appreciation. Her eyes rolled over every inch of the other witch, taking in every detail of her dress and appearance as though saving it to memory for later. I didn't understand why. Beverly looked so much better and more natural.

Dolores stood stiffly, like a soldier at attention, and I wasn't even sure she was breathing. I'd never seen her look more nervous than at this very moment. All the more reason why I was glad I came.

"Thank you for inviting us," said Dolores with a grin that was way too large for her face. It almost looked painful.

The witch flashed a fake-looking smile, the kind that showed too much bottom teeth and never reached her eyes as her gaze flicked to my left where Iris stood. For a fraction of a second, it looked like she was going to acknowledge her. Sensing the same, Iris's expression changed to a surprised delight, and she opened her mouth to say something, but the witch had already lost interest and was staring at my aunts with open curiosity.

"You must be the Davenport witches I've heard so much about," said the pale witch, her voice odd with a forced housewife's good cheer into it, as fake as her smile. "You're not what I expected." She was still smiling, though I noticed the slight narrowing of her lips. "It's a pleasure to finally meet you. I'm Jemma." The witch gestured with her hand, her expression placid and enigmatic. "Please. Come join the others. They're dying to meet you."

I looked at Iris, and seeing her face flushed with embarrassment, I clenched my jaw. I already disliked this witch, and I was still standing in the foyer. It could only get better from this point.

We all filed in behind her and crossed the entryway, me following the others after Iris. Something was creepy about this place, and the fakeness oozing off this witch had my witchy instincts meter pinging off the charts. I found it curious that my aunts didn't sense anything, still fangirling over this coven of witches.

Me? I wanted nothing more than to leave and take Iris with me.

My shoes clicked loudly on the wood floors as we walked into a hallway. The space was at least two stories high, lit with an enormous iron chandelier. We passed a grand stairway off to the right, and I stuck my head through a doorway to see a display of coffins. Different-sized urns filled the back wall, on open shelves.

"This is so wrong on so many levels," I mumbled.

"I think it's cool," said Iris, which really didn't surprise me.

Jemma strolled into a large room, which I assumed was probably where the mourners assembled for funerals. Only now the room wasn't cramped with rows of uncomfortable pews or groups of sad-looking people surrounding a casket.

The room was sparsely populated with witches standing in little knots, talking while drinking from their glasses. Some even sat in comfortable chairs as soft music played with a steady rhythm. The smell of cigarettes reached me, and somewhere in the middle of all that, I felt a quiet, quivering pulse—witch magic.

It hummed through the walls and the floor like a living, breathing beast as though the house itself was made of magic, like Davenport House. But this wasn't from the house. It emanated from the witches in the room.

My eyes found a familiar, plump witch in her early sixties, her dark hair piled on her head in a pyramid shape. Her long, flowing dress of loud zebra patterns, in a mix of black and white, grazed her feet. Martha. I'd never seen her face this red before, and even from where I stood, I could see the sheen of sweat covering it. Her bejeweled glasses had slipped to the tip of her nose.

"Oh, that sounds fabulous, hon," said Martha to the short witch next to her, whose name I couldn't remember, though I knew I'd met her. Martha's voice was loud and her speech a little wobbly. "I'll get on him when I get home."

I did not want to know what that was about.

Only a few other witches from town were here. In fact, only seven more that I could spot, and none of the male witches.

A waiter walked by Martha, and she snatched up another glass of red wine. His black shirt was unbuttoned, exposing his tan muscular chest and rows of abs. He looked like he belonged on the cover of some fashion magazine, with white pants that were two sizes too small, exposing the shape, size, everything about his manly package.

I pulled my gaze from his equipment and looked around the room. The only males in here were the hot waiters with the too-tight white pants defining their meat twinkies.

"Cocks and Broomsticks," I muttered with a smile on my face, making Iris snort. "I get it now."

"What?" laughed Iris and I gestured to the waiter's groin as he moved past us.

The Dark witch's eyes widened and kept staring until he was gone. "Wow. That was... wow... Those are some hot pants. Oh my God," shrieked Iris. "You can see all their..."

"*Genital* direction."

Iris slapped a hand to her mouth, which I suspected was to keep her from crying out.

If this place didn't give me such a sour feeling, I might have hired them for Beverly's birthday bash. This was just the kind of thing she'd love.

31

It was my turn to laugh. "I hope they're getting paid well for this." Obviously, they were eye candy for the witches, like a pretty south pole display. Whatever. No judging.

"Sisters of the Circle," called Jemma with a childlike eagerness in her voice. "May I present the Davenport witches."

Again, the slight of not acknowledging Iris. It was my turn for a flush on my face, but mine wasn't from embarrassment. It was from anger.

And then something odd happened.

A group of about five witches stopped whatever they'd been doing and all turned to look at us. That in itself wasn't odd. It was *how* they looked.

Every single witch had the same dress as Jemma's, though in different colors. Even their hair and makeup were styled in the same fashion, all the way to the pearls around their necks and their false smiles.

This was all kinds of creepy.

I leaned my head next to Iris. "Is it me, or did we just step into another season of the *Stepford Wives*?"

Iris shrugged. "I think it's cute. It's like their own signature look. Their trademark or something."

"Hmm." If the Stepford Wives were witches, these would be them. It was clear I was the only one who thought this coven was off their brooms. I saw them for what they were—false.

"Don't you feel something odd about them? Something… off?"

"Like what?" Iris was staring at them with open admiration, clearly not sensing the same thing I was.

And when I cast my gaze around to my aunts, I saw the same thing there. Nervous body movements and wide eyes, like teenage girls meeting some college boys.

The next thing I knew we were surrounded by the Stepford witches.

"I'm Candice," said one of the wives—I mean, witches.

"Joan, delighted to make your acquaintance."

"Yasmine, pleased you could come."

"Gretchen… you all look so lovely…"

I kind of tuned out after the fourth one. I'd already forgotten their names. I blamed it on the overwhelming stink of strong perfume and that other scent I couldn't put my finger on that even their perfume couldn't mask.

I felt myself taking a step back, away from all the crazies and the buzzing of their fake hospitality. I couldn't take any more of the falseness that made my skin crawl over my bones. I cast my gaze around the room, noticing how Martha and the other witches from town had a weird, glazed look in their eyes, almost as though they were under a spell—the Stepford witches' spell. My aunts didn't have that look about them: well, at least not yet. I didn't like it.

Iris turned her head my way, seemingly only now realizing I had stepped away, and joined me.

"I know that look," she said to me, her eyebrows high.

"What look?"

"The one where you want to hurt someone," replied the Dark witch. "Your face never lies."

I laughed. "You got me." I lowered my voice and said, "Do you think these witches cast some sort of spell that was activated once everyone entered the house?"

Iris thought about it a moment. "I didn't feel anything other than the entrance ward. Just a soft tingling. Why? Did you feel something else?"

I shook my head. "Not sure. Something. A spell, maybe?"

"What kind of spell are we talking about?"

I felt the weight of someone's eyes on me. When I looked up, Jemma was watching me, her expression calculating. It turned into a smile, and my own expression hardened further.

"One that would enable them to control anyone who entered this house," I answered.

Iris shifted her weight next to me. "I know what you're thinking, but you're wrong. See, the wards on the door are like a full-body scanner machine. What you felt was just the wards screening you, making sure you're a witch. I felt them too. It doesn't mean you were spelled. Besides, I'm sure Dolores would have spotted a spell of that magnitude if there was one. She's the most experienced witch here. She would have called it."

"Not if she wasn't paying attention. Look at them. They look *way* too happy. They're not arguing while in the same room. It's not normal. Not for my aunts."

Iris laughed. "Well, I don't think so, but I can go back and do a revealing spell. It'll tell me if there's anything unseemly. I'll have to go and fetch Dana. I don't have any of my magical tools with me."

Dana was the name she'd given her album of paranormal DNA she'd collected over the years and stored for future curses and hexes. I couldn't ask her to leave the party, not for something I still wasn't sure about.

"Forget it. It's fine." Not really, but I didn't want to cause a scene. And what Iris was saying did make sense. If there'd been a spell, my aunts would have felt it.

Yet, I had felt something…

One of the Stepford witches, the shortest one, pinched one of the waiters' butts. She threw back her head and laughed while Martha fanned herself with her free hand. The waiter's face was hard as he ventured our way and lowered his tray of wineglasses for me and Iris.

It was hard *not* to stare at his pork sword. I mean, the guy was wearing tight white pants, which was enough of an anomaly. The bulge had no choice but to say, "How's it hanging?"

Isn't it true when you know you're not supposed to look at something, you end up always looking at it anyway?

He caught me staring at his appendage and my face flamed. Embarrassed, I didn't know what to say to him, so I just thanked him for the wine and watched him disappear through a doorway to the right.

Iris took a sip of her wine. "I'll admit. They are a little eccentric." Iris finally saw reason.

"Maybe they're robots."

Wine sputtered out of Iris's lips, winning a glare of the century from Dolores. Once seemingly satisfied that Iris wouldn't spit up again, she turned around and continued her conversation with Jemma.

Hello, Tessa…

"Hello, Iris," I said to the Dark witch, smiling.

Iris squished her pretty face into a frown. "Huh? Are we pretending we've only just met?"

It was my turn to frown. "Didn't you just say hi to me?"

"No."

I shook my head. "Weird. I swear I heard you just now."

A smile pulled Iris's lips. "Maybe they put something in the wine."

I stared down at my glass. "Maybe I shouldn't be drinking this."

I'm right here, Tessa.

I jerked, and panic swept me for a moment. That was definitely *not* Iris's voice. Worse, the voice had come from *inside* my head. *My* head. The only voice I'd ever heard inside my head was my own. This wasn't it. This voice was different.

Holy crap.

Someone was speaking to me telepathically.

CHAPTER

4

"**Y**ou okay?" Iris searched my face. "You look a little spooked."

I swallowed, my heart thrashing in my chest like I'd just shoveled the driveway for fun. "I'm fine."

This was definitely *not* okay, and I was most definitely *not* fine.

I've heard the stories. Once a witch, wizard, sorcerer, or any magical practitioner invaded your mind, they proceeded to take control of the rest of you. It was the only reason they did it in the first place—to control you, own you, and force you to do their bidding. Basically, you were their puppet, like a parasite taking hold of its host.

And just like a parasite, once they were inside you, it was hard to get them out. Sometimes the parasite could never be removed. And when that happened, the victim ended up going mad and eventually killing themselves.

I felt eyes on me again and caught Jemma staring at me once more. I knew at that instant the voice I was hearing was Jemma's. Somehow, she'd managed to get inside my head.

I'm so happy to finally meet you. I've heard so many juicy things about you, all of them good. Don't you worry, whispered the voice inside my head.

The initial fear turned into anger. I knew I'd felt something, stepping through that threshold when my head had felt like it wanted to leave my body and run away. I should have trusted my gut. I should have listened to my witchy instincts and pulled back. But it was too late.

Jemma had put a spell on me.

That Stepford witch was trying to control me or something, and like hell was I going to let her do it.

"Tessa!" Iris jumped in front of me, shielding my body with hers. Her eyes were as wide as I'd ever seen them, and they were staring down at something.

I looked down, following her gaze, and my breath caught. Sparks of black energy pooled around my fingertips like dozens of tiny flickers of static electricity.

Whoops.

The scent of sulfur and something like burnt hair rolled up my nose, but somehow this time it didn't bother me. You might even say… I liked it. Yup, something was definitely wrong with me.

"You need to calm down," warned Iris, still shielding me from the others with her body.

"Easier said than done," I mumbled, wishing I had pockets to stuff my fingers in. Still, I didn't think pockets could hide the demon magic. It wanted out.

"Think happy thoughts," encouraged Iris. "Marcus and you on a beach… Marcus and you *naked* on the beach… Marcus and you naked and *running* on the beach… Marcus and you naked and running on the beach *covered* in whipped cream…"

"Okay, okay." I laughed. And laughed harder. "You crazy witch."

But it had worked. I checked my fingers, and no demonic magic sparks were shooting out of them. Had anyone seen me? I couldn't be sure, though perhaps the dim lighting had saved my ass.

Maybe not.

I looked up to find Jemma on her way over, her dark eyes studying me. "Tessa, the rest of the coven would love to meet you. Your friend needs to learn to share." She smiled that false smile again that made me want to slap her, her white teeth looking practically fluorescent. "Come," she gestured with her hand, "come meet the others."

I didn't know much about mind-controlling or mental-manipulation spells, but following my witchy instincts, the longer I stayed in this house, the stronger the hold she'd have on me.

Yeah, not going to happen.

I plastered my face into one of her false smiles. "May I use your bathroom? I really need to go, you know what I mean?"

Jemma looked a little ticked off for a brief second, and I got a glimpse of the real witch with hard lines pressed around her mouth and her eyes. But then she smoothed out her expression. "Of course. Up the stairs. First door on the right."

"Thanks."

I grabbed Iris by the hand because we all knew women traveled to the bathroom in pairs and tugged her along with me and out of the party room.

"We're leaving," I told her, once we were out of earshot. "I don't like this place at all. Something's off about this coven. They feel... false, somehow. Wrong. I don't know why my aunts can't see that."

Iris was unusually quiet, and I hated it.

41

Once we passed the staircase, I whispered because with witches, sometimes the walls *did* have ears. "Screw them. You don't want these witches to like you anyway. Think of it as a good thing. Imagine being invited to this again? I'd rather go out to dinner with Gilbert." I eyed her carefully for a smile but saw none. "This was a complete waste of time."

When we reached the front door, Iris's face transformed into a smile as she pulled her hand from her black leather clutch. Pinched between two fingers was a strand of dark blonde hair.

"Not a complete waste," she said. "I've got what I need. With this, we'll see if she put a spell on us."

I grabbed her face and kissed the top of her head. "What would I do without you?"

"You'd be a mess," replied the Dark witch, looking smug.

I could always count on Iris to fix up a hex when I needed one. "Can you call Ronin to pick us up? I'd call Marcus, but he's busy with Grace."

Now wasn't the time to inform Iris of the voice inside my head. We needed to get out of here and as far away as possible from the Stepford witches.

"Yeah. Sure." Iris pulled her phone from her clutch and began dialing. "What about your aunts?"

I cast my gaze down the hallway in search of them, but I couldn't see anyone. "They'll be fine. Even if they do notice we're gone, which I doubt, they'll probably figure we got bored and left."

Running away scared, came the voice in my head again.

I stiffened, not appreciating the mind invasion by a stranger. I tried to ignore the voice as I searched for my boots, found them, and slipped them on.

The voice laughed. *Stay! There's so much we need to discuss.*

"Screw you," I muttered, not sure if she heard me or not. I wasn't sure how this telepathic communication worked.

Iris was speaking to Ronin, but I barely heard her over the voice that kept talking.

You and I are going to get really close. How do the young people say it, again? Ah, yes. Besties.

I gritted my teeth. "Get out of my head."

The thing with friends, continued the voice, *is that they look after one another. They help each other.*

"Stop talking," I hissed.

And you're going to help me. Aren't you, Tessa?

I focused and yelled with my inner voice as loudly as I could.

Fuck off!

The voice laughed again, more like a giggle that sounded very girly and young. She was enjoying this.

You can't leave, Tessa. You must stay… stay…

"He'll be here in five minutes."

I turned to find Iris slipping her phone into her bag. "Good. Thanks, Iris."

Letting out a frustrated breath, I eyed the front door, hesitating. Walking through the first time had done something to me. What were the chances that stepping out wouldn't do something again? Or worse?

Iris stepped closer to me. "What's wrong?"

"What if we can't leave?" I told her. Anger and frustration bubbled up again, and I had to strain to keep it from manifesting my new demon mojo. What else was I supposed to call it? It kind of had a nice ring to it.

Iris's pretty features creased in a frown. "What do you mean?" Worry flashed in her eyes. "You mean, you think we're trapped? Like they put a ward on this house that'll keep us inside?"

I nodded. "That's exactly what I think."

Iris stiffened, and her chin quivered in anger. "We'll see about that."

And then she did something that truly surprised me.

With a determined look on her face, Iris pushed me out of the way, grabbed the door handle, and yanked it open. Before I had time to blink, she was standing on the front porch, glaring at the shadows, like she was expecting —

no, hoping—something was out there so she could hex it.

After a few beats, she turned to look at me. "I only sensed the same magic stepping through the first time. Now, you try it."

I made to move but halted.

I'll see you soon, Tessa Davenport…

I turned my head, feeling a presence draw near me.

Jemma stood in the hallway, her expression stiff, with anger sparking in her eyes. That only solidified my confirmation that Jemma was communicating with me telepathically.

Holding my breath, I spun back around the door and stepped through.

A wash of magic fell over me as though I'd stepped into a warm shower, only the water was replaced by a trickle of energy. But this time there was no pain, no head pounding, just tiny little pricks of energy that crawled over my skin and then were gone.

I jerked as the door slammed shut behind me. So I did what any well-mannered witch would. I flipped it off.

"Come on," I said, hooking my arm in Iris's. "Let's wait for Ronin at the end of the driveway. I want to put as much distance as I can between us and this house." If I could blast it to the Netherworld, I would.

"You still think they spelled you?" asked the Dark witch as we strolled down the driveway.

I nodded, my chest tightening at what I was about to tell her. Every witch in the universe knew hearing voices in one's head was bad. Nothing was worse.

When we reached the end of the driveway, we stopped, and I pulled away from Iris slightly so I could see her face when I told her the news.

"I have to tell you something," I started, watching her puzzled expression. I needed Iris. I needed her skills in the Dark arts to help me rid myself of this parasite. I needed my friend.

What I wanted more than anything right now was to go home and put some food in my belly until my head felt better. But that wasn't an option for me.

My head was stirring, and my thoughts were a frantic current I couldn't calm or control. The one question that took power over all my other thoughts was why the witch Jemma was doing this to me?

I was going to find out.

CHAPTER

5

"You sure this is going to work?" I asked Iris, sitting crossed-legged on her bedroom floor next to her, my muscles stiffening with anticipation.

"I'm sure." The Dark witch's eyes crinkled at the corners as her knees pressed against the hardwood floor. "If she put a mind-controlling spell on you, or any mental manipulation spell, *this* will destroy it." She reached over and flipped the pages of an old book, using two fingers to manage the unwieldy tome. Some of the binding had been torn off the spine, and the smell of dust and leather rose to my nose as I watched her eyes move over the pages.

I let out a breath and pushed my anxiety down. "Good."

A startling, loud chorus of hisses soaked with rage filled the room. I looked over at the tiny, orange gremlin demon standing in a chalk-drawn circle on the floor three feet from us. Her lips pulled back, revealing a mouth filled with fishlike teeth. Gigi.

The size of a house cat, she had bright orange fur, large batlike ears, tiny purple horns, and a short tail like you'd see on a bobcat. She had that cute but deadly look going for her.

I knew most Dark witches needed the help of demons to call upon their powers, more like borrowing their magic, and Gigi seemed to be Iris's go-to demon. And by the constant hissing and the flipping of her fingers, Gigi wasn't a happy demon.

"Thanks for helping us, Gigi," I told the gremlin demon, trying to soothe her.

Gigi stopped hissing. She fixed me with her abnormally large, black eyes, and then she raised a taloned hand and gave me the finger.

I grinned. She was my kind of demon.

I turned my attention back to the old tome. "Where did you get the book? I don't recognize it."

Iris shrugged. "I stole it," she answered, winning a snort from her half-vampire boyfriend sitting at the edge of her bed.

"I don't know why, but I'm really aroused right now," said Ronin, and I spotted a faint rose color tinging Iris's cheeks.

I rolled my eyes and leaned over, trying to read the Latin on the pages. Some of the words had worn off, and she needed to read the spell right. I just hoped Iris was the skilled witch I knew her to be. Too many times I'd heard the stories of witches trying to debunk hexes and spells, and too many times things had gone wrong.

"So, Tess…" Ronin leaned forward, resting his elbows on his knees. "You're showing demon magic, *and* you're hearing voices?"

"Lucky me, huh?" I needed to speak to my father. Part of me wondered if he'd disappeared on me because he knew the consequences of giving me his blood. Yeah, he knew it would change me. And when I found him, because I was going to go looking for him after this, he was going to answer my questions.

I had several. How the hell did I control my demon mojo? How long would it last? And how did I get rid of it?

"Do you still hear the voices?" asked Ronin, pulling me out of my thoughts. "Are you hearing someone speaking to you now?"

"It's just the one voice. And no. Not since we left that house."

"You do know that witch is only doing this to control you. Right?" said the half-vampire, his voice carrying a new edge to it.

I met his troubled gaze, knowing he was thinking back on those sorcerers who had controlled the minds of his family and used them to kill for them.

"I know," I told him, watching his face tighten with some past memory.

"But why you?" continued the half-vampire. "Why not Dolores or Iris?" I wondered the same thing.

I'd thought about it a lot, actually. "I think it's the ley lines." It was the only thing that made sense. "Since I've been using them, things have had a strange way of finding me. My father. Demon hit men. Now this coven. Somehow they found out I could manipulate them."

"It's that guy Silas," announced Ronin. "He's probably telling every witch he can about you. You said he threatened to take your Merlin license. Right?"

"That's right."

Ronin was nodding, his face tight. "He's making damn sure everyone knows who you are and what you can do. The whole damn witch community—White and Dark—know all about you, Tess. I'd bet good money on that."

"Ronin's right." Iris met my gaze. "After what you did to him with his amulet, you can bet your ley-line skills are not so secret anymore."

My face screwed up in thought. "And now Jemma wants to use me for my ley lines."

"How?" Ronin's face grew worried. "I thought you could only use them yourself? Could she jump a ley line with you?"

"She wants the power," I told him. "She wants to use the ley lines' power through me. Like a conduit. She'll use me to wield it. If she controls me... she controls the ley lines." It reminded me of Samara, the High priestess in the Church of Midnight. She, too, wanted to use the power of the ley lines, though it didn't end well for her. But knowing Ronin's sensitive history with sorcerers, I decided not to mention it.

"Shit," said Ronin as he raked a hand through his hair.

"Shit is right," I answered, my gut tightening. "It's why we're doing this right now. Why I want that witch out of my head." Before she used me to do something terrible because that's exactly what my witchy instincts told me she wanted.

Iris's chin lifted. "We're going to get her out of your head," she answered, her confidence absolute, and I took comfort in that.

But I was still nervous. This was *my* head we were talking about. *My* mind. I kinda liked the orb that sat on my neck. It was normal to be a little nervous.

"Don't worry. Iris's got this," informed Ronin, seemingly having noticed the tension I was giving off.

I pressed my lips together tightly. "I'm not worried."

Ronin scoffed. "Yeah, you are. You're wound up tighter than a two-dollar watch."

I was.

Iris reached out and took a piece of chalk from her bag on the floor next to Dana, which was stocked for curses, much like this one.

My heart slammed in my chest as I watched the Dark witch draw two circles, one around each of the two ceramic bowls she'd positioned on the floor in front of her. Then she drew a few runes and symbols around the outside of each circle.

Next, she flipped open Dana, peeled away one of the plastic page covers, and carefully pulled something off the page. Between her fingers was a strand of dark blonde hair. Jemma's hair.

Iris placed the hair in the bowl on her left and leaned back, admiring her handiwork.

"Is that it?" Ronin's eyes were wide with curiosity.

"Not quite." Iris's gaze fell on me. "I'll need something of you as well."

My eyebrows shot up so high they about flew off my forehead. "Me? Like what?"

"Hair. Fingernail or toenail. Skin. Blood. Just something with your DNA on it."

Yikes. "Here." I reached up, pulled out a single strand of hair, and gave it to the Dark witch. It was the easiest and the least creepy option of the bunch.

Iris gave me a tight smile. Without a word, she placed my strand of hair in the bowl to her right. Next, she leaned over the two bowls and chanted, "Invoco tenebras," channeling her energy from the tiny demon gremlin she'd summoned.

Gigi let out a cry out of outrage. "Witch! Hate! Witch! Hate!" she screamed, kicking out her legs and thrashing around in her circle.

Iris's hair lifted in a breeze that touched only her. She'd gone still, gathering intent and power about her.

Gigi stopped thrashing as her fur turned yellow and then white. The demon's face was creased in hatred, and a flash of guilt hit. I hated doing this, but I didn't see any other way.

The bedroom lights flickered off and on again as power soared through the room. Gigi's eyes were now closed, and her fur kept switching from orange to white, and then it turned blue.

"Per manus magicae!" cried Iris. "Cor meum cruentum proieci in aeternum. Maledictam tuam ab hac maga aufer!"

Energy spilled into the room, cold and fast. It hummed and crackled like an electrical storm, and my body tingled from my center to my fingertips. My head throbbed with the pressure of my blood, making me dizzy. A wind that came from inside the room, with all the windows closed, lifted strands of my hair. The ceiling light flickered again, sending looming, twisted shadows to dance on the walls.

And then the power settled.

I stared at the bowls, not sure what to expect.

I definitely wasn't expecting them to burst into flames or the sound that followed.

A tall, green flame rose from each bowl, and then a peal of laughter echoed around the room, magnified like the voice had come from an amplifier.

Okay, now I was a little freaked.

A chill crawled neatly down my spine and then back up again. The flames flickered and went out, leaving the stench of burnt hair with nothing else. The bowls were empty.

I glanced over at Iris, my pulse throbbing. "Guess that wasn't supposed to happen, huh?" By the look of utter bewilderment on Iris's face, I was going with no.

The witch shook her head. "That's never happened to me before. Ever."

I looked at Ronin's worried expression before turning back to Iris. "What? The flame? Or the voice?" Iris just sat there looking stunned, so I pressed. "What does the green flame mean? And the voice? Does this mean Jemma knows what we tried to do?"

Finally, Iris blinked and turned to look at me. "I'm sorry, Tessa, but…"

"She knows," I answered for her. "Jemma knows. It didn't work. Did it?" My pulse leaped, fueled by anger and fear. Now that she knew, what was that witch going to do about it?

Iris shook her head, looking defeated. "No. I'm sorry."

"Okay, so we try again." Ronin was next to Iris on the floor, his arm around her shoulder as he rubbed her arm gently. "Just try again. No harm done. We do it again."

At that Gigi hissed and spat. "Iz'tuk sk Hzud'tk!" she growled in some guttural language.

I looked over at the tiny demon, seeing that her fur was back to its original orange color. I was with Gigi on this one. I didn't want to use the poor demon, but I also didn't want some creepy witch in my head controlling me and using me for her personal gain.

"Try again," encouraged Ronin. "You can do this. You're the most badass Dark witch I know. Not to mention the sexiest. Your ass does look amazing in a thong."

"We can't." When Iris's eyes met mine this time around, they were laced with fear. "You don't understand. I made things worse."

My mouth fell apart. "What do you mean, worse? Worse as in what? What could be worse than having a Stepford witch inside my head? Iris? Iris, please answer me."

Iris didn't speak for a moment. "I could be wrong, but... I'm afraid I made the connection… *stronger*."

The hair on the back of my neck prickled, and for a second, I just stared. "I'm sorry. Say that again?"

Iris shook her head solemnly. "I think… I think I just opened the door to your mind and threw away the key."

Well, slap my ass and call me Sally.

CHAPTER

6

I sat on the hardwood floor, barely hearing Gigi's cries over the noise of blood pounding in my ears.

Well, *this* was unexpected.

I'd expected Iris's counterspell to work or even not work, just not make things worse. Just goes to show how my life always seemed to be pulling me back down the crapper when I thought things were finally looking up.

"I'm so, so, sorry, Tessa," came Iris's voice.

When I looked back at her, my heart gave a tug at the pain I saw on her face. "It's not your fault. I asked you to do this. You were only trying to help."

"And now I've made things worse." Iris's eyes welled with tears.

"You don't know that," I told her, though my voice sounded harsh, and clearly I didn't believe it myself. "There's a chance you could be wrong." Though that loud laugher seemed to say otherwise.

Iris wiped at a tear, looking angrier at herself. "I don't understand. It should have worked. I've done this counterspell four times before, and it always worked."

I sighed. "It's okay, Iris. This is not your fault."

"What's not her fault?" came a familiar, stern voice.

Dolores stood in the doorway with her hands on her hips and her expression firm with disapproval. Next, came Beverly, pushing her way forward, followed by Ruth, whose face transformed into a brilliant smile at the sight of Gigi.

"What's going on here?" demanded Dolores. "We heard a strange noise?" As she stepped into the room, she wrinkled her face. "And what's that smell?"

"Burnt hair," I offered, not that it was any of her business. I was a grown-ass woman. I didn't need her permission.

Dolores stared at me. "Burnt hair?"

"Did you girls try that Twist-Me-Pretty curling hair spell from Martha's?" Beverly eyed the bowls on the floor. "I could have told you it didn't work. The last time I tried it, I nearly went bald."

"That's not it," I answered, though I was pretty sure my Aunt Beverly could rock it bald too.

Beverly looked at me and raised a knowing brow. "I mean bald… *everywhere*."

Okay. Too much information.

"Really?" Ronin was staring at Beverly like he was trying to see through her clothes. Usually, at that precise moment, he'd get a whack from Iris, but the Dark witch just sat there looking ill.

Oh dear.

It was bad enough that I had a mind-robbing witch on my case. I didn't want Iris to feel guilty about something that wasn't her fault. The thought of that coven brought a bitter taste to my mouth.

I pushed myself to my feet. "Iris was trying to help me remove a spell one of the Stepford witches put on me."

At that, Dolores's face went three shades darker. "Am I to assume by Stepford witches, you mean the Sisters of the Circle?"

Oopsie. "That's exactly who I mean." I wasn't about to cower from Dolores's frown. I could conjure up a deep frown on a whim too. It just wasn't as impressive since I had to look up at her while doing it.

"Who's this cutie?" Ruth was bent over Gigi, her hand resting just above the demon's head like she was contemplating whether or not it was safe to pet her. I'd go for the not.

"Ruth. I wouldn't," I warned, just as Gigi pulled back her lips and showed Ruth her rows of supersharp teeth.

But Ruth didn't seem to want to give up, or she just chose to ignore me. She picked a spot next to the tiny demon and sat, muttering in a soft tone I'd heard her use with Hildo and other small creatures.

And Gigi? Well, Gigi spun around and bent over.

Ruth rocked back and clapped. "Oh look. She's showing me her bum!"

It was hard not to smile.

"What spell are you talking about?" asked Dolores.

My attention snapped back to her. "When I first entered the house. When I walked through… I was spelled."

Dolores tsked and dismissed me with a wave of her hand. "That was just usual wards that keep the unmagical from entering. To make sure only those invited could enter. Only those with acute magical talent," she added, her chin held high in the air.

Ruth rolled her eyes. "Here we go."

"That's not what I mean." I cast my gaze over my aunts, my chest tightening because I knew they were going to throw a fit with what I was about to tell them.

"What *do* you mean?" asked Dolores, annoyance in her tone.

"Jemma put a mind-control spell on me—a mental manipulation curse. Whatever. The point is, she did." I figured I should just come right out and say it. When the three sisters all looked at me like I was mold on last week's sandwich, I continued. "She's in my head. The witch is speaking to me through my mind." I took a breath. "She's trying to control me. She wants to use the ley lines through me. Use their power."

Dolores let out a laugh. "Don't be ridiculous. The Sisters of the Circle might not be what you were expecting, but they don't sneak around spelling minds either. It's absurd. I won't allow you to speak of them in this way."

"I'm speaking about them in *this* way because it's the truth." Anger soared, and now that I knew I had some demon mojo in me, I could feel it itching to get out like my own monster on a leash that I could barely contain. Who was I kidding? I couldn't contain it even if I wanted to. "You don't believe me. Do you? She did something to me. This Jemma. And now I can hear her voice in my head. She spelled me the moment I stepped through those doors. You have this illusion of the perfect coven. Well, let me tell you something. If it spells unsuspecting witches, it isn't perfect. Something's not right about them. I felt it. You would have felt it too if you weren't so in love with them all."

It seemed my anger was nothing compared to my Aunt Dolores's.

Her face twisted into something ugly and terrifying. The room even seemed to take on a darker cast, and I swear she grew like two inches more. All she needed was a beard and a pointy hat and she could be Gandalf's twin.

"I will *not* have you ruin this for me," she spat, and I jerked back like she'd slapped me. She pointed a finger, which could easily have been a knife the way she was slicing the air with it. "I've waited my *entire* life to get an invitation," she went on, foaming at the mouth, for real. "You won't take this from me. I won't let you."

I raised my hands in surrender. "Whoa. Ease down, soldier. I have no idea what—"

"I've always been overshadowed my whole life. Beverly has her looks." Dolores was pacing now. "She's never had to wait for a man, never been without a date on Friday night since she was old enough to flirt."

"Very true." Beverly smiled and looked down at herself. "As soon as I had my boobies, well, the rest is history. The goddess knows where to put her efforts."

"And Ruth's got potion making," continued Dolores. "Everyone loves her. She's like that sad puppy in the pet store window. She's just so goddamn loveable it makes me sick." She stared at the wall for a second, like she was gathering herself. Then she spun around, her eyes filled with anger. "And what do I have? My brain. My intellect. A tongue like a razor. I've never been good at making friends like Ruth, never been attractive—"

"Also true," said Beverly.

"But this is *my* time to shine. This time it's about me. The Sisters are interested in making me part of their coven, and I will *not* let you ruin it for me."

Dolores stormed out of Iris's room, leaving me to pick up my jaw off the floor.

"Really, Tessa?" Ruth was up on her feet, giving me her version of narrowed eyes, but they came off looking like she was trying on new contact lenses. "You didn't have to say those things. You don't know how much this means to Dolores."

"But I didn't…"

Ruth walked past me and left.

"Sorry, darling," said Beverly. "But this time, I have to agree with my sisters." She put a hand to her brow. "I can't believe I just said that. But making the coven out to be some evil, conniving lot of old spinsters that have no sense of style— though that part is true—well, it's just plain mean." And with that, Beverly left the room, swaying her hips like she was on a catwalk.

I stared at her, fists clenched and my anger stirring, too upset to even trust myself to comment.

Ronin clapped his hands once. "That went well." He sat on the edge of the bed again and stretched out his long legs. "Why do I have the sudden need for popcorn?"

Iris let out an exasperated breath. "That's not helping, Ronin."

"He's right." I rubbed my temples. "They don't believe me. They think I've made this up to hurt Dolores. It's crazy." I could hear my aunts' voices carrying back from downstairs. They were probably opening the vodka to drown their anger and disappointment in me.

Well, I was disappointed in them too. I was pissed. They thought I made it all up? And for what? It's not like I wanted to be involved with these Stepford witches. And seeing what Jemma *could* and *would* do, I didn't want my aunts anywhere near that group.

It left me with just one option. I needed to get proof that this group of witches was as fake as their fake smiles. The only problem? I had no idea how to do that.

Worse? Now my aunts would never agree to help me. Not if they thought I was lying and trying to sabotage Dolores's chances of joining this coven.

It stung. I'll admit that. It stung that my aunts refused to believe the truth. They never stopped once to ask themselves why I would lie about something like that. I thought they knew me well enough. Guess not.

A shrill yowl sounded in the room, and we all looked at Gigi. The poor, tiny demon was in a fit of being forgotten, still a prisoner within her summoning circle.

I glanced over at Dana, Iris's book. "You wouldn't happen to have any more of Jemma's hair. Would you?"

Iris shook her head. "I had only the one. Without some of Jemma's DNA, I can't do the counterspell again. Sorry."

I gestured toward Gigi. "Then no point in keeping her here. You should let her go."

Gigi met my gaze for a second, and then she flipped me off. I didn't blame her.

Iris waved her hand over the little demon, muttered a few Latin words, and with a pop of displaced air, Gigi was gone.

The room fell into an uncomfortable silence, and my shoulders tensed. I might not have heard Jemma's voice since we left their party, but it didn't mean she wouldn't resurface again. I knew she would before too long.

I had to get her out. Now, before it was too late.

"There has to be another way," I said, looking at Iris. "I'm not going to have some stranger in my head, telling me what to do. I won't."

Iris looked a little uncomfortable before answering and shifted the weight on her knees. "There is another way... one that I didn't mention... but..."

"But what?" Ronin and I asked together.

Iris stared at her feet before answering. "You're not going to like it."

"I'll probably like it a hell of a lot more than having a witch invade my headspace," I answered.

Iris lifted her dark eyes at me. "You won't."

My heart leaped at the tremor that reflected in her voice. "What is it?"

Ronin leaned forward. "The suspense is killing me, and technically, I'm half dead."

The Dark witch's eyes flicked over to the half-vampire and then back to me. She studied me a moment, her expression one of warning. "The only way to stop Jemma from controlling your mind is to kill her. Kill the navigator."

I cursed. "Fuck me."

CHAPTER

7

I woke up the following morning with my mind free of any parasites, meaning said parasite Jemma. In fact, I hadn't heard her voice inside my head since I left the party last night. I wasn't sure what that meant. Could Jemma only invade my mind in that house? Or did she need to be in proximity of me for her mind-control spell to work? Or maybe, she just wanted me to think that. All were plausible.

I never thought murder was up there on my list of achievements after I hit thirty. Went to show you never knew what the world would throw at you—apparently lots of crap.

Desperate people facing mounds of pressure were essentially stupid creatures. But murder? I wasn't that desperate or stupid.

It might be the only way Iris believed I could rid myself of this mind-snatching, but I was certain there was another way. It wasn't the first time a witch or any magical practitioner tried to invade another's mind to control them. And it wouldn't be the last. I was willing to bet someone had figured how to remove a mind-control spell or block it so it wouldn't happen again. It was just a matter of finding that counterspell, counter-curse, or potion. Whatever it took, I *was* going to find it.

If my aunts wouldn't help me, I would figure it out on my own. I was a grown-ass woman. I could do this.

Feeling restless, I could only admire the ceiling for so long, so I grabbed my phone: 7:23 a.m. I thought about texting Marcus, but I knew he'd stayed up late working with Grace. I didn't want to wake him up. Besides, I didn't need him for what I was about to do.

With my heart pounding in my ears from excitement, I leaped out of bed, crossed my room, and cracked open my bedroom door. Voices trailed up from downstairs—the three distinct voices of my aunts.

"They're up," I whispered to myself. Perfect!

After listening for another three seconds, I pulled open my door and darted down the stairs as quietly as I could. When I reached the second floor, I tiptoed to Dolores's room and snuck inside.

I only needed about thirty seconds if I didn't get caught.

Pulse racing, I crept to the back of her room, where a bookcase lined the entire wall, and snatched up three of her tomes from her private collection, *Black Grimoire, Hexes & Jinxes for the Modern Witch,* and *Ledger of the White Witch.* With the three books in my arms, I darted out and tiptoed back into my room. Once I'd closed the door, I began reading.

Black Grimoire was my first choice for obvious reasons, and I was rewarded by three chapters devoted entirely to mind-control spells.

Apparently, the ability to control minds— mental manipulation as well as psychic possession—was an ancient skill that had been around for centuries. No surprise there. The more I read about it, the more shocking details I discovered.

Not only could you hear this mind-controller's voice in your head, but they could also infuse their thoughts, perceptions, memories, and emotions into you until you couldn't tell the difference and had lost yourself over to them, leaving you completely subjected to the navigator's control. They could also manipulate you into a semiconscious state, where you had no recollection of any actions that you performed while under the navigator's control. That was a scary thought.

Apart from witches, mind control was an extremely difficult spell to perform and actually have it stick. Sometimes it didn't work, and both parties ended up dead or with magical lobotomies.

I spent all morning and most of the afternoon reading. I still had so much to learn about the paranormal world and all its wonders. Once I started, I found I couldn't stop until I'd fulfilled my curiosity. I didn't bother going downstairs to fetch anything to eat. The two protein bars I'd packed in my bag were enough to satisfy my stomach until they weren't.

I sat on my bed, feeling both angry and excited. I was angry that Jemma, this stranger, had invaded my mind, getting a glimpse at my most private thoughts. But I was also excited because I'd discovered something important.

According to these books, witches were by far the least accomplished in this skill set. In fact, they rarely performed it because most of them never got it right.

Only one brand of magical practitioner was skilled enough at mind manipulation to navigate another person's mind and body. And that, my friends, was a demon.

Luckily for me, my father was one.

Feeling marginally better, I took a quick shower and went in search of my aunts downstairs, hoping a good night's sleep had erased some of their feelings from the fights last night. I didn't want to call it a fight. It was more of pointing the finger at me and with lots of accusing stares and glares.

"They love me," I told myself, making my way down the stairs. "I'm their only niece. What's not to love?"

I stepped into the kitchen. The air smelled of old coffee and something like toast. No late-afternoon snacks were laid out for me like there had been nearly every single day since I'd arrived a few months ago. My eyes found the coffee machine. The lit ON/OFF switch was off, and the glass carafe was empty.

"Definitely *not* feeling the love," I mumbled to myself.

I cast my gaze around the kitchen. Dolores was acting like I didn't exist, her eyes glued to her newspaper. Beverly, sitting at the table across from Dolores, kept giving me tiny, covert smiles while sipping her coffee, like I'd been caught cheating on my husband. And Ruth… well, Ruth kept staring at me with her version of sad puppy eyes, like I was on my deathbed dying from some incurable disease and she couldn't do anything to help me.

Hildo was sprawled on the kitchen table next to Ruth. He caught me staring, and he moved a finger, very slowly, across his throat. Nice.

"Hello, ladies," I said, looking at Dolores to see if she'd make eye contact with me. Nope. Both Ruth and Beverly picked a spot on the kitchen table and stared at it as though answering me would betray their sister.

I cleared my throat and tried again. "So, what's going on? Anything happening that I should know about?" I waited for a response but still nothing.

Four women living together, we were bound to have a few fights, but the cold shoulder? I hated those.

"Really?" I told them, my irritation and anger stirring. I glared at them, my lips pressed together. "You're not going to speak to me? Wow. Real mature. Surprising for *mature* ladies."

"Better watch who you're calling a mature lady," threatened Beverly, pointing a red manicured finger at me. "I don't look a day over thirty."

At that, Dolores would have normally ripped into her, but my aunt didn't even move or blink. Not even a facial muscle twitched.

Shoulders stiff, I walked over to the coffee machine, grabbed the glass carafe, moved to the kitchen sink, and filled it up with water.

"You could apologize to Dolores," offered Ruth. "That's a start." Her blue eyes moved to Dolores, but the witch's attention was still glued to her newspaper.

I turned the tap off, moved to the coffee machine, and dumped the water in it. "I'm not going to apologize," I growled, shoving the carafe on the burner with a bang. "I didn't do anything wrong. I'm not the one who mind-spelled someone—which is an illegal spell, by the way." I had just read that. "Jemma did. The moment I stepped through that door, she was in my head."

At that, Dolores slammed her newspaper on the table, stood, and stormed out of the kitchen.

I braced and gritted my teeth. I didn't know why, but she made me feel guilty. And the more I felt guilty of speaking the truth, the angrier I got.

Shaking my head, I turned on the coffee machine. "Unbelievable."

Beverly shifted in her chair until she faced me. "I'll tell you what's unbelievable. You."

"Me?"

Beverly let out a frustrated sigh. "You couldn't just leave it alone. Could you?"

I tried to keep my emotions from getting the best of me, but I could feel my control slipping. "Not when I'm being accused of being a liar. I didn't make this up. Why would I? I'm not that psychotic." Though the voice in my head said otherwise.

"You just had to push her again," continued Beverly. "Wasn't last night enough? Don't you see how important this is to her? Being part of this coven means the world to her."

I narrowed my eyes. "It's a bad coven."

Beverly lifted a shoulder. "I'll admit. I don't see Dolores in any of those clothes. She's got such a masculine body. Those dresses'll never fit over those manly shoulders. But it doesn't give you the right to mock them or her."

I took a breath to try and calm my nerves. "I didn't mock anyone."

"You kinda did," said Ruth. "Making things up is mocking." Her eyes met mine, and she turned away at my glare.

Beverly pushed her chair back and stood. "Why can't you just leave it be? Let her have this. You don't have to like this coven. Just stop belittling them. It's not an attractive quality. Makes you out to be an old spinster one day. Nobody likes those."

This conversation was going nowhere fast. It didn't matter how many times I told the story. If they choose not to listen, what did it matter?

Emotions swelled, and anger made my face burn. I pushed away from the counter, away from the coffee machine. I didn't want their coffee. I didn't want anything from them. Not anymore.

"I thought we were family," I said.

Ruth looked shocked. "Of course we are, silly. Why would you say that?"

My face twisted, and I forced the bitter emotions away. "I thought you'd be different from my mother. Thought I'd finally found where I fit in. I thought we could trust each other."

Beverly pressed her tiny hands on her hips. "Don't you go comparing us to your mother. We are *not* the same."

"Maybe not the same… but close."

Ruth was shaking her head. "I don't understand."

I knew I should be controlling my emotions better, but I couldn't. I was tired and scared. Things were happening to me that I didn't understand. And those I thought were closest to me, my beloved aunts, didn't even believe me.

When I needed them most, they weren't there for me.

This wasn't a need for a shoulder to cry on or hugs. Hugs weren't my thing anyway. This was more of a trust issue. Just as Marcus had said, if there was no trust, how could there be a relationship? And that went for family too.

"Maybe living here was a mistake." As soon as the words came flying out, I regretted them. But it was too late. There they were.

Both Beverly and Ruth seemed taken aback by my comment.

Ruth's face paled, and her mouth was hanging open. "You don't mean that." She hesitated a moment, looking at me as though she hadn't heard me right. "Tessa? You don't mean that?" she repeated.

My chest tightened at the hurt in Ruth's voice, and I made sure to look away. If I made eye contact with any of them, I knew the waterworks would start.

I didn't trust myself to answer. I'd already made things worse. But maybe leaving Davenport House and finding a place of my own was the right thing to do.

But why did it feel so... wrong?

I stared at the basement door, knowing I could just call out to my father, and I had a fifty-fifty chance he'd show up. But I didn't want to have *that* conversation with him in front of my aunts—the one about me having this new demon mojo. He might not want to talk about it either or might want to discuss this in private.

Besides, I think we all needed a break from one another. I'd jump a ley line and see him later.

Without another word, I stormed out of the kitchen in a much similar fashion to Dolores because I needed to talk to someone else. Someone who'd been good to me and respected and trusted me.

I needed to tell Marcus everything.

And I needed to tell him now.

CHAPTER

8

"**A**nd now, Dolores hates me," I told the chief of Hollow Cove, sitting across from him in a leather chair in his office.

The uber-sexy chief's gaze rooted to mine with those stupid mesmerizing gray eyes framed by incredible, thick, black lashes. He was off the hotness scale, hands down. If there was a word for such hotness, it was superstud. I even glanced behind him to see if he was wearing a cape. Or tights. Tights would have been awesome.

"Dolores doesn't hate you. She's just upset." A tiny smile crept along his full lips. "Families fight. I don't know of any family that doesn't. She'll get over it."

I'll admit. It was hard to concentrate with such a hot specimen only a few inches across from me. Said specimen which I'd seen naked, multiple times, who'd seen me naked, multiple times, and which we'd done multiple, naked things together.

Was it just his hotness, or was it the older I got, the hornier I became?

My eyes drifted down to his chest, which was covered in a low V-neck black shirt, causing the heat on my face to increase.

Marcus caught me staring and gave me a smug smile, the kind that sent my nether regions pounding. When those gray eyes pinned me, and I saw a flicker of desire in them, it was all I could do not to dive over his desk and rip his clothes off so I could rub my face all over his hard chest.

Yeah, I wasn't a lady. Never said I was either.

I cleared my throat, trying to rid myself of those hot flashes, but it wasn't working. "You believe me. Right? You don't think I'd make this up?" If he did, we were going to have a serious problem.

Marcus watched me a moment and then leaned forward, interlacing his fingers on his desk. "Of course I believe you. It's all over your face, in your eyes. You wouldn't be so upset if you were lying. I know you didn't do this to hurt Dolores."

I scoffed. "Can you tell her that? She thinks I did. To ruin her chances of being selected for that coven. It makes no sense. Why would I do that? I don't care about that stupid coven. I'd never even heard of it. But somewhere in that big brain of hers, she thinks I did."

"What about Ruth and Beverly?"

"They think I made it up too." My chest clenched at the memory of what happened, the shock and disappointment in their eyes. I gave a short laugh. "I never thought they'd react this way. I thought… I thought they'd believe me." Here I thought I knew my aunts. Guess I didn't. Guess I didn't know them at all.

The chief's face went serious. "Are you still hearing her voice? This Jemma?"

I shook my head. "Not since I left the funeral home she's renting."

"Is it possible this spell only works inside the house? You said you felt it when you first walked in. What if she can't reach you if you're not in there?"

"Yeah, I thought about that. Maybe? Guess we'll find out if I can't figure out another way to get rid of it."

Marcus's brows rose. "You've *tried* to get rid of it? When?" His face was both serious and a little anxious.

"I did. Well, *we* did. Me and Iris. We tried a counterspell last night."

"And it didn't work?"

"Noooo." I hedged a bit. "And Iris thinks maybe she made it worse."

Marcus let out a sigh and rubbed his jaw. "Damn it, Tessa. Why is it that trouble always seems to find you?"

"If I knew the answer to that, I wouldn't be in this mess." And what a giant mess it was. I slumped back in my chair and let out a breath before rubbing my eyes. "I think I might have kicked myself out of my house," I said with a laugh.

The chief's handsome face scrunched up in a frown. "What?"

"I got angry, and when I get angry, it comes with buckets of stupid—"

"I know." The chief smiled.

"Well," I added, and with my own smile. "I might have *implied* that I was moving out. Which would have been fine if I had a place to live."

"You can move in with me."

I stared, too shocked at what he'd just said and how easy and quickly it had come out.

"Uh… I… uhhh…" Yeah, I was incredibly eloquent in times of indecision.

The chief's gaze lingered on my face, and I felt my cheeks flame. "Move in with me," he repeated. I looked for traces of a joke in his tone or his expression but saw none. He was serious.

Marcus wanted *me* to move in with *him*…

Move over office furniture! I was about to do some major cartwheels.

I know it. You know it.

I opened my mouth, but before I could answer, a knock sounded on the chief's door.

"Come in," he called, straightening in his chair, all businesslike and sexy as hell, which had my hormones doing a jig.

The door to his office opened.

Oh. Hell. No.

Allison walked in—yes, *that* Allison—all leggy and irritatingly gorgeous. She held a tablet in her hand with her head high. Her usual long, blonde hair was tucked neatly into a bun. She was trying to go for sophisticated and smart, but with the white shirt that was way too tight to hold on to those massive boobs combined with her black pencil skirt that looked painted on, she looked like she was auditioning for the lead secretary role in a porn movie. Still, she was beautiful. Still, she was a pain in my ass.

Allison saw me and looked me over. Her face twitched like I smelled bad or something, as a satisfied smile spread over her perfect face.

My face flamed with embarrassment. That's when I realized I hadn't put on any makeup or bothered to brush my hair. I had bed hair. Ooops.

I looked like a homeless person, and Allison looked like *that*. I could never look that good, even with every spell in Martha's salon.

Well, I could run away embarrassed and mortified, or I could own my disheveled appearance.

I decided to own it.

"What the hell are you doing here?" I asked and made a show of tossing my hair, feeling a knot in the back. It seemed Allison had ditched the idea of having a witch spell me. She'd opted for a better, *closer* approach. Damn. She was good.

She eyed me with amusement in her eyes. "I work here, *witch*," she said, emphasizing the word witch. She'd said witch, but all I heard was bitch.

Could my day get any worse? Of course it could. We were talking about yours truly here. And we all knew how that went.

I looked at Marcus, and he frowned at what he saw on my face. He was clueless. Men.

Yet, I was comfortable enough in my skin with my insecurities to let it go. Though Allison looked like sex on a stick, Marcus had picked *me*. Me. Me. Me.

Mine, he'd declared. Still, knowing that Allison would probably see him more than me was, needless to say, irritating.

Alison put her free hand on her hip. "Why? Does that bother you?"

"Give that chest a rest. Would you?" I told her.

"Excuse me?"

"Excuse you?"

Allison lost some of her composure, her smile faltering.

"Allison started working here today, as our new HR coordinator," announced the chief, apparently only now realizing that perhaps he should have told me, though that was really not my business.

I pulled my eyes away from the blonde wereape. "That's nice."

Marcus was staring at me like he wanted to say more but wasn't sure he could. "What is it, Allison?"

Allison beamed at the chief and moved around my chair so she was practically leaning over Marcus's desk, her hips swaying and giving me a close-up view of her ass.

"I'm helping Grace with some citizen complaints," she said, her features pulled in a radiant smile. "Did you look into Gilbert's complaint about the height of the sidewalk next to his store in relation to the sidewalk on the other side of the street? He's claiming his is two inches shorter. And hazardous to the public."

Marcus shook his head. "Yes. And you can call Gilbert and tell him his sidewalk is fine."

Allison swiped her finger across her tablet. "Okay. Anything else I can do for you?" she purred, and I didn't miss the way she'd said "do" either. She was practically bent over his desk, waiting.

For my boot up her ass.

"That'll be all. Thanks, Allison." Marcus's eyes moved to mine and held them. It was like she didn't even exist.

Allison, being Allison, didn't even notice the obvious dismissal. "My pleasure," she responded.

My *pleasure*? If her butt was still near me, I would have kicked it.

I kept my eyes on the chief as Allison pulled away from his desk and walked out the door. He was watching me like he wanted to rip my clothes off. Let's see how long that would last after what I was about to tell him.

I swallowed hard, suddenly nervous. "There's something else I have to tell you."

A flicker of tension washed over his face, barely visible, but I saw it. "What is it?"

My chest was doing a tug-of-war with my intestines. "Remember when I told you about the demon hit man, Vorkan, how he'd cut me with his poisoned blade the first time and that to save me, my father had to give me some of his blood?"

The chief nodded. "I remember."

"Well. Something's happened to me. Is happening, actually."

Marcus leaned forward on his desk, and his shoulders went steely with tension. "What is it? What's happening?"

I tried to smile to lessen the tension, but my facial muscles just twitched, probably making me look like I was constipated. I looked over my shoulder before saying, "I have demon mojo. Demonic magic."

Marcus's lips parted, but he didn't say anything.

Hmm. Not the reaction I was going for. "Did you hear me?"

"I did." His gray eyes narrowed as he studied me. "Are you sure?"

"Pretty sure. Remember those black tendrils Vorkan hit you with? Well"—I hooked thumbs at myself—"yours truly got them too."

The chief eyed me then—not in an "I want to take you on my desk right now" kind of way but in more of a "Is there a demon inside my girlfriend?" kind of way. I wasn't so sure I liked it.

"How do you feel?" asked the chief.

"Same." I shrugged and added, "I'm not about to change into a demon, if that's what you're worried about." Hell, that's what *I* was worried about.

Marcus shook his head. "No. I'm worried about you. Your mental health. It's a lot to happen all at once. A lot to process."

"I'm not going to pretend that I'm fine. Though technically I *feel* fine, I'm not fine. The demon mojo I can handle. Seems to only surface when I'm angry, so I think I can control it. But the head invasion worries me."

"Because this Jemma might be able to control you."

"Exactly."

"And you think she wants to control you to access the ley lines' power?"

"It's the only thing that makes sense," I answered. "I mean, I'm nothing special apart from being really good at wielding and manipulating the ley lines. I don't see why she'd be interested in me except for the lines."

Marcus was silent for a while, but I could see the storm of emotions brewing behind his eyes. "We need to figure out a way to get her out of your head." He leaned forward again. "We need your aunts. They're the most capable witches I know. I'm sure they can do it."

I laughed. "Good luck with that."

"I'll talk to them," said the chief. "I'll make them understand. Make them see reason. This is your life we're dealing with. They'll come around."

"I doubt it, but you're free to try." I was glad he believed me. "Could you do something else for me?"

"Sure. What?"

"Can you do some digging on this coven? The Sisters of the Circle? I'll do my own, but I'd appreciate some help. Without my aunts' help, I need all the extra help I can get."

The smile the chief flashed had my pulse rising. "I will. I'll also have Jeff tail them. See what they're up to."

"Thanks." Jeff was one of Marcus's deputies, though I'd barely spoken to the guy since I moved here. I wagered he was very good at his job, and I was grateful for the extra help.

Another knock came from the door, but this time Grace's white head appeared in the doorway. "Your four o'clock is here," she said, as usual completely ignoring me.

"Thanks, Grace." The chief stood as Grace shut the door behind her.

I shot to my feet. "I better get going."

"Where are you off to?" he asked, coming around his desk. He slipped an arm around my waist and pulled me against his hard chest, sending a spike of desire to my core. I breathed in his scent. I didn't know what it was about it, but it made my lady regions go all out of whack.

"I have something to discuss with my father," I answered, staring at his lips.

I let my entire body mold into him, relaxing and letting go of all the tension I'd been carrying. He tilted his head, desire heady in his gaze. His fingertips slipped down my lower back and tightened against my ass, pulling me closer.

He dipped his head. His lips traced a path along my jaw, and then he kissed me. His lips were soft and warm, and the desire behind his kiss had my pulse hammering. Need dove to my middle and sent me alight.

Damn, this wereape could kiss. He could light my panties on fire too.

"Don't forget about my offer," said the chief before pulling away. Heat still shone in his eyes, fervent and unashamed. "Think about it." He traced a finger along my jaw, teasing. And then he left.

Leaving me staring into space, knees rubbery and loose.

The chief wanted me to move in with him.

Holy witch farts.

CHAPTER
9

I jumped the ley line.

I rushed forward with the propulsion of the ley line, feeling like I was piloting an F-16 while standing up and without the hassle and constriction of a metal contraption. I sped forward in a howl of wind and colors, though mostly whites and blacks since we were still in January, and the sun had already disappeared for the evening.

Energy careened through my head, my body, and everywhere. It was a rush. And after abstaining from using them because of the Vorkan thing, I'd nearly forgotten how much I loved riding the ley lines.

Yeah, it was pretty awesome.

Once I reached Sandy Beach, the only public beach in Hollow Cove, which was completely covered in snow, I pulled back on the ley line's power. I felt a sudden release as the images around me slowed until they weren't blurred anymore and I could make them out clearly. I slowed until I was almost at a standstill.

"Dad?" I called, searching and only seeing a sea of white around me from the piles of snow that covered the golden dunes on the beach. I always wondered about this connection thing. If he could sense me using a ley line, following that logic, I should be able to do the same thing. Right? Only, I had no idea how.

A shadow stepped into the line with me. It solidified into the shape of a man—tall and fit with silver, shimmering eyes. His graying hair and beard were trimmed perfectly, matching his expensive, dark business suit.

His eyes sparkled with delight. "Tessa. How wonderful to see you."

"Cut the crap." I pressed my hands on my hips and leaned slightly forward, a posture Dolores would employ to get answers that always seemed to work. "Why did you leave like that the other night? After you said you'd wait?"

Obiryn watched me for a long moment. "I know you're upset. I had things I needed to take care of. I only left when I knew that you were safe."

"How did you know? How did you know I was safe?" I demanded.

"A feeling."

"A feeling?"

My father nodded his head. "Yes." He shrugged and added, "A family thing."

I gritted my teeth, staring at the man, demon, who'd saved my life twice already. "You know. Don't you? You knew what would happen to me?"

His silence was my answer.

"And what?" I pressed, my voice rising with my anger. "You didn't think of mentioning it to me? Oh, by the way… you might sprout demon mojo out of your ass when you're mad."

A smile tweaked my father's face. "Demon mojo? Is that what you're calling it?" he said, looking pleased, way too pleased.

"Don't even try."

My father sighed. "I wasn't certain it would manifest. Not all offspring manifest powers from both parents. You didn't as a child. You took more after your mum as a witch. It was a fifty-fifty chance that it would reveal itself after the transfusion. I didn't want to worry you in case it never happened."

I got that part, but still. "You should have told me."

My father's face wrinkled in a clutter of worry and guilt, and all my anger evaporated. "I'm sorry. You're right. You're absolutely right. I should have told you."

I blinked, not used to hearing that. "Now what?"

The demon's brow furrowed. "Now what... what?"

My shoulders rose. "What do I do with it? Will it go away? Or will it stay with me forever? Am I a demon now?" I wasn't going to lie. That was the one question that I needed answered.

"Ah. I see." My father smiled, but his eyes held a trace of sadness because I'd just basically declared in not so many words that being a demon like him was a horrible thing.

Damn. When I screwed up, I screwed up big.

"You needn't worry," answered my father. The softness and kindness of his words made me feel worse. "You're not a demon in the sense of a full-fledged demon like me. You'll always be part of both worlds. You'll never become a full-fledged demon if that's what's worrying you. You are uniquely you. Part demon. Part witch."

"Now *I* should apologize," I told him as a rush of guilt swept me. "It came out all wrong. I'm just... a little overwhelmed. I don't know what's happening to me or how to control it."

My father took my hand and squeezed it. It was warm, and I wasn't sure why that surprised me. "You're still you. Nothing's changed apart from a tiny improvement."

"Improvement?"

My father grinned. "Think of it as a new skill set. It will set you apart from all the other witches."

"No kidding."

"You're more powerful than them now. You have the ability to choose." He let go of my hand. "You can either use your witch magic" — he gestured with his right hand — "or you can use your demon magic." He gestured with his left. "It's marvelous. You have the best of both worlds. Literally."

"Another reason for them to hate me."

My father's eyebrows shot to his hairline. "Hate you? Why would they hate you?"

Just the thought of what Silas did to Marcus with that amulet set my anger rising again. It made me wonder what other witches were capable of?

"You forget the whole demons and witches thing," I said. "Just like in your world, demons sleeping with witches is like a bad omen. The same goes for here. The White witch or Dark witch courts won't be too thrilled if they hear about my demon mojo. I still might lose my Merlin license because I used the ley lines. I'm under investigation, apparently. Imagine what they'd do if they found out I can manipulate demon magic? Look what your own council did to me. They wanted me dead." Maybe they still did, but I wasn't going to get into that right now.

My father rubbed his beard, deep in thought. "I see your point. Perhaps you should hide it for the time being. Make sure no one sees it. Yes. I think that's best."

I snorted. "That's going to be tough. The thing is, I don't know how to control it. It seems to jump out when I'm upset. It's very different from my witch magic, which I control with elemental power or by power words or ley-line energy. It seems pretty... wild."

My demon father was shaking his head. "Not wild. Just different from what you're accustomed to, though it has similarities to elemental magic. Not in the way of the elements, like water and fire and such. But how you can draw upon them. Call upon them. Think of it as a dark-force manipulation. Dark-elemental manipulation, dark-energy manipulation."

"Okay, I think. I still don't know how it works."

My father stared at me. "I'll teach you. I'll teach you so you can hide it. Keep your demon mojo at bay until you need it. You already have a great understanding and grasp on ley-line magic, so it shouldn't be that difficult for you to wield it."

I let out a breath. "When can you start?" The sooner the better.

A smile spread across my father's face. "I'm free tonight."

"That works for me too. Great. Thank you," I said, feeling some of my tension leaving me. That was one thing out of the way, but I still had the issue with the mind-control thing.

"What do you know about mind-control spells?" I figured it was a shot. My father seemed very knowledgeable in all things supernatural, so he might know something.

He frowned thoughtfully and then said with a smile, "You mean a Jedi mind trick?"

I grinned. "Exactly, Obi-Wan."

My father looked smug. "Well, from what I know of your laws on magic, on your side, it's illegal. But not so in my world. Mental manipulation is quite common with demons, usually to get information." He watched me carefully, his silver eyes pensive.

"What can you tell me about it?"

My father's brow lowered skeptically. "Why? Are you trying to control someone's mind? Jedi mind tricks sound like fun, but I would strongly urge you not to try them. They're dangerous and difficult. Sooner or later, while you control them and manipulate them, you start changing too. The link starts to bleed both ways if it's not severed properly and quickly. It's a dirty business."

Damn. That didn't sound good. "Okay. But it's the other way around." I let out a breath. "I'm not the one trying to use a mind-control spell. *I'm* the one they've done it to."

I told him everything—from the moment I stepped into that house to the Stepford witch look-alikes, which he thought was a nice touch, to finally Jemma's voice in my head.

When I was done, my father's face was set in a hard cast. "Mind-control spells or any kind of mental domination are like a targeted mark," he said. "You create a link, a channel to the target, which in your case could have been the door, and then you pour energy into that channel. The continuous channel of energy follows you around once it's in you, like a tick riding on your back."

"Nice."

"It robs people of their free will. This witch wants to use you and not it a good way."

"Tell me about it."

My father was silent for a while, his fingers stroking his beard thoughtfully. "Are you sure it's a mind-control spell and not something else?"

"Yes, I'm sure. What else could it be? I can hear her in my head." I searched the frown on his face. "Why?"

"Yes, hearing voices is never good," answered my father. But I was very aware he'd ignored my question.

"According to my research," I began, realizing we were still hanging in a sort of time-freeze way in the ley line, which I'd forgotten about, "witches aren't very good at mind control. In fact, they're terrible at it. This Jemma might have been able to spell me, but I'm willing to bet that she had help."

"From a demon?" offered my father.

I nodded. "That's what I think. Just like you said, demons are the experts behind mental domination. I need an expert to help get rid of that parasite inside my head."

"Like me," said my father, looking smug.

"Yes." My heart was doing a drum solo. "Can you do it? Can you reverse the spell?"

My father studied me. "Usually, demons don't need to reverse the spell since they most always end up killing whatever being they were using. You need to extract the spell from your mind. It's a critical and complicated process. A lot depends highly on what magic she used. Think brain surgery. One mistake and you could end up a vegetable."

"Great."

"But yes, I can do it. It'll take time to prepare. I can teach you to block your mind from her until the counterspell is complete."

"Thank you."

My father clasped his hands behind his back. "It would be a lot simpler if you just kill her. That would sever the link."

"Yeah. I don't think I'm ready to murder someone just yet." Especially since I had zero proof she was actually doing it. The proof was in my head, and I didn't know how to extract that.

"Hmm. Have you told your aunts?" asked my father. "What do they make of all this? They must be worried sick about you."

I sighed through my nose. "They're not exactly speaking to me right now. They think I made the whole thing up." I pointed to my head. "The voices? Dolores thinks I'm trying to sabotage her chances of joining the Stepford witch's club."

"Oh dear," said my dad.

"Oh shit," I agreed.

My father laughed. He was so easy.

"You get some rest before tonight," said my father. "I'll be there at seven. We can start with basic controls for your demon mojo and see how that goes. Preferably in a room that can sustain some damage. And I'll teach you some techniques to keep Jemma from entering your mind."

I smiled. "Sounds like fun."

"Good." My father straightened his jacket. "It's temporary, but if you can master it, it will help."

"Thanks," I said and smacked him on the arm. "See you later, Dad," I told him.

My father waved. "You'll see me later, Daughter."

I laughed, and he laughed. There was no denying we shared DNA.

With a smile, I watched his image fade as he jumped or teleported or whatever he did to get out of the ley line and back to his world.

A sense of relief pulled on me. Now I could go home and relax. Yeah, who was I kidding? There was no relaxation for me any time soon. My nerves were shot.

Because I knew now, more than before, if I didn't get Jemma out of my head soon, I'd need a straitjacket.

CHAPTER
10

Apparently, wanting to rid oneself of a mental parasite was harder than it looked. And it looked like it was going to be a real nightmare.

After my meeting with my daddy demon, the realization of what removing the mind-control spell entailed had left me feeling drained and tired. Brain surgery was scary as hell. It didn't matter if it was magical or non-magical. There were no guarantees when it came to surgery. Things could go terribly wrong for me, and I wasn't ready to give it a go. Well, not yet.

The knowledge that my father could help me block out Jemma's voice temporarily gave me more time to find proof that this coven of witches was up to no good. Then my aunts would be on my side and even help me.

Wishful thinking? Maybe. Yet I knew it wouldn't be easy.

When I'd arrived, my aunts were in their usual spots around the kitchen table, almost like old times. Except for one thing. They were giving me the cold shoulder—still.

That was until Dolores decided it was time to speak to me.

"So, I hear you're moving out?" Dolores had said to me, her voice dangerously low and aggressive as I stepped into the kitchen. "Shouldn't you be packing boxes? You don't have much, so it shouldn't take you that long."

My heart sank. I was sort of hoping they'd forgotten about that.

I stood there like an idiot, not knowing what to say yet knowing I'd done this to myself. I had a temper. Sue me. And I hated being accused of something when I was innocent.

My gaze moved to Ruth, and she quickly looked away, her face a deep red. Guess I knew who told Dolores, but I wasn't angry with Ruth. Knowing her, she was probably worried that I was going to move out and told Dolores. Dolores wanted me out, no mistaking that frown.

I clamped down on my teeth. "I'll be gone as soon as I can find a place."

With my face probably the same color as Ruth's, I spun around and climbed up the stairs to my room.

Marcus's offer had started to sound really good to me. Maybe I should take it.

The only problem with that was, other than the ley lines, Davenport House provided safe access for me to see my father. And there was the question about training my demon mojo. I didn't think training in a ley line was going to work. What if I accidentally shot my father out of a ley line? Would he survive that? I had no idea, and I wasn't going to take that chance, not with my father's life.

I'd been in the attic in my room since then, counting the hours until seven, when my father would arrive. We could use my room for training. It was away from the other rooms and big enough, thanks to House's magical renovation. If I could slap House a high-five, I would.

A loud growl emanated from my stomach. My protein bars had run their course. With supper around the corner, I was a famished beast. But this beast was too stubborn to go downstairs and fix herself something to eat.

But if I wanted to train my demon mojo with my dad and not pass out from exhaustion and lack of sustenance, I needed food. I needed protein.

I grabbed my phone. Iris was still with Ronin, so I'd ask her to grab me a three-bean salad from Witchy Beans Café on her way home. That is *if* she was on her way.

A knock came from my bedroom door.

"Yes?" I called, looking up and thinking maybe it was Iris. I'd texted her earlier that I had barricaded myself in my room.

Ruth's face appeared, followed by her body and then a tray with something that smelled amazing.

"I don't care what Dolores says," said my aunt defiantly as she made her way inside my room and set a tray of what looked like a glass of water, a plate with cheese, crackers, olives, and you guessed it, a three-bean salad. "I won't let you starve in my own house. You need to eat."

I just about hugged her to death as I squeezed her tiny frame in my arms. "Thanks, Ruth," I said to the top of her white head, and some of her hair found its way into my mouth.

Ruth beamed as I let her go. "You're welcome," she said and straightened her apron, which read IF THE BROOM FITS, RIDE IT.

"I'm famished," I told her and stuffed in as many cubes of cheese as my mouth allowed.

"I'm not surprised. You haven't eaten all day." Her grin grew as I made a three-bean, cheese sandwich with two crackers. I didn't mention the protein bars because I didn't want to take away her thunder.

"Well, I better get downstairs. This should hold you until supper." Ruth turned around. "I've got mounds to do before the dinner party. Let me know if you need anything else."

The cheese melted in my mouth. "Mmm. Is that balsamic vinegar?" I said between chews, my eyes rolling in my head. "Love, love, love balsamic vinegar."

"I know." Ruth giggled and made it to the door when something she'd said before came back and slingshot me in the face.

"Wait? What party?" I held on to another three-bean cheese cracker sandwich in midair, causing a kidney bean to slip and fall.

Ruth turned and said, "The dinner party we're throwing for the Sisters of the Circle. It's going to be a *blast*," she added with wide eyes. She lowered her voice. "My butternut squash is going to *explode* when they least expect it." She slapped her thigh and laughed.

I stiffened. Oh crap.

My earlier cheese was knocking on my stomach wall, threatening to get out. "Wait. What? You've invited them? Those witches are coming here?"

Fear constricted my breathing. Jemma was coming here.

Ruth wrinkled her brow. "Now, you wait just a minute—"

I shot to my feet, rushed past her, and raced down the staircase two steps at a time. I hit the bottom, ran to the kitchen, and skidded to a halt.

The counters and kitchen table were topped with an assortment of food: canapés, bite-sized cheese quiches, mini-veggie pizzas, brussels sprouts, roasted-black-bean burgers, risotto, roasted squash—which I assumed were the exploding ones—couscous salad, tomato, and mushroom linguini, veggie noodle stir-fry, and one of my favorites, spicy veggie chili. The scent of spices and cooked veggies rolled off my nose. The kitchen smelled like a busy restaurant and looked the part too. Dirty pots and pans and dishes were piled in the sink and on the counter.

"I've never seen so much food," I said out loud.

"Isn't it wonderful?" Hildo lay on his back in the center of the kitchen island with a dreamy look on his face. His belly was swollen to the point he looked pregnant or like he had a nasty beer gut.

"Maybe, if it wasn't for the Sisters of the Circle," I said.

"And why's that?" said Dolores's voice behind me.

Great.

I turned around. Her glare was even more pronounced than before. It made her look crazy.

She'd done her hair up and painted her eyes with blue shimmering eye shadow that was in style in the eighties, along with pink lips, and she'd penciled in her eyebrows with black, which only made her look more severe—kinda like Morticia Addams with gray hair. A long, flowing blue dress draped her tall frame. Now, I got the blue eye shadow. She gave off a bohemian look, and if you erased the eye shadow and the eyebrows, she looked quite nice.

Dolores's face twisted into a mask of lines and frowns.

Maybe not so nice.

"I'm warning you," she hissed, sticking a long finger at me. "You try anything. Anything at all, and I'll hex you!"

I leaned back from her finger before she poked me in the eye. "Hey! What's the matter with you? You need to lay off the caffeine, sister. You're acting crazy."

"Dolores!" Beverly appeared and pulled me away from her sister. "Get ahold of yourself. I know you don't have a feminine bone in that masculine body of yours, but please try to control your temper. The coven will be here any minute. You don't want to look flushed and bothered, like you haven't been laid in decades. You look like that every day. This is a special day. So, behave."

Dolores retracted her menacing finger and pressed her hand to her hip. "She's going to ruin this for me. I know it."

106

Okay, now I'd had enough.

"What is your problem?" It was my turn to press my hands to my hips. "Ever since this coven came to town, you've been acting weird. It's like all you care about is them. Guess what? I don't care about your stupid coven. Okay? Let me do you a favor by staying in my room all night. I won't even show my face. Happy?"

Dolores raised her overly drawn brows. "Yes."

"Good." I let out a breath. "Besides, my father'll be here soon to help me with my new demon magic—"

"Obiryn is coming here? Now?" shouted Dolores, outraged, her hands in the air like she was offering herself as a sacrifice to the goddess.

"Yes," I shot back, not appreciating her tone. I narrowed my eyes and took deep breaths to try and stifle my anger. It didn't help. "We're not going to bother anyone, if that's what you're worried about. We'll be in my room. He's here to help me—"

"Absolutely not." Dolores stomped her foot, actually stomped it. "That demon is not coming here."

"Careful," I practically growled. "That *demon* happens to be my father. Who saved my ass—twice." I took a step toward her, looking up into her overly done face. I hated that she was taller than me for times like this, but I wouldn't back down now. Besides, she started it.

107

From the corner of my eye, I saw Hildo jump off the island and felt him brush my legs as he hurried out.

Beverly gave a tiny, forced laugh. "That's right. He did. And we all love him. Right, Dolores?"

"Who do we love?" Ruth came into the kitchen, all smiles. One look in our direction, and her smile faded. "Not this again," she muttered as she moved to the kitchen stove and began stirring whatever was brewing in her four pots.

"Obiryn," commented Beverly and moved to stand next to us. "We all love and respect him. Isn't that right, Dolores?"

"We do," Ruth answered for her.

Towering over me, Dolores just scowled, her frown speaking volumes of disapproval. "He's not coming here tonight, and that's final."

"Yes, he is," I countered, and part of me was astonished both at her behavior and that we were both acting like children.

Dolores's frown deepened further, nearly covering her eyes. "No, he is *not*."

"Yes. He. Is."

"Dolores." Beverly pressed her hand on her sister's arm. "Don't you think you're overreacting?"

Dolores yanked her arm from her sister. "I am most certainly *not* overreacting."

"You kind of are," mumbled Ruth, though Dolores didn't seem to hear.

Dolores threw her hands in the air. "What would happen if they discover that we are harboring a demon in our home? I'll never be accepted. Never."

"Maybe that's a good thing," I said and then quickly regretted it at the shades of red that materialized over Dolores's face.

"You know nothing about the Sisters of the Circle," she said, seething.

"I'm okay with that." Anger warmed me, and I gritted my teeth.

Yes, I was angry, furious at my aunt, but I was also sad. I didn't recognize her anymore. Was this some underlying fear of the coven discovering that I was part demon, thus ruining her chances to join? That sounded about right.

Dolores kept glancing at the digital clock on the stove and then back at me. Yeah, she wanted me gone.

"Don't make me hex you, because I will," threatened Dolores again, her face red with moisture.

I snorted, half in resentment, half in bitter amusement. "Try it, old lady, and see what happens."

"Enough!" shouted Beverly. "I've had enough of you two. You're being ridiculous. You're acting like children. You're supposed to be adults. Act like it."

My pulse pounded like I'd just used a power word. I watched Ruth walk out of the kitchen, balancing a plate topped with canapés as she headed toward the living room at the front of the house.

Dolores turned on her sister. "You know how important this is to me."

"I know," answered Beverly.

"Then how can you be on her side?"

"I'm not on anyone's side. I just want you to stop fighting. Your arguing is giving me a headache."

"I want this dinner to be perfect." Dolores glanced over toward the kitchen. "I can't risk anything going wrong."

"You mean me. Right?" I said tightly, and then the metallic bong of the doorbell vibrated through the air.

The three of us stiffened.

Before we could move, Ruth's voice floated from the front door.

"Come in. Come in. Let me take your coats."

Dolores rushed out of the kitchen followed by Beverly after checking her reflection in the toaster, her red kitten heels clonking loudly.

I watched them go, feeling alone and unbelievably annoyed.

"You're not going to attend the dinner party?" asked Hildo, who'd appeared back in the kitchen.

"I'd rather do a walk of shame naked through the town," I told him. It was the truth. No way in hell was I going to sit through this dinner with a bunch of fake witches, who clearly had a different agenda than what Dolores believed.

Voices and laughter—my Aunt Dolores's loudest of all—drifted from the entrance. I tried to listen to what they were saying, but with Dolores's loud cackling, I couldn't make anything out.

My head bowed, I walked down the hallway toward the stairs, trying to be as inconspicuous as I could. I even stayed on the left side of the wall, practically trying to blend in. I'd sneak up to my room, and they'd never even see me.

I'd made up my mind. I was not going to stay in the house tonight. I was going to pack a bag and stay with Marcus.

The idea of him and me living together had my insides doing some flip-flops. It was nice to see that our relationship was blossoming and heading in a more serious direction. I wasn't complaining. The idea of waking up every morning next to that man would make me leave right now without packing. Maybe I'd just bring my laptop.

I was seriously falling for him, and fast. It was a tentative, quiet love, with a promise of something that would grow if I didn't screw it up. This was also our chance to see if we were compatible living together. From what I could see, Marcus kept his place clean, just like his person. And that was sexy as hell.

I smiled. I was going to enjoy living with him.

I looked up when the soft conversation from the entrance gave way to clipped steps as Jemma appeared in the hallway.

Shit, I'd been so enthralled about living with Marcus, I'd forgotten about the damn witches.

Maybe if I ignored her, she'd go away.

Jemma's face split into a grin. "Hello again, Tessa. Glad you could join us for dinner tonight."

Maybe not.

CHAPTER
11

I didn't even have to look in Dolores's direction to feel the depth of her scowl. "Sorry, but I have work to do that can't wait. Maybe some other time." I gave the witch a blank stare.

I'm onto you, I told her in my mind, narrowing my eyes for good measure. I figured this telepathic thing went both ways.

The slight arch in her perfect brow was my answer. "Well, how disappointing. We were expecting you to be with us for dinner. We were all so excited."

"Of course, she'll stay." Dolores joined us, and I didn't miss that flash of panic across her face. "Your work can wait. Can't it, Tessa?"

My lips parted. How quickly she'd changed. "You want *me* to join you for dinner? Really?" I didn't care to hide the harshness of my voice.

Dolores threw back her head and gave a loud laugh that sounded forced. "Always joking, our Tessa. Her mother was just like that at her age." She patted my shoulder, hard. "Of course, silly. We wouldn't want it any other way." And then she laughed again, the wrongness of it making me cringe.

I wasn't giving up. "Hmm. That's odd. Because a minute ago you were practically throwing me—"

"We're also celebrating your eight months as a Merlin," Dolores blurted, all smiles.

Wow. She was good.

"Excellent. How wonderful." Jemma smiled. The light in her eyes spoke of a possessive strength that made me stifle a shiver.

The last thing I wanted was to share air with this witch, but then again, maybe this was my opportunity to show my aunts just what she was capable of. Maybe they'd sense the mind-control spell she put on me. Maybe she'd slip up. Better yet, I was going to cause that slipup.

Going against my witchy instincts, I bit back my ire and followed Dolores and Jemma into the living room where the rest of the Stepford witches were gathered. The same six that I'd met at the party, including Jemma. I'd imagined there'd be more of them. Guess these were the elite, the top bitches.

Ruth was back, balancing a tray of wineglasses sloshing with red liquid. Smiling, she offered them to the guests. It hit me that Ruth's smile was the only genuine one in the house tonight. It would make for an interesting dinner party.

Looking around, the Sisters of the Circle were wearing their usual fake smiles and their evening best. Jemma was in a blood-red, full-skirted, tea-length, 1950s' swing dress. Another of the Stepford witches wore the same dress, only in orange with black stripes running through it. It seemed to be the theme since the last four were in the same style of dress, one light blue with white polka dots, one metallic silver, one black, and the last one in a bubblegum pink that looked more like what a Barbie doll would wear.

The sounds of conversations drifted around me, and the chime of polite laughter made me sick to my stomach. I wished Iris was here, but she was out with Ronin. I doubted she knew about the dinner. If she did, she'd be here. It would only look suspicious if I texted her now. Besides, I didn't think she was invited. Being snubbed by the coven once was bad enough. I didn't want Iris to have to go through that a second time.

My gaze slid to Jemma, and I rolled the possibility around that she had invited herself over, finding Dolores to be an easy and grateful subordinate. As if feeling my gaze, she turned to me smugly as she chatted with Beverly. Her expression shifted as Ruth entered.

"Dinner is served," said Ruth, bending over from the waist and lowering herself in a curtsy. Then she skipped into the dining room, her bare feet slapping on the hard wood.

The Stepford witches all moved to the dining room, following Dolores and Beverly. I waited until they all took their seats and grabbed the chair at the far end of the table, the one closest to the entrance in case I needed to make a quick exit.

Tessa… why are you so angry? said the voice in my head.

I flinched and gritted my teeth. I would never get used to having someone share the space in my head. Well, for one, that was my space. My head. And it only had room for one of us—me.

Guess my theory of being able to control me only when I was inside that Victorian funeral home went out the door.

I flicked my gaze to Jemma, who was sitting at the other end of the table, chatting it up with Dolores. I had no idea how she could manage to speak to me *and* Dolores at the same time. The witch had some skills, but so did I. And I was still going to take her down.

What you need is a little sex to loosen you up. How about that sensual, intense male you keep thinking about, with the gray eyes? I bet he's spectacular in bed. All those large, hard *muscles.*

I tried to shut my mind off, pushing out all other thoughts, and focused on one thing. Ruth's presentation.

The table was gorgeous; no doubt the three sisters had had a hand in it. Above a crisp white tablecloth sat a stunning winter centerpiece. A tall, three-foot branch sat in a glass vase immersed in pine cones. Tiny candles hung from its branches along with a few silver star ornaments. Six candles in glass jars were spaced out evenly. It wasn't as elegant as Mrs. Durand's presentation. It had a more cozy, rustic feel, but it was still stunning. And I liked it even better because of it.

Especially after I spotted three unsuspecting gnome figurines hiding behind some candles. The one bent over, showing us a butt crack, was my favorite. Gotta love my Aunt Ruth.

Utensils, napkins, water, and wineglasses were all placed perfectly in front of each designated spot. All that was missing were the dinner plates.

Ruth stood at the head of the table, her eyes wide and her cheeks pink as she watched the pleased faces, listening and smiling to every compliment on her presentation. Her expression was as warm and pleasant as a steaming cup of hot chocolate.

"Wait for it," she announced suddenly, her blue eyes shining with determination. Ruth spread out her hands before her, and I felt a tingle of energy over my skin. Then with a clap of her hands, plates topped with polenta lasagna with roasted pepper sauce next to a serving of tomato risotto materialized on the table.

Okay, that was cool. And by the smug smile on Ruth's face, she knew it too.

"Enjoy," announced Dolores, sitting at the head of the table, like the captain of her ship.

The Stepford witches all gave their thanks, and then, one by one, at the same time and in the same way, they picked up their knives and forks and delicately started to slice into their lasagnas.

My mouth parted. It was the strangest thing I'd ever seen. Like puppets being pulled on invisible strings by their master. It was creepy and cringeworthy but also hilarious.

A snort escaped me before I could stop myself. Oops.

I winced and jumped in my seat. My breath caught as pain erupted from my arm like I'd been pinched, hard.

I'd just been pinched by magic. And I knew who'd done it.

I lifted my gaze across the table to Dolores's daring glare, her dark eyes piercing and merciless. She'd just struck me with a spell.

I refrained from using my demon mojo to pinch her back. She might think me a liar, but I wasn't about to embarrass her or ruin her dinner party. I'd find a way to prove it to her. I just didn't know how yet.

But that didn't mean I couldn't hit back.

You're on, Gandalf.

Smiling on the inside, I pulled on the elements around me, ever so slightly, as I drew in my will and focused on the incoming energy soaring through me from the elements.

You should burn off her eyebrows, said the voice in my head. *They look ridiculous. Trust me. You'd be doing her a favor.*

Ignoring the voice, I focused on the black olive on my plate, flicked the fingers from my right hand, and whispered, "Inflitus."

A soft push of kinetic force lashed out from my outstretched hand.

The black olive sailed across the table, dogging the centerpiece, and hit Dolores in the forehead.

Beverly gave a little "oh" of surprise but quickly regained her cool and took a sip of her wine, her eyes crinkling.

Half of the Stepford witches never looked up from their plates while the other half remained engaged in polite conversation. They didn't notice. Too bad. They were missing all the fun.

Frowning in indignation, Dolores didn't even bother peeling off the olive that was surprisingly still stuck to her forehead as her lips moved in what I knew was another spell.

Uh-oh.

I barely had time to react as I felt the wash of magic.

A wave of energy pushed from Dolores, and I jerked as something slapped me in the face, hard, and not unlike someone's hand.

Dolores had just invisibly bitch-slapped me.

Oh, no she didn't, laughed the voice inside my head. *What are you going to do about it?*

The sound of silverware hitting plates echoed around me. Then the table went silent. The Stepford witches all watched with stunned expressions, though Jemma had a weird smile on her face like she'd expected it and wanted more.

I didn't know the spell Dolores just threw at me. She was a much more skilled and accomplished witch than I was, but after tonight, I was going to make sure I knew it.

Come on, Tessa, said the voice. *You can't let her get away with that. Go on. Do your worst.*

I stared at Dolores, the muscles from her jaw clenching, and she had a crazed look in her eyes like she was barely in control of her actions. She was losing her cool. I'd never seen her like this before. And yes, we were behaving like teenagers.

But she'd started it.

"This is delicious, Ruth," said the bone-thin, blonde Stepford witch I remembered, was named Gretchen. She seemed to have noticed the tension growing between me and Dolores. "You must give me your recipe. It's absolutely to die for."

Ruth hurried into the dining room with her apron crumpled in her hands. Her face flushed as she said, "Oh, it's nothing really. The secret's in the sauce." She leaned forward, her eyes wide, and whispered, "Brownie pee."

Gretchen's face wrinkled in disgust. I smiled. Ruth's Brownie pee was the name of a rare mushroom that only grew in Ireland. But Gretchen clearly had no idea. Let's see if they'd want to come to dinner again after that.

I turned my attention back to Dolores, her long face calm and her eyes daring me on in our war. Daring me to do better.

Obviously, I obliged.

With my irritation growing, I tapped into my will. Careful not to call on my demon mojo by mistake because, let's face it, it could happen. I summoned the elements with my gaze on a huge asparagus in my plate.

Holding on to the energy, I raised my right hand—

"Oh, hello. Is this a bad time?"

My asparagus dropped on top of one of Ruth's gnomes.

I looked up. My father stood in the dining room.

CHAPTER

12

Well, this was a pickle.

Busy playing war with Dolores, I'd completely forgotten that I'd set a time with my father to train my new demon mojo and help block Jemma from my head.

Shit. I blinked, my heart pounding, my breath held. "Da—"

"David!" Beverly jumped from her seat and rushed over to my father, her hips swinging. Color high, she looped her arm in his. "So glad you could join us, darling."

Damn. Beverly had just saved my butt. Apart from my aunts, Marcus, Iris, and Ronin, (and my mother obviously), no one knew my real father was a demon. The paranormal community still believed my father was Sean Sanderson, the human musician with a giant ego, who no one had ever heard of, and who my mother married.

Having a demon father would probably make me an outcast. Not to mention the damage it would do to the family name and my aunts.

Who's the silver fox? said the voice in my head.

I flicked my eyes at Dolores. Alarm cascaded over her as she straightened. The panic in her eyes was obvious. Her face took on a greenish tint, not unlike the asparagus I was just about to smack her with.

My father's brows rose in surprise. "Why, yes. Thank you, Beverly." He wore a different suit from the one I saw him in earlier. This one was a teal, three-piece suit. With his hair and beard trimmed expertly, he looked like a middle-aged model for Polo Ralph Lauren. The best part was, he was dressed for dinner, all the time.

Yet, something was different about him. His eyes. His eyes were blue. Not their usual glowing silver. Interesting.

He scanned the table, his new eyes moving quickly over the witches and his features unreadable. His gaze settled on me for a brief moment, and I saw the recognition in them. To anyone else, it just looked like he was politely acknowledging everyone. They wouldn't have caught it. But I did.

My father was on board.

Beverly steered my father closer to the table. "Everyone. This is David."

"Yes, you said," declared Jemma, looking highly amused, her smile widening as she inspected my father like she wanted to take a bite out of him.

"I invited him to join us," said Beverly.

My father looked at Beverly and gave her a warm smile. "Sorry, I'm late. Traffic."

"Of course, darling," Beverly purred and slid her free hand up and down my father's arm.

"Here we go." Ruth appeared with an extra chair and set it next to Beverly's. She hurried off and came back with a plate filled with the same polenta lasagna and an empty glass of wine.

"Ladies," greeted my father as he pulled out Beverly's chair for her and then sat next to her once she was seated.

I smiled. They actually made a nice couple. It made me wonder what my life would have been like if he'd chosen Beverly over my mother.

Some of the tension left Dolores's shoulders as she grabbed her water glass and took a sip.

Next to my father was the red-haired Stepford witch I knew as Candice. She had her eyes set on him, calculating. Her nostrils flared like she was trying to guess his cologne or the paranormal scent he was giving off.

"Are you a witch, David?" asked Candice, not caring to hide her curious yet contemptuous tone.

The glass in Dolores's hand shattered with a loud pop.

Beverly picked up a piece of glass that had landed on her plate. She shrugged and said, "Man hands. She takes after our father."

My pulse hammered in my chest.

Shit. Shit. Shit.

Dolores twitched in her chair, her hand, though not scathed or bleeding from the broken glass, plopped on the table as though she'd lost all motor functions. She looked gray now, almost like a corpse. I didn't think she was breathing.

My father gave a snap of his fingers, and a flock of white butterflies appeared above the table, fluttering up all around us with silver dust sprinkling down like soft snow. The scent of his magic filled the air with a wisp of pine and earth, the White witch scent. *Damn, he's good.*

"Oh!" Ruth clapped her hands. "Oh, look how wonderful. This is lovely, David." And then she jumped in the air, arms flailing, trying to catch one.

Next, my father just pointed to the glass shards scattered over the table. They lifted in the air, and with a white spark, molded back together until they were a solid, perfect glass again. The glass drifted and settled down on the table next to Dolores. Nice.

I glanced around the table. Candice's face was pulled in esteemed approval. So were the others. This dinner would have taken a different turn if they thought he wasn't a witch. He'd passed their test.

I felt myself relax. I hated this group, but at least my secret was safe.

He's not a witch. Is he, Tessa? No, he's something else...

I stiffened. Jemma had access to my mind. It shouldn't be a surprise that she knew what he was.

The voice tsked. *Keeping secrets, are we, Tessa? Afraid of how the world would perceive you if they knew? Knew what you are?*

If Jemma knew what my father was, she wasn't sharing with the others. Why? Why didn't she just come right out and say it?

I waited for the voice to answer, but it didn't.

With a slight *pop*, my father's butterfly exhibition disappeared. I glanced over at Jemma again. She was watching the interaction between my father and Beverly. Her eyes were glinting, but I couldn't tell what she was thinking. No, she wanted to take Beverly's place. That's what.

With his attention still on Beverly, I watched as my father's hand rose slightly above the table. And with a flick of his finger toward

Dolores, the olive on her forehead vanished. If she felt his magic, she didn't show it. I didn't even think she remembered it was there. Her bottom lip quivered as she let out a shaky breath that no one noticed but me. She looked so uptight, so sad, defeated.

Guilt hit. I'd been selfish. I was an asshole. I should have controlled my temper.

Surprisingly, the rest of the night went well. If you counted having a bunch of robot-like witches constantly watching you with a type of knowing curiosity like there was something about you they didn't know.

Still, Dolores had relaxed, and some color had returned to her face. She was all smiles when Jemma paid her *special* attention. If the Stepford witches weren't a bunch of mind-controlling freaks, I would have been happy for my aunt. But I just wanted them gone—from my house and my head.

I jammed the fork into my mouth so I wouldn't have to talk to anyone, which conveniently kept the coven from speaking to me.

Dessert was melted chocolate over a cyclone of vanilla ice cream that kept spinning in their bowls. Now Ruth was just showing off.

When Ruth finally served coffee, I felt myself unwind a little. The dinner hadn't gone so terribly wrong. Jemma hadn't forced me to do something I didn't want to do. In fact, she'd barely spoken inside my head after my father had shown up. Maybe her magic was running out. Maybe trying to control me was harder than she thought.

"I have an announcement." Jemma wrapped her hands around her coffee mug and waited to get everyone's attention before continuing. Her eyes flicked around the table, fixing on each of her coven members before saying, "My sisters and I have come to a decision. We've been expressing our wish to grow our coven, to share our love of the Craft. But we must be careful who we include, as it takes lots of time for the new witch to learn our traditions and become established in our coven. The goddess has blessed us with so many wonderful sisters, and it is time to welcome another." Her gaze rested on Dolores. "But not just any witch. As you well know, only the true proficient and those with a true gift can become a Sister of the Circle."

From the corner of my eye, I saw Dolores straighten in her chair, her expression heavy with pride and her mouth twitching as she tried to hide the smile on her face, but it made her look like she was trying not to fart.

I narrowed my eyes at the coven. If they made Dolores part of their crazy-ass coven, I was about to throw up all of Ruth's hard work.

Jemma's eyebrows rose, and she took on a formal stance. "We would like to extend an invitation to join our coven to a witch here in this lovely house," said Jemma, her voice echoing around the now silent dining room. Her eyes met mine and she said, "To Tessa Davenport."

Ah... crap. Guess I should be packing my bags.

CHAPTER
13

I know I shouldn't have looked, *really* shouldn't, but I couldn't help myself.

My gaze settled on Dolores.

Her scowl was nothing short of terrifying. She leaned forward, slowly, her long face creased into something truly feral as her lips twitched into a snarl. I even spotted some drool. Her face darkened, along with her eyes, making them appear almost black.

If looks could kill, I'd have exploded like a Tessa piñata.

Yikes. My stomach clenched, and a chill rolled through me. There went any hope of mending my relationship with my Aunt Dolores.

Beverly looked uncomfortable. She kept throwing worried glances at Dolores, like she thought her big sister was about to spell my ass. I wouldn't doubt she would. Ruth's head tilted in confusion with a deer-in-the-headlights expression on her face.

My father was also frowning, but his frown was aimed at Jemma as he sat silently in thought. I could see ideas and schemes formulating behind those blue eyes. Yeah, he knew she was up to something.

What hurt and surprised me the most was the accusation in Dolores's eyes. It was almost as though she thought I'd made this happen on purpose. Like I had planned it all along. That I'd gone behind her back and made sure the Sisters of the Circle asked me to join their coven instead of her.

Boy, she couldn't be any more wrong.

"Tessa?"

I turned to the sound of Jemma's voice and looked at her.

"Do you accept?" asked Jemma, smiling as though I'd already said yes, as though saying no was not a possibility. "To become a ? Be a part of the most famous coven in all the witch communities?"

Everyone's attention snapped to me, and a sick feeling sank to the bottom of my stomach.

If I knew a spell to make myself disappear, I would have done it by now.

Okay, people. I knew what I *had* to do, not what I *wanted* to do. I also knew I was about to hurt someone I loved by doing it, but I didn't have a choice in the matter.

Beverly caught my eye. She must have recognized something on my face because she was shaking her head, her eyes wide in a silent "no."

Ruth shifted from foot to foot, a dish towel twisting in her hands, and I was hoping she wasn't imagining wringing my neck.

I couldn't look at Dolores. If I did, I'd lose it.

Instead, I met my father's gaze, full of determination and encouragement that gave me the courage and support that I was doing the right thing. I needed that even though I felt like I was betraying my family. Even though I felt I was going to lose them.

My face warming with a mixture of guilt, frustration, and fury, I finally said evenly, "Yes, I accept." I strained to keep Ruth's fantastic cooking right where it should be. I heard the quick intake of breath from Ruth and the tiny moan escape from Beverly. Bet she'd never done that without being naked and in the presence of a man.

Still, I wouldn't look at Dolores.

I felt like crap, horrible. But being one of them meant I could get close to them and finally figure out what the hell they were up to. And why Jemma felt the need to put a mind-control spell on me.

Jemma reached out and grabbed my hand. Her skin was warm and clammy, and I had to resist pulling back. Even the feel of her skin was creepy and wrong.

"I knew you couldn't refuse," she said. "You'll make a wonderful addition to our coven."

I flinched and snatched my hand from her, focusing on keeping my mind blank and free of my plans. She'd been able to break through the vaults of my mind well enough to know about Marcus. I didn't want her knowing about this.

A chorus of approvals ushered from the coven, and the six of them clapped enthusiastically, their teeth flashing and eyes bright.

I was in hell.

Finally, I moved my gaze over to my tallest aunt.

She narrowed her dark, flashing eyes at me. A burst of jealously passed over Dolores, and I swear I could almost see hate there. It was nearly palpable. I knew she'd never forgive me for this, but I was going to do it anyway. I had to.

Slowly, Dolores pushed back her chair and stood, her lips and fingers moving in a silent spell. Dolores was the fastest spell caster I knew.

She could draw a spell faster than any gunslinger in the Old West could draw his gun and shoot you.

The happy chatter across the table vanished. Everyone froze, including me.

Shit. Now, I *was* going to get it.

But I was saved from Dolores's wrath by the bell, literally.

Knock, knock, said the voice in my head, surprising me since she'd been silent for so long.

"What?" I said before I realized I'd spoken out loud.

The ringing of the front doorbell cut through the voice in my head.

"I'll get it," called Hildo as he padded out the kitchen and hurried down the hallway.

I didn't know how he could open doors, but I didn't look. I kept my focus on Dolores, I mean the witch who wanted to kill me. Or so that's what her face told me. I needed to be ready to protect myself. It sounded insane when I thought about it, protecting myself from the aunt who used to love me, the aunt who always had my back.

Voices drifted but I couldn't make them out over my concentration.

"Tessa. It's your lover," announced the cat, making me cringe. I hated when he called Marcus that. But it seemed to lessen Dolores's fury for a second as her focus moved behind me.

Once I judged that she wouldn't burn me on the spot, I turned from her, stood—a little too fast—and made my way to the front entrance.

Marcus stood in the entryway with a smile that still made me weak in the knees, and that was a good thing. He wore a pair of dark jeans that fit his muscular thighs and thin waist perfectly. His black puffer jacket accentuated his wide shoulders and hid most of what was underneath. But it didn't matter. I knew what was under it. Been there. Done that.

"Hey," I said as I joined him. "You got something for me?" Like those manly hands rubbing me all over to take some of the tension off.

Marcus's smile turned suggestive at what he saw on my face. "I do." His attention lingered on me for a moment, rolling over my waist and my face to my breasts. But then he turned to the voices in the dining room. "You've got company. Sorry, I should have called first." He leaned sideways, trying to get a glimpse, or more like listening to the voices. "You invited the coven here?" he asked me, his voice low though his brows were up in surprise with a side smile.

"More like they invited themselves."

Marcus let out a sigh through his nose. "Well, you're not gonna like what I have to say."

I crossed my arms over my chest. "It's one of those nights. Might as well say it." It couldn't be as bad as Dolores wanting to flatten me like one of Ruth's buttermilk pancakes.

"I did some investigating," said the chief, careful to keep his voice low again. "I even reached out to some of my sources and called in a few favors."

I leaned closer, taking in his musky scent and wishing I could rub my face all over his neck. "And?"

Marcus flicked his gaze over to the dining room area and then back to me. "They're squeaky clean. There's nothing on them. Not even a parking ticket, a late payment on their taxes, or even a phone bill. Nothing."

I hissed out a breath. "Figures. Doesn't that make you a bit suspicious?"

The chief's gray eyes flashed. "Absolutely."

If Marcus couldn't get any dirt on them, I would. And now being part of their coven enabled me to do so. And then, hopefully, Dolores would believe me. That's if she hadn't murdered me in my sleep.

"I have to tell you something. The coven just…" The rest of my sentence was lost as Jemma and the five other Stepford witches stepped into the hallway, with Ruth hurrying to get their coats.

Yasmine, the black-haired witch and the shortest of the coven, which she made up for with her voluptuous body, rolled her eyes over Marcus with a sort of sly sensuality that made my blood boil. No doubt she was wondering what he'd looked like naked or in those white, skin-tight pants their waiters wore.

I slinked my body before his, so all Yasmine could stare at was my face or my breasts. I didn't care which, as long as it wasn't Marcus.

She saw what I'd done, and she gave a soft laugh, which only made my cheeks burn in irritation. Marcus wasn't a piece of meat. Well, okay, he was *my* piece of meat.

Jemma joined us, and with only a stare had Yasmine flicking her eyes away from Marcus and drifting away from us.

Oooh, you're going to love this, said the voice inside my head.

Jemma was nodding as she took me in. "We'll see you tomorrow at midnight for your fitting."

My anger vanished, replaced by my confusion. "My what?"

Jemma reached out and touched my hair. Her fingers grazed my cheek as she tucked a strand on my shoulder. "For your new clothes, silly. Being part of the Sisters of the Circle, one must look the part. It's expected of you."

I wanted to die.

They wanted me to dress like them? What kind of backward coven was this? One with a dress code. The thought hadn't occurred to me. This was going to suck. But I'd have to do it. Apparently, the clothes came with the coven.

It wasn't that the clothes were of bad taste. Hell, I loved Audrey Hepburn's style—she rocked capris and ballet flats—just not six Audrey Hepburn wannabe robots.

Jemma's dark eyes studied me, flicking over my face. "A fitting is part of the initiation ritual, a ceremony all new members must partake in order to join our coven. Your rite of passage. Your rebirth."

It sounded horrible. "Sure." I heard Marcus's soft snort, and I turned my head so he could see my glare. "Yes, okay," I forced myself to say and looked back at Jemma. "I'll be there."

Jemma's smile was way too toothy to be genuine. She said nothing as she hooked her arm with Yasmine's, and they walked out the front door, which Ruth was holding open for them, behind the other four witches.

A dull, sulfurous scent wafted in, and I found myself wrinkling my nose.

Then it hit me. My demon mojo was beginning to smell. Self-conscious, I took a step back from Marcus. We all knew how sensitive his nose was to smells. The last thing I wanted was for him to get turned off by my rotten egg smell. I'd have to ask my father about that too.

Ruth shut the front door. "Well, that went better than expected," she said happily, though I couldn't understand why. Ruth being Ruth, always managed to find something good in the worst situations. "Don't worry about Dolores," she added, seeing my confusion. "She'll forgive you." She stared at me a moment. "No. She won't. Sorry."

"Forgive you for what?" asked Marcus.

"I'll tell you in a minute."

"Come on, Hildo," Ruth said to the black cat sitting quietly in the hallway. "I've saved you some dessert."

The cat spread his lips into a smile. "I love me some dessert."

Beaming, Ruth walked past us and disappeared into the dining room with Hildo bounding next to her, his tail high. I could hear my father's voice as well as Beverly's.

"What happened with Dolores?" Marcus's voice was filled with concern.

A sick, twisted feeling exploded in my stomach as I told him about the dinner with the coven and my acceptance of their offer.

"I only accepted to get close to them," I whispered. "Now that you couldn't find dirt on them, I know I did the right thing. I feel like an ass. The biggest ass. But I don't have a choice."

"Do you still hear her voice inside your head?" asked the chief.

"I do. But it's all talk. She hasn't made me or asked me to do anything." I really didn't get that part. What was the point of invading someone's head if it wasn't to make them do stuff?

Marcus watched me for a long moment, his expression pinched in deep concern. "Have you thought about my offer? With everything that's happening, I don't think you should stay here. Not unless you want to." His gray eyes grew intense, and I felt warmth spread through my core.

I knew what offer he was referring to. And right now, it was the best offer of the night. Just the idea of me going home with him had most of my tension easing out of me. Perhaps the night wasn't ruined after all.

My eyes moved to his lips—I couldn't help it—and when his lips quirked, heat rushed to my face. "I have thought about it. And I acc—"

Marcus bent over and let out a howl as if he were in pain.

"Marcus!" I reached out and pressed my hands on his back, only to be shoved away by his strong arms. I hit the side of the wall and winced in pain as my head hit the hardwood panel.

Still bent over, Marcus thew out a hand. "Stay back!" he warned. "Something's… not… right… I'm… shifting… can't… stop… it…"

Another howl erupted from him just as my father, Beverly, Ruth (with Hildo on her shoulder), and Dolores rushed into the hallway.

"What's happening?" cried Beverly.

I couldn't answer. All I could do was stare as the sound of tearing material filled the air, and then in a flash, Marcus had shredded his clothes until he stood in the entrance in all his naked glory.

Marcus's face and body rippled, a sort of slithery motion just beneath the surface of his skin that stretched his features. He let out a growl as his mouth opened, showing carnivore teeth the size of my fingers. There was a flash of black fur, a roar, another horrible tearing sound, and the crack of breaking bones.

And then, instead of a man, stood a four-hundred-pound, silverback gorilla.

Seeing Marcus change into his beast form was always a pleasure, well, first because I got a glimpse of his naked body, but the powerful creature that stood before me was also extremely terrifying and exciting at the same time.

Only this time, it was different.

"What's going on? Why did he change?" came Dolores's voice.

Ruth whipped out her pink spatula. "Where's the threat?" she voiced, moving the spatula as though it were a sword or a wand.

I pushed off from the wall, staring at the massive silverback gorilla whose shoulders practically grazed the side walls of the entrance. I breathed in the scent of a mixture of musk, sweat, and animal.

"I'm not sure. I think something's made him change." The way he looked both angry and terrified certainly seemed like he couldn't control it. It reminded me of the amulet Silas put over him, taking away his ability to heal.

Fury rumbled my core. Was this Silas again? Did he put some sort of curse on Marcus to get back at me? If he did, I was going to kill that tatted bastard.

With my pulse racing, I moved toward the gorilla until his massive head came up. The muscles on his chest flexed as he stood on all fours, his front hands resting on his knuckles in a posture I had become very familiar with when he was in his beast form. The confusion in his gray eyes tightened my gut.

"Don't worry about it," I told him, not knowing what else to say. "We all mess up our magic sometimes. It's no big deal."

"Speak for yourself," mumbled Dolores.

I kept my eyes on Marcus. "Go ahead. Change back." I was fully aware he'd be buck naked in front of my family, but I didn't care. Something wasn't right.

"Don't worry, darling," said Beverly. "I've seen your father naked many, many times." As though that was supposed to make it okay. She leaned into me and whispered, "You are a very lucky woman."

The gorilla nodded his head and then took a deep breath and closed his eyes, seemingly focusing on his wereape magic and calling it forth. My skin tingled with a sudden influx of power, Marcus's power. It felt warm, pooling over my skin like sunshine.

Marcus's eyes snapped open.

My heart lurched in my throat.

And then nothing happened.

"Nothing's happening," noted Ruth, filling me with irritation.

Marcus's gaze snapped to mine, his eyes narrowing in fury and agitation. His lips pulled back, revealing canines that could chomp off a man's head from his neck in a single bite.

I felt pressure on my arms just as I was hauled back and crashed into my father's chest, his strong grip on my arms.

"He's not himself," warned my father.

My lips parted, and I looked back to find the gorilla shaking his head as a wild panic flashed in his eyes. He was afraid. I needed to get to him. He blinked, and all I saw was a blood-rage fury.

With an earsplitting roar, the gorilla pounded his fists on the hardwood, over and over again, smashing a massive hole. The ceiling, the walls, and the floor sang in resonance with the impact. Splinters of wood and plaster dust showered around us, and I gasped as the ceiling cracked. Damn. He was going to bring the house down.

I wiggled free from my father's grip. "Marcus! Stop!" I shouted.

The front door flew open. Marcus was hauled in the air by an invisible force, and the gorilla was thrown out into the night.

That's what happened when you assaulted a magical house. It fought back.

Crap. "Marcus!" I ran out into the cold night and rushed over to the end of the walkway where Marcus the silverback gorilla pushed himself up on his back legs and began pounding his great fists at the frozen ground in anger.

Okay, so he had a bit of a temper. I did too. I could work with that.

But that's not what caught my breath.

People were screaming. No, wait. Not people. *Animals*.

I cast my gaze down the street, and everywhere I looked, animals were fleeing in the streets in a mindless panic.

I blinked as a white-and-black llama came bounding into view, followed by a beautiful palomino horse and a black horse. Next, three large grizzly bears and three black bears came careening toward Davenport House. About twenty wolves—grays, whites, blacks, and browns—sat in the snow at the border of our property. I spotted another silverback gorilla, smaller than Marcus, which could have been Allison, but there was no way of telling. She or he was tearing up the asphalt, just as pissed as Marcus.

The sound of wings flapping reached me, and I could make out a large bald eagle perched on a branch of one of the oak trees in front of the house. I spotted more birds of prey perched in the same tree, their yellow eyes fixed on the house. A loud growl sounded to my left, and I spotted three cougars (the animals, not the ladies) their ears low and their tails lashing behind them.

Something came at me from the dark sky. I ducked as a tawny owl flew over my head, screeching.

I threw my fist in the air. "I swear. One of these days, you're going down, Gilbert!"

Something small dropped next to my foot in the snow. "If that's poop, you're a dead bird!"

"What in the cauldron?" Dolores appeared next to me, hands on her hips as she took in the scene. "The whole town's gone to hell."

"You can say that again." The whole damn town was a mess. It looked like the entire town's shifters and weres had shifted to their beast forms.

And judging by the collective panic in their eyes, they couldn't change back.

CHAPTER
14

Okay. Hollow Cove was now Open Season.

It was as though the zoo in Maine had opened their gates and let all the animals out, in the middle of winter no less.

But this wasn't the body language of animals frolicking happily in their newfound freedom. I was looking at ears flattened against heads, tails between legs, and the whites of their eyes showing in the moonlight. Eyes gleamed in utter, raging panic.

These weren't the cute zoomies puppies did around the yard. This was a frightened scurried run.

Every shifter, were, and paranormal creature had changed into their beast form and gathered here at Davenport House. Clearly, they expected my aunts were going to fix whatever was happening.

Now that I was paying attention, the scent of sulfur was a hundred times worse outside, more potent. The stink hadn't been me.

I turned back to Davenport House. My father stood in the doorway, a frown on his face. I knew he couldn't step outside or maybe even the porch. I wasn't exactly sure what would happen to him if he did, but I knew it would either hurt like hell or even kill him.

"Rain check on that training?" I called out.

My father's silver eyes had returned, and they surveyed the scene around him. They were hard, somehow frightening, a look I'd seldom seen on his face. "I'll come back tomorrow night," he answered, though not looking at me.

"Okay. Thanks." I watched as he continued standing in the doorway. He didn't look like he was planning on leaving anytime soon. Weird.

Whines, growls, barks, calls, hoots, and the sound of Marcus pounding on the ground echoed in the night air. The beasts were restless. Like I said, a zoo.

"Oh my God. They're all here."

I turned to the sound of Iris's voice and saw the Dark witch walking toward me with Ronin.

"It's like this all over town," said Iris as she joined me. "The weres and shifters are all acting crazy. I've never seen anything like this before. They're half-mad with fear. We followed them here."

"It's a damn freak show, and it's not even a full moon. At least that would explain some of the crazy, but not all." Ronin turned to me and smiled, revealing his flat human teeth. His eyes met mine, and he shrugged at what he saw on my face. "No control. Like their shifter wires are all messed up."

"You're not affected?" I asked, looking over him but not seeing any signs of his vampire alter ego.

Ronin stuffed his hands in his jeans pockets. "No. I'm not."

"Hmmm." I gestured to Marcus, who'd finally stopped pounding the ground and opted for pacing instead. "Looks like only the shifters and weres are affected."

"Not witches either," commented Iris. "I feel fine." She flicked her gaze at my aunts. "You guys all look fine too. I think it's some sort of spell or curse that only affects some paranormals."

"You can feel magical energies?" I hadn't felt anything yet, but Iris was a lot more experienced than I was.

The Dark witch nodded. "I can. Something's here all right. It's well-hidden, but not well enough. The residual magic is cold." Iris looked at the snow-covered ground. "It seems to be coming from the ground. Can't you smell it?"

"Yeah." I felt a sudden thrumming in the air near my feet, but when I tried to pinpoint where it was coming from, it vanished.

"Okay, okay. Calm down, everyone. No need to panic." Dolores moved past me and stood at the edge of the walkway with her arms in the air. "This is what we call a magical conjunction, the crossing of energies. It happened before in 1978. Some of you were here then. Gilbert, you remember."

The owl perched in the tall maple tree ruffled its feathers and gave out a loud screech.

"It's when the Earth's magic crosses with paranormal magic," continued Dolores. "Think of it in terms of crossing the wrong electrical wires. You get a short circuit. It just means that both forms of magic crossed and need to be separated."

Iris leaned over. "You think she's right?"

I shrugged. "No idea. I've never heard of this before. But it makes sense." My eyes went back to the house where my father still stood, watching everyone with something like caution in his expression.

"Let's everyone take a moment to calm down," Dolores was saying with confidence oozing out of her. "I'll have a counterspell up and running in no time. The energies will be separated, and then you can all go home and back to your lives."

At that, most of the anxious paranormals, including Marcus, stopped fidgeting and stilled, accepting and believing that Dolores could fix this, fix them.

I met Marcus's eyes, seeing the traces of heated rage, but also a hint of anxiety and confusion. My heart gave a tug. I shook my head and smiled, trying to tell him that it was going to be okay.

But the gorilla pulled his eyes from me, the muscles on his neck bulging with tension.

I stood back like the others and watched as Dolores started to chant in Latin. Most of the words were lost on me, and I reminded myself that I really needed to study more if I ever wanted to get better and be as good as my aunts.

Power thrummed as the air grew thick with energy and wind blew around us. Beverly and Ruth appeared next to Dolores, and the sisters all joined hands to combine their power.

Energy brushed along my skin as the White witches' magic poured over us and the paranormals, before stretching out into the streets and covering the entire town like an invisible warm blanket, which smelled of cedar and pine and felt like sunrays on my face. I smiled. It was an amazing feeling, like running barefoot in a meadow of wildflowers.

A sudden burst of light blinded me and then was gone.

The chanting stopped, and my aunts let go of their hold on each other.

"The spell is done," declared Dolores, and I couldn't help but notice how she pretended I didn't exist. "You can change back into your human forms at will now." She wore a satisfied smile on her face. "See, there was truly no reason for all this panicking."

My attention snapped to Marcus. The silverback gorilla, though still visibly shaken by this ordeal, had his eyes closed as he concentrated on bringing forth his magic.

Chilled, because I ran out without a coat, I wrapped my arms around myself. I held my breath, waiting, and I sensed that Iris and Ronin were doing the same thing.

When the massive silverback gorilla let out a roar, I knew it hadn't worked.

That triggered frenzied howls from all the paranormals, and a large group of wolves, cougars, bears, and a few deer came surging forward like crazed beasts with one controlling mind.

I didn't think they wanted to hug us.

"Oh crap," I muttered as the shrieks rose, a frenzied chorus of berserk rage. They were going to trample us to death.

"Back to the house!" cried Dolores as she sprinted up the walkway and ran to the porch with Beverly and Ruth in hot pursuit. I was last since Ronin had picked up Iris and with his vamp speed was already at the door when I hit the first step.

And yup, my daddy dearest was still there, in the same spot as before, leaning in the doorway. I wanted to ask his opinion, but I didn't have any time.

Once I reached the top of the porch, I spun around with a power word on my lips. I was going to propel them before they trampled us.

But I didn't even need to.

With a sudden influx of magic, a massive boom shook the ground and air, which made me jump as my heart lurched in panic.

A huge gust of displaced air burst from Davenport House and hit the oncoming horde of panicked beasts.

The paranormals were thrown back forty feet, most of them landing in the street across from the house. Some rolled down to the end of the road, disappearing behind snowbanks.

Smiling, I let out a breath. "Thanks, House."

The sudden loud screech and twisting of wood as though the exterior siding was expanding was my answer.

My smile faded at the look of horror on Dolores's face.

"I don't understand," she said, standing next to me on the front porch. "That counterspell should have worked." Concern shifted on her features as she flicked her gaze over the crowd of paranormals, toward something in the distance.

The three sisters exchanged an uneasy sidelong glance that only lasted a few seconds, but I'd caught it. Something was definitely wrong, and they weren't sharing.

"Oh, I don't like this at all. Not at all." Beverly's green eyes were wide, her pretty face wrinkled in worry as she wrapped her arms around herself. "Did you see them? They've all gone completely mad! They wanted to kill us. They think we're responsible for this."

"I know. I was here," snapped Dolores, her dark eyes scanning the paranormals, who were shaking the snow from their fur.

I looked across the front snow-covered lawn. Marcus the silverback gorilla was pacing again, his eyes wide and wild, and my heart sank at the confusion and unease I saw on his face. He looked trapped, confined in an invisible cage. He also looked like he was about to pound on some parked cars or take down some of the electrical poles.

"If it's not a magical conjunction, what do you think this is?" Ruth was shifting from foot to foot, looking like she needed to use the ladies' room.

Dolores raised her chin. "It has to be a curse. There's no mistaking that. Could be the Twilight coven from New York. They've always been envious of what we have here. I remember Francine saying that one day they'd take down our town and make it their own." Dolores let out a labored breath. "But this is more sinister. My guess is the Guild of Dark Wizards."

Beverly let out a sharp breath, and Ruth crossed her legs, looking extremely uncomfortable. Yeah, she needed to pee.

"You can't be serious!" exclaimed Beverly, shaking her head.

"Who are they?" I'd never heard of the Guild of Dark Wizards, but from the concerned expressions shared by the sisters, I didn't think they were good guys.

Dolores looked at me, and I was surprised she actually answered. "They hate all shifters and half-breeds of any kind. It's no secret they want to remove them from our world. They've done it before too."

"What do you mean?"

Dolores paused and said, "They've destroyed communities of paranormals, just like this one. It started in Europe back in the twentieth century, and I've heard the rumors that they're in North America now. They eradicate all shifters. Anything that is part animal or has a beast form, they kill. And this curse only affected them."

Ruth nodded, her face wrinkling in distress. "That's right. We weren't affected."

"I've heard of these bastards," commented Ronin, leaning on the porch post closest to my father. "They hate vampires too, not just shifters. Yeah, it's gotta be them."

But I wasn't buying it.

"Oh, come on." I threw my hands in the air. "Isn't it obvious? Who's new in town and has the skills and the means to do this?" I stared at their blank expressions. Jeez. I was going to have to spell it out. "The Sisters of the Circle."

Iris's attention snapped to mine, worry lines wrinkling her forehead. "You think so?"

"Yeah, I think so," I answered. "I don't believe in coincidences." Somehow, I knew the coven was involved. The question was why?

"What is this madness?" It was Dolores's turn to throw up her arms. "You just can't stop, can you?"

"Apparently not if you still think this coven is all rainbows and unicorns."

Dolores's long face darkened. "You're one of them now. You accepted the invitation to join their coven. How do you think they'll feel when they hear you're blaming them for this?"

"They'll know I'm onto them." Which wasn't ideal since I wanted to keep those suspicions to myself until I found proof, but Dolores was pushing my buttons.

"You're being ridiculous," shot Dolores, and from the corner of my eye, I saw Ruth, wince. "Your logic has no merit. Give me one reason why the Sisters of the Circle would want to put our community at risk? What would they gain from performing a curse like this?"

Okay, she had me. "I don't know." Yup, I sounded lame, but I didn't know. However, that didn't mean I wasn't going to do my damnedest to find out.

Dolores scoffed. "I don't know who you are anymore."

"Right back at you," I snapped. I could be just as nasty as her.

Beverly stomped her foot. "Would you two just stop it! Stop. How about we stop this bickering and figure out how to help these poor souls."

"It's them," I repeated. "The coven did this."

"If you hate them that much, why did you accept their invitation?" asked Dolores. I heard her teeth grinding, and the sudden flush of anger on her face was truly savage.

I clamped my mouth shut, knowing that even if I tried to explain, she'd never believe me. "I…"

Beverly let out a breath. "Leave it alone, Tessa. Just stop it."

My mouth fell open. "That's not fair. I didn't ask to be part of their coven."

"But you accepted." Dolores looked away from me and stepped to the edge of the porch. "Go home," she called out. "Go home and rest. We'll figure this out in the morning. No need for

157

all this nonsense. Get some sleep. It'll all be okay in the morning."

None of the shifters moved for a long while until one of the cougars got up and padded away. Then all the other shifters followed, everyone except for Marcus.

"Let's go, ladies." Dolores gestured toward the door. "Looks like we have a lot of work to do tonight."

Without another word, my aunts turned and walked back into Davenport House, leaving me, Iris, and Ronin staring back at them.

I realized, then, that my father had disappeared, and I hadn't even noticed.

Anger fueled me. How could they be so blind when it was right there in front of them?

I stared back at the street. "Guess I can't count on them to help now."

"Dolores seems pretty pissed." Ronin leaned on the porch railing next to me. He folded his arms on his chest, his eyes reflecting in the porch light and searching. "I'd hate to be on that witch's bad side. She scares me."

Iris let out a long breath. "For what it's worth, I believe you."

"You don't think it's that wizard guild?" I'd forgotten the name already.

Iris shook her head. "It's like you said. It all started when the Sisters of the Circle came to Hollow Cove. The voices in your head. This curse. Now they've offered you a position in their coven. It has to be connected."

Ronin made a sound of agreement in his throat. "Yeah. Makes sense."

Relief and gratitude washed over me at the loyalty of my friends. At least I could count on them.

"Besides," said Ronin. "The wizard guild wants us dead, period. They don't want me or the shifters to stay in their animal forms. They want us gone, like we never existed. These bitches are just playing with us."

Stay in their animal form.

I stared out into the night until my eyes met that massive silverback gorilla who was the chief in town. Guess I couldn't stay at his place tonight. The gorilla was full of rage. He felt powerless, which fueled his rage. He needed an outlet for it, or he was going to hurt someone, possibly kill.

He was in no shape to have company. I didn't think Marcus would want that either, and I didn't blame him. The thought of having to stay in Davenport House tonight after the continued animosity between me and Dolores made me sick to my stomach.

But I didn't have a choice.

Yet that wasn't the reason why my heart wouldn't stop pounding. "What happens the longer they stay this way?" The gorilla stilled, and I knew his hearing was just as good as it was in his human form, probably better. He wanted to know the answer too.

"Depends on a lot of things," said Iris, worry pinching her features, "including age and type of shifter. But the longer they stay in their beast form, the harder it will be to turn back to their human form." She hesitated, and I knew she was holding something back.

"What is it?"

A flicker of unease crossed her face. "Well, if they don't change back soon, I mean, some might never change back."

"What?" Ronin pushed off the railing, his eyes catching the light of the porch. "Are you saying that these poor bastards are going to stay this way for the rest of their lives if we don't find a way to reverse this?"

Iris nodded.

Shit. The worry that had wrapped around my guts grew stronger and stronger until it blossomed into full-blown anxiety. "How long do we have?"

Iris's face looked pale as tension marred her expression. "Depends on the curse. Forty-eight hours, maybe? Possibly less? After that, it'll be too late. Their beast will take over. They'll forget about their human part and succumb to their animal." Iris took a breath and said, "They'll never be able to change back."

CHAPTER

15

Never change back...

I clenched my jaw to keep the panic that was trying to overwhelm me, back down. "I'm taking these witches down," I hissed.

"I'll do it," said Ronin, and he flexed his hands, exposing his talons like he was getting ready to slice them up. "No one does this to my town without answering to me."

I stared at the half-vampire. I'd never heard Ronin talk like that before, so violent and excited about it. I glanced at Iris and could see the worry lines around her eyes.

"No," I told him. "They're probably back inside that house. It'll have all kinds of wards and spells that'll protect them from intruders. Let me think about it. We can't do anything tonight. They're not stupid. They're prepared. We need to be smarter." I looked out toward the street and saw that only Marcus was still there now. All the other shifters were gone. "But there's something I have to do first."

Iris squeezed my hand. "I'm staying at Ronin's tonight. Call me if you need me."

I nodded. "I will. Thanks."

I watched Iris and Ronin get into his BMW parked at the curb and drive off.

Then I took a deep breath, willed myself down the front porch, and walked straight to the waiting gorilla.

Coils of white smoke shot out of his nostrils as they flared. Fury wrapped his face into an ugly grimace, and when his lips pulled back, fear iced through me.

But I kept going.

I walked and only stopped until we were face-to-face.

"You heard all that. Didn't you?" I asked, my pulse throbbing.

One glance at his expression told me he had. His face was calm and cold and still as if carved from stone. But his eyes. His eyes were like storms.

A muscle in his jaw twitched.

Oh crap.

Marcus burst into motion. He flung himself at the nearest car, thankfully not my aunts' Volvo, and flipped it over like it was a toy, the muscles bulging from his back, neck, and arms. He leaped on the car, fists pounding. Glass snapped and steel groaned as he smashed and pulled at the underbelly of the car, like pulling the innards from a beast.

Next, Marcus lunged at the nearest tree, a tall ash. He thrust his fist at the tree trunk, and it exploded like he'd punched through a paper wall.

Holy gremlin balls, he was powerful.

The top part of the tree tipped and began to fall. He grabbed it and snapped it in half. He raged in the street like a tornado, smashing, pounding, and tearing, so wild and primal in his fury that he was both frightening and hypnotic at the same time. He was dangerous, deadly, and mine.

Okay. Now I knew to never be on the silverback's bad side. He was more terrifying and stronger than I thought. But this was enough.

"Enough," I called out. And when the gorilla kept thrashing at parked cars, I yelled again. "Stop it! Or I'll never have sex with you again!"

Yup, that did it.

The massive gorilla lowered his fists and turned slowly. He let out a long breath but then moved away from the parked car. He joined me on the curb, his chest rising and falling, the tension still visible over his body. Coils of white mist rose from the sheen of sweat covering his body. His breathing was ragged and hard.

I pressed my hands on my hips. "Are you finished?" I waited for him to answer but then realized he'd never once spoken to me in his beast form, or his King Kong alter ego.

Marcus the gorilla made a disgruntled sound in his throat before giving a single nod of his head.

"You can't talk. Can you?" I guessed.

His silver eyes reflected in the streetlight like tiny moons. He shook his head.

"Well..." I sighed. "I've never learned sign language, so bear with me."

The gorilla's nostrils flared as a quiet growl reverberated in his throat that I understood as a yes.

I watched his face, seeing the underlying anger that could erupt any second. Alone, he'd go mad and probably wreck his apartment or even his building. He'd either hurt himself or someone else in the process. And when this was over, that's *if* we figured out how to remove the curse, he'd hate himself for it. He'd never forgive himself.

Which meant I couldn't let him out of my sight until I'd figured this out or he learned to calm his ass down.

I reached out and touched his shoulder.

The gorilla jerked back as though I'd hit him. A warning growl slipped from his throat, his teeth bared as he kept shaking his head.

Fear clawed through me, but I pressed it down and took a step toward him.

The gorilla leaped back again, growling and thrashing his head back and forth in caution.

Now he was just irritating me. "You need to calm down. If you don't, you're going to hurt yourself or someone else. Is that what you want? I get it. You're pissed. I'm pissed too. But acting like a deranged gorilla isn't going to help anyone."

Silver eyes stared at me, narrowing, but he didn't move.

"Good. Now I'm going to touch you, so don't freak out. Okay?" My heart hammered as I took another step, my hand trembling ever so slightly as I reached for his muscled, yet furry shoulder. Was I mad to do this? Probably. Would he rip my hand off? We were about to find out.

My fingers touched dark fur, surprisingly soft and silky. I felt him wince under my touch, but still, he didn't move. Feeling a little braver, I pressed harder until I felt the firm muscles of his shoulders against my fingers. I kept pressing and rubbing until I saw the visible tension lessen from his posture, his body, and even the muscles of his face. And he hadn't killed me. I took that as a win.

I slipped my hand down his arm and clasped his hand with mine, my skin riddling in goose bumps at the rough, yet warm gorilla skin.

"I'm going to tame that wild beast of yours. Got it?"

Marcus the gorilla looked away and gave a long sigh through his nose.

"You're not going home tonight," I told the beast. "You can't be alone. Not like this. The best place for you now is with me. Here. In Davenport House."

The gorilla whipped his head back at me, glaring, and tried to pull his hand away, but I clung on, though I could feel my hand slipping.

Finally, Marcus stopped tugging. With his free hand, he pointed to the house and then slid his finger across his neck.

"I get it," I told him. "House threw you out, but that was your fault. You did attack him. He was only defending himself." Yes, to me House was a butler of sorts.

The gorilla's eyes disappeared under his heavy frown, but he didn't pull away from me.

He was a stubborn, furry bastard. "You *are* coming with me, and I'm not taking no for an answer. It's the only place you can rip apart who can fix himself. But don't get any ideas. House won't let you break things again. So, you need to behave. Will you behave?"

The gorilla grunted and eyed Davenport House like it was an enemy.

Yeah, this was going to be fun.

"C'mon." I pulled on the massive gorilla's hand until he let himself be dragged by me up the front porch and faced the front door. "So far so good. Now, let's see if House still has some issues with you."

I reached out to grab the handle, and the door swung open on its own, warm air brushing against my face.

I glanced back at the gorilla. "See? House agrees that you should be sleeping with me tonight." My face flamed. "Uh… you know what I mean."

I realized how that sounded, but it was too late to take it back. Can you say awkward?

The gorilla's eyes sparked with what I guessed was laughter. He raised his brows suggestively and my face burned even more.

Pretending that I didn't just humiliate myself, I went through first. Though I couldn't see him, I could sense the huge gorilla right behind me, and we hit the staircase just as I heard the front door close.

Voices drifted from the kitchen. My aunts were hard at work with whatever spell or counter-curse they thought was going to reverse the situation that kept the shifters from changing back into their human forms. Emotions tightened my chest. I wouldn't lie and pretend that being pushed aside didn't hurt. I knew accepting the coven's offer would eventually bite me in the ass, hard. I just hadn't really thought about the consequences until right now, at this moment.

Part of me knew I had gone too far, just far enough that perhaps Dolores would never truly forgive me. But it was something I had to accept. Live with. I needed to do this—for me and for them, for all of us. Even if they didn't realize it.

The stairs groaned and squealed under the gorilla's weight. I spun behind me, certain the wood under his feet was about to give way.

The gorilla, Marcus, caught me staring, shrugged, and then actually raised both his arms and flexed, his muscles bulging.

"Okay, there, hot stuff. Keep moving."

Smiling, I led the way upstairs, cringing every time Marcus took a step, but we eventually made it up to the attic and my bedroom.

I hit the small landing, my heart hammering madly in my chest. I didn't know why I was so nervous. It wasn't like I hadn't been with Marcus in this very bedroom before, naked and doing all kinds of naked acrobatics. Only this time it was different.

He had that primal wildness in his eyes as a gorilla that wasn't there in his human form. Not always, and only in flashes. But I'd seen it. It was there.

And it made me extremely nervous.

What if he couldn't control himself?

I wasn't sure what we were going to do once we were inside my bedroom. Guess I'd just wing it.

I pushed my bedroom door open and walked in, waiting for the gorilla to step inside before I closed the door.

My gaze flicked to my bed, and when I looked back at the gorilla, he was watching me with a knowing look on his face.

In a blur, the gorilla dashed across the room, powerful muscles on display, leaped in the air, twisted around, and fell flat on his back on my bed, his arms crossed behind his head.

Okay, then. Time to panic.

The bed groaned and bowed and the bottom grazed the floor. I held my breath, expecting it to collapse. But then the bed bounced back up with the gorilla still in the same position.

If not for magic, that bed would have looked like a pile of match sticks under his weight.

"Ha ha. Very funny," I said, trying to brush off my nerves. "I think you'll be better off on a cot or something. Maybe a couch? I'm sure House can find something comfortable for you."

The gorilla rolled to his side, propped himself up on his left elbow, and with his right hand, tapped the spot next to him.

Cauldron help me.

"Uh…" Yeah, I was totally panicking.

Marcus the gorilla arched his brows, flashed me a mouthful of teeth with a sly grin, and again tapped the spot next to him and waited. It was amazing how similar a gorilla's expressions were to us humans. It was eerie, but I could also read his meaning just as I could from his human face.

Rooted to the spot, I had to physically will myself forward. My heart throbbed in my ears as I neared the bed with the massive gorilla waiting for me in it. I was nervous, but if he tried anything, I'd have to defend myself.

I didn't realize I was visibly shaking until I brushed a strand of hair away from my eyes and caught sight of my trembling hand.

In a flash, the gorilla sat up. His sly grin and smiling eyes gave way to concern and a little disbelief. He turned his head, searching my room, and then the next thing I knew, he leaped off the bed, grabbed my notepad and a pen from my desk, and sat on the edge of the bed.

He flipped the notepad to a blank page and started scribbling. I was surprised how he managed to handle such a small pen with such big gorilla hands. When he was finished, he moved closer to the edge of the bed and pushed the notepad at me.

I gave a nervous laugh as I looked down at the wobbly letters. "You write like a five-year-old."

The gorilla sighed through his nose and shoved the pad at me again, his gray eyes pinched in concern.

I stared at the squiggly lines that were actually readable, just messy.

ARE YOU AFRAID OF ME?

My lips parted and something in my core shook. I felt tears threaten to make their appearance. My emotions were already paper thin because of what had transpired with my Aunt Dolores.

When I looked up and saw his eyes shimmering, I recognized the sadness there, and my heart just about exploded.

"No. Of course not." I shook my head, though it wasn't entirely true. His strength was truly mesmerizing and exciting but also terrifying. Especially if he lost control.

The gorilla began writing again and showed me the pad.

YOU'RE LYING.

Damn, that gorilla was perceptive. Marcus could always see through my bullshit. Guess in his beast form he was no different. Maybe his perceptions, his wereape senses were heightened.

I didn't know what to say, so I just stood there like an idiot. The truth was I was scared that he would lose control. Iris's comments were still very fresh in my mind. The longer they stayed this way, the deeper the pull of their beast. The thought of losing him had fear squeezing my throat until I felt I couldn't breathe. I couldn't lose him.

The gorilla began scribbling again.

I WOULD NEVER HURT YOU. HURTING YOU WOULD BE LIKE HURTING MYSELF.

Okay, I was *not* going to cry. Nope, not crying. Crap. I was crying.

My eyes and throat burned. I didn't trust myself to speak. Now I was about to lose control. I wiped my eyes and nodded.

The gorilla jotted something down again.

IF WE DON'T FIND A WAY TO BREAK THE CURSE, I WON'T BE THE MAN YOU KNEW. I WON'T BE MARCUS ANYMORE. I'LL BE AN ANIMAL.

Alarm shot through me, and my pulse thundered. "We will," I swallowed hard. "We're going to break the curse. You have to have faith."

His face grim, the gorilla wrote something new and flicked the notepad at me.

I WILL LEAVE TOWN. I WON'T HURT ANYONE.

"Don't say that." I sniffed, staring into his sad eyes again that were ripping pieces of my heart. "Just don't." The thought of never seeing Marcus again was unbearable. Not when we were finally in a really good place and moving forward in our relationship.

The gorilla didn't look at me as he wrote again on the notepad.

YOU HAVE TO HEAR IT. IF THINGS DON'T WORK OUT, I WANT YOU TO BE PREPARED.

My heart throbbed in my throat, and I moved to sit on the edge of the bed next to him, my shoulder brushing against his. "I'm going to fix this. I promise. Even without my aunts' help. Because, let's face it, they hate me right now. *I* hate me right now. But believe me. I'm going to break this curse. I swear it."

The gorilla watched me for a moment and then scribbled on the pad again.

ARE YOU STILL HEARING THE VOICE?

"Not since she left the house," I answered. "Whatever spell she put on me seems to only work when she's near me. I think that's good. Well, not *good*, good, but it tells me that her spell is weak if she can't communicate with me when we're far apart. Weak spells are easier to break."

The idea that someone could invade my mind so easily didn't settle well with me. It made me angry. It was a violation. But so far, it was just a voice—a nagging, stupid voice, but a voice nonetheless. She hadn't forced me to do anything.

But it didn't mean she wouldn't.

The gorilla made a sound of agreement in his throat and scribbled a few words.

YOU'RE SEXY WHEN YOU'RE MAD.

173

I smiled. I knew he was just trying to loosen the mood and help me cope with what was happening to me, to him, to us. He was more worried about me than himself. Marcus was truly the very best of men and the best thing that had ever happened to me. No way in hell was I going to lose that or lose him.

Marcus the gorilla shifted his posture, and I felt the warmth of his body through the touch of his furry shoulder as an ache pooled in my core. He wrote something else down and showed me.

I CAN SLEEP AT MY PLACE TONIGHT. YOU DON'T HAVE TO WORRY ABOUT ME.

A flash of guilt took me, and I stared into those mesmerizing gray eyes that seemed to see into my soul. But the sadness I saw in them now nearly did me in.

"Stop. You're sleeping here with me tonight," I told him, hating how weak and shaky my voice sounded. I reached out and clasped his big, black hand into mine. I'd never really realized how big it was compared to my own. His skin was warm, rough, and not unlike his hands in his human form, maybe just hairier and twice their size. "Besides. I won't be able to sleep if you're not here. I'll worry. And I'll stay up for hours. And I need my beauty sleep." I smiled at him, and he smiled back, though weakly.

Okay, time to kick my lady balls into high gear.

I let go of his hand and pushed the gorilla as hard as I could on his chest toward the bed, which moved him exactly one inch. "God, you're a heavy bastard. Scoot over. I like sleeping on the left side of the bed."

This time the gorilla's smile was genuine, and it transformed his face, making it soft and cute, not at all scary and wild and unpredictable.

With a powerful thrust of his legs, the gorilla bounded up on the bed as he did as he was told. He moved over to the right side, on top of the light-gray comforter. He crossed his hands under his head and waited.

"If you fart, I might have to kill you," I warned and pulled off my boots, jeans, top, and bra and tossed them on the nearest chair to the bed. I peeled away the comforter and sheet and slipped in.

The gorilla snorted, and a deep series of rumbles sounded from his chest. He was laughing.

I didn't realize how tired I was until my head hit the pillow and a wave of drowsiness overcame me. Though the beast next to me did not smell like the sexy, musky male scent I was used to but more of an animal scent that resembled a dog. It wasn't a bad smell at all. I found it soothing in a way.

The sheets pulled, and I felt a warm, callused hand wrap around mine. The two of us lay still in the bed, holding on to each other like that for what felt like hours, both lost in our thoughts.

Anger and fear sparked through my body. I was both enraged and terrified. Enraged I might not break this curse in time. Terrified this was as close as I'd ever get to be with Marcus ever again.

And terrified I was about to lose him forever.

CHAPTER
16

I stood on a black dressing puff—not sure what else to call it—while the entire Stepford witches' clan goggled at me like I was a hot item on sale at Macy's. I'd arrived an hour ago, and after useless small talk, they stuffed me with pastries and tea that was so sweet it was practically syrup and then yanked me up onto a puff.

I was in the same elegant room with lots of drapery and large, expensive Persian carpets, where they had held their little dinner party a few days ago. But now, instead of a room packed with witches and sexy waiters with their meat twinkies on display, it was just little me and the Sisters of the Circle.

When I woke up this morning, Marcus was gone. In place of the massive four-hundred-pound gorilla lying next to me was a note scribbled on my notepad.

Gone to check on the town. It's complete madness.

I hadn't understood his meaning entirely. But when I had made my way downstairs after a quick shower, I understood why.

A wolf was lying on the kitchen table, a deep gash across its middle, staining its light silver fur with bright red.

"What happened?" I asked as I rushed in.

As soon as I had entered the kitchen, Dolores had stood up and left without even a glance in my direction.

Hey, at least she was consistent.

Ruth had looked up, her hands stained with the wolf's blood, holding a needle and thread. "Abby's been in a fight. She came to us early this morning looking like this. Poor girl."

I didn't know Abby, but Ruth knew her well enough to recognize her as a wolf. "But who would do this to her?" I asked.

"Looks like it was another wolf," answered Beverly. She had dark circles under her pretty green eyes. "Probably wanted to mate with her, and she wanted nothing to do with that beast."

"She's the fifth shifter we've healed since this morning." Ruth wiped her brow, leaving a long blood smear. "The town's gone mad. They keep coming in, and we keep having to fix them."

"It's like they can't control their beasts," answered Beverly. "The wildness is slowly taking over. And it'll only get worse the longer they stay in their animal forms." She echoed what Iris had told me last night. "If we can't find a counter-curse to break this curse, there's no coming back from this."

I shifted uneasily. "How is that going? I mean… did you figure something out? Are you closer to finding something to break the curse?"

The silence that followed was discouraging.

"Dolores is still working on a counter-curse," Beverly finally said. "She believes she can break it." But by the doubt in her voice, I didn't think she believed it.

"How was Marcus with you?" asked Ruth, the concern in her tone and her face had my tension thumping in my veins.

"He's fine. He left early this morning. Why?" I knew what she was asking. But so far, Marcus was just fine. He was still him. But for how long?

Ruth pinched the skin around the wolf's wound, stabbed the needle through it, and began to stitch her up. The wolf didn't even flinch. "Umm… just wondering how he's doing. He was here, you know," she said. "He helped us pin down Yuri—a werecat, a cougar. His right eye was scratched, and his left ear was bitten right off. If it wasn't for the gorilla's strength, we wouldn't have been able to help Yuri."

Damn. And I'd slept through it all.

I rolled up my sleeves. "What can I do to help?"

Ruth pointed to the kitchen. "You can start by bringing me more of my organic honey over by the kitchen island. We have to rub it on her wound, so she won't get an infection."

And that's how my morning went. And afternoon. And evening. And most of the night.

Twenty-five more shifters had arrived at Davenport House for aid, and by the time the last one was fixed up, it was time for me to go to my midnight "fitting" appointment.

Gretchen, the tall, skinny blonde in a white dress with a pink flowered print took a step forward, her pink pedicure showing from her white, high-heeled sandals.

She gave me a pleasant and false smile as she said, "Time to begin. Clothes off."

The face I made probably made me look constipated. "Right. About that…" I wasn't about to take my clothes off in a room where I knew everyone was looking directly at me. I wasn't a prude, but a girl had her limits. "Do you have a bathroom where I can change?" I asked, remembering Jemma mentioning one upstairs somewhere.

At that, all the witches giggled, cementing the reasons why I didn't like this group.

The fact that they didn't even mention the crazed paranormals running through town, which was impossible to miss if you stepped outside, made them all the more guilty in my book.

Gretchen kept that phony smile on her face and raised her manicured hand that matched her feet as she twirled her finger in the air. A ring with a large ruby circled her finger, which I'd never even noticed before, and glowed like hot coal.

A hushed sound was followed by a dull rustling of clothing and then a tug. With a flash of light, the air around me hummed as I felt Gretchen's magic sizzling. I heard a sound like a distant wail I couldn't pinpoint, and in another rush, I felt the spell leaving me.

And then… I was buck naked.

Well, not entirely. My jeans, sweater, cami, and even my socks were gone. I stood, wearing only my bra and underwear and the frown of the century.

"Oh look. She's got cellulite all over her back thighs," commented Yasmine, and my face felt like I'd stuck it in an oven.

Yes, I was humiliated, but my anger was the winning emotion.

I didn't know how I managed to control my demon mojo, but somehow I did. The goddess must love me.

"She could use some tightening up here… and here… and she'll need a lift too," I heard Candice say as she moved behind me.

"Are you talking about my ass?" What the hell was wrong with these witches? Marcus happened to *love* my ass.

Jemma let out a breath and joined Candice and Yasmine behind me. "She's got a little back fat and some hair right over here on her love handles."

Kill me now.

"We need to remove at least twenty pounds."

"Well, ladies," said Jemma. "Let's get to work."

I turned on the spot, tempted to jump down from the puff, and glared at these witches. "You're not touching my body. Forget it." I'd heard about some glamour spells that could nip and tuck your imperfections for a few hours, but I'd never been a vain enough person to even want to try. And why bother? They didn't last.

It was obvious they all did this to their bodies, morphing and changing them until there was probably nothing left of the real them.

I realized now why they looked so fake because they *were* fake. Through and through.

Jemma's face split into a creepy smile. "Don't worry, Tessa. We're going to make you beautiful," she added, her voice dripping with more falseness. At this rate, I was going to need a mop.

I glared at her more. "Oh, really?"

Jemma's eyes widened as she said, "We're going to remove all that cellulite and give you the legs of your dreams."

Oh, hell no.

I straightened and pressed my hands to my hips. "No. I happen to like my cellulite, thank you very much. In fact, I love it." Damn, never thought those words would ever leave my mouth. But there you had it.

"We've all done it," soothed Joan, mistaking my reluctance for nerves. "It's nothing. I removed fifty-five pounds from my body. Gave myself new breasts, a new butt, a tight stomach, new lips, and a few face lifts. I have the body of a twenty-year-old."

I wanted to puke. "You could just diet and exercise like the rest of the world," I practically growled. "What's wrong with a few wrinkles and flabby arms? Nothing, that's what. Aging is a natural part of life. You should embrace it, not shun it."

The witches all screwed up their faces like they'd just tasted something unforgivably sour. Yasmine retched like she was about to throw up.

Jemma pinned me with her eyes, which seemed to glow with intensity. "Don't you want to be a better version of yourself?"

"I don't think we agree on what a better version of oneself *is*." In part because, to me,

183

that was your spiritual part. Not your physical. Embracing who you were and accepting it.

Jemma's face twisted, losing some of her composure. "Tessa. Don't you think you're being a little excessive? There's nothing wrong with changing one's appearance to make it more… attractive."

I stared at each witch in turn, slowly. "You're not changing the way I look. And that's final. If you don't like it, I don't care." I knew I was stretching my luck. They could tell me to leave and cast me out of their coven. But this was where I drew the line. I'd just have to figure out another way into their schemes.

I wasn't sure how long I stood there in my panty and bra glory while they all looked like I'd slapped them across the face. I wished I had.

I just wanted to leave. Problem was. What the hell happened to my clothes?

"Fair enough," announced Jemma suddenly. "If Tessa doesn't wish to improve herself, that is her choice."

I narrowed my eyes at the witch, hating how she was making it sound like I was lesser now that I didn't want my cellulite gone. Like it made me less significant somehow.

"Let us continue." Jemma walked back around and faced me. "What's your favorite color?"

My lips twitched. "Black."

Jemma's eyebrows flew to her hairline. "Another color, perhaps?"

"Blue, I guess."

"Ah, yes. Blue is fine. Though with your complexion, red or even burgundy would look marvelous."

"Sure. Whatever."

With a satisfied smile, Jemma raised her hands, and I spotted a similar ring on her finger, though hers had an emerald stone cast in it. "Sisters. Let's get Tessa ready."

Together, the witches all raised their hands above their heads and began chanting. The language was strange. I'd never heard it before, or maybe I had, but having them all chanting it at the same made it difficult to grasp.

Their voices grew steady and strong. My heart shuddered in sudden unease. I knew I was about to be hit with their magic, but I still jerked when I felt it.

A gust of their combined power hit me from all sides, and I gasped at the pressure I felt against my body, like a giant hand was squeezing the air out of me, or possibly popping my head off like a dandelion. The pressure lessened, and a mist of reds, oranges, yellows, blues, and pinks rose around me. The mist quivered and formed a vortex.

And you guessed it, I was in the middle of it.

Colors spun around me until I couldn't make out any of the Stepford witches. Though I could hear their voices as they continued to chant. Power rolled, and their voices screamed—no, wait a minute—those weren't the steady, clear witches' voices. These were different. The voices were faint, as though distant, and too high pitched. It almost sounded like the voices of haunted spirits as they screamed and wailed their tormented replies while trapped in the maelstrom just like me.

What the hell was this? Who were those screaming voices?

The power made it hard to breathe, and the roar of the wailing spirits, and the chanting voices of the witches grew steadily stronger until their voices and the spirits became part of the vortex as it boomed and echoed all around.

And then it stopped.

My ears rang in the sudden silence that followed. My balance wavered, but I managed to stay upright.

Yeah, something was up with their magic. This wasn't White magic. If I had to guess, I'd say these ladies were dabbling in the Dark arts. Which was fine. Hell, I dabbled in both. But why were they hiding it? Why pretend to be conjurers of White magic when it was clear it was Dark?

The screaming voices were gone, replaced by a loud chorus of applause from that sicko coven.

"Oooh! She looks amazing!" cried Holly, clapping her hands the way Ruth would.

"That color looks incredible on her," commented Joan. "Definitely makes up for the other imperfections."

Candice beamed, her eyes sparkling. "A bit more cleavage would have been better, but nothing a good push-up bra can't fix."

Gretchen and Yasmine had commented as well, but I didn't care to listen.

I stared down at myself. A burgundy dress hugged my hips and flared out hitting just above my knee. Black, open-toe shoes peeked at me from below, and I noticed my toes had been painted in the same color as the dress. And when I reached up and touched my hair, well, I nearly screamed.

It was rock solid like I'd used five cans of hair spray.

Cauldron help me. I was wearing a stiff on my head.

I met Jemma's gaze. "Do you have a mirror?"

Jemma raised her jeweled hand, her lips moving, and with a snap of her fingers, a tall, antique standing mirror appeared in front of me. One glance at myself, and I kinda wished I hadn't asked for it.

"I feel like I'm stuck in a rerun of the movie *Hairspray*," I said, staring at the height of my hair piled on top of my head in a beehive style. The dress was off the shoulders, and I hated to say it, but it fit me perfectly and molded to every curve, bump, and lump of my body. I had more

187

makeup on than Martha, and she practically used up one lipstick every day.

"Such an improvement to what she looked like before." Holly, a beautiful black-haired witch, with Asian features, was staring at me with a toothy smile on her pretty face. But was it really hers? I mean, look what they did to me. Who knew what they truly looked like?

"She's like Cinderella." Candice beamed. "And we're her fairy godmothers."

"An ugly duckling transformed into a swan," stated Gretchen.

Nice. I glanced away from my reflection before I vomited over this dress. My anger rebounded in me, matching my thrashing heart. I could feel my demon mojo wanting out, and it took a huge amount of self-control to tame it and push it back down. Sprouting black tendrils from my fingers wouldn't win me any pointers with this coven. I had to play it cool.

Aren't you adorable, mocked the voice in my head.

I frowned. *Go to hell*, I told her in my head.

Now, now, why so angry, Tessa? You accepted the invitation. Part of you must have known you'd have to play dress-up.

I closed my eyes and sighed through my nose, trying to keep all those pent-up emotions from bubbling out of me. I was so filled with guilt and anger that it was a miracle I hadn't blown up by now and strangled a few of those Stepford witches with their dresses.

I wonder what Marcus would say if he saw you now...

I clenched my jaw until it hurt. I didn't want to think about Marcus right now, of what was happening to him. If I did, I was definitely going to lose it.

My eyes snapped open, and I focused on Jemma, her eyebrows high as she spoke softly to Joan.

You know what? I told her. *It seems to me that the other members of this backward coven don't know about our* special *connection. Do they? Seems to me that's why you're talking to me in my head and not out loud in front of them. I think I'm going to tell them. Yeah. I think I'm gonna. I wonder how they'll feel when they find out you've been doing this behind their backs.*

The voice giggled. *Oh, do it. I dare you. Let's see what they do. Go on. Do it.*

Hmm. I didn't like how happy she sounded at the prospect of me blabbing. Looking at her now, I couldn't even fathom how she could talk to two people at once. And I hated her for it, for doing this to me.

I stared at my reflection again. To cozy up to this coven, I needed to play the part. And that included making me look ridiculous.

"Now what?" I asked. If they were going to parade me all over town, I might have to kill myself.

"You're done for the night," said Jemma, looking pleased with my transformation. "We have an important meeting in Cape Elizabeth, and we mustn't be late."

That, my friends, was music to my ears. It meant the house would be empty.

I didn't know and didn't ask who they were meeting up with so late at night. Trying not to smile, I stepped off the puff, tripped in my new shoes, and managed to stay upright by a miracle.

I looked around. "Where are my clothes?"

Jemma wrinkled her face at me. "We destroyed them."

"You *destroyed* them?"

"And by the looks of it," said Jemma, pointing at my shoes, "you need to practice walking in those. We can't have a Sister falling all over herself. Can we? You need to familiarize yourself. Stand straight. Shoulders back. Chest out and walk."

Jemma and all the other Stepford witches walked in single file out of the room, like they were parading on a catwalk with carrots up their butts.

I managed to follow them to their foyer in those shoes. Heels that high should be illegal.

Holly wrapped her pink, wool winter coat around her shoulders. "Do you need a lift?"

My eyes found my boots lying at the entrance where I'd tossed them. "No thanks. I can walk." When Jemma raised her brows at me, I added, "I'll practice at home. That way, no one will see me if I fall."

Apparently, that was the right thing to say, as Jemma looked positively pleased when she stepped out the front door.

Once my boots were on, I walked out onto the platform with them.

"See you later," said Jemma as she shut the front door behind us.

But before I could ask her what she meant by that, she hurried away with her coven and made their way to the parked limo at the curb waiting for them.

I stood in their driveway, smiling and waving them off as the limo disappeared.

My smile was genuine as I reached for my phone and began texting Iris.

With them gone, it was perfect. It meant that I had at least an hour to search the funeral home.

Starting now.

CHAPTER
17

"**W**hat the hell are you wearing!" Ronin's rich laugh echoed around him as he shut his car door. He could barely walk he was laughing so hard.

I narrowed my eyes and pinched my fingers together. "I'm about *this* close to punching out your vampire teeth," I hissed. "I'll beat the vampire out of you."

Ronin clamped his mouth shut, his face twisting as he tried hard to keep his laughter inside. He raised his hands in surrender. "I'm sorry. But what did you expect? You look like an overdone housewife from the fifties. I mean, look at you!" He studied me a moment. "You think I can get an outfit like that for Iris—ouch!"

Iris punched him on the arm, though a tiny smile curled her lips. "Leave her alone. Don't you think she's been through enough already? Having those witches do her up like a doll? It took a lot of self-control to let them. I wouldn't have been able."

The half-vampire rubbed his arm. "I didn't say she didn't look hot. She looks hot. Like *vintage* hot."

I shook my head at him. "He's right." I touched my hair and cringed. "I look ridiculous. I feel ridiculous. You can say it. I've said it." I was glad Marcus wasn't here to witness my humiliation. I had a sudden feeling of being dirty. All I wanted was to go home and jump in the shower to wash away the layers of the Stepford witches' magic off my skin.

"I think you look cute," said Iris, grinning encouragingly and showing the dimples in her cheeks.

I laughed and checked the street one last time. "C'mon. We need to hurry." I shot forward, running as fast as I could in a dress, which was more like an awkward speed walk, and climbed up the stairs of the funeral home.

I pulled on the door handle. "Locked. Figures they wouldn't leave it unlocked." I hadn't even seen any of them lock the door.

"Stand back." Iris joined me on the porch. She tapped the messenger bag that hung across her chest. "I've got Dana with me," she said as though that would solve all our problems. Working fast, she knelt and pulled out Dana. She flipped through the album and peeled off what looked like mud or something else I didn't want to think about. She then stuffed it inside the keyhole on the handle, mumbled a few Latin words, stood up, and yanked the door open.

My eyebrows rose, impressed. "Now, that'll come in handy."

Iris beamed. "I always come prepared."

I set out my witchy senses, looking to feel any curses or magical energies, but felt none. I hadn't felt any when I came in for my fitting either. I traced the edges of the door carefully, not seeing any visible wards, but that didn't mean there weren't any.

"I'm not sensing any wards," said Iris, reading my thoughts and searching my face.

"Me neither. I thought maybe they'd have put up a curse or something for burglars."

Iris raised her hands around the doorframe. "I'm not feeling any energies or any magic residue. We're good."

I took a breath and stepped through with Iris and Ronin right behind me.

None of us combusted into flames. I took that as a good sign.

"How long do we have?" asked Ronin as he shut the door but not before glancing down the street one last time.

I exhaled. "An hour maybe? But let's give ourselves a half hour. Just in case."

"So, what's the plan?" asked Iris, as she curled a lock of black hair behind her ear. "Do you know what we're looking for?"

I whipped my boots off on the rug in the foyer. "We search the house for clues. Anything that'll prove they're behind this curse. With a curse of this magnitude, this level, there's got to be some kind of magical materials around somewhere. Something I can show Dolores."

"She still won't believe you?" Iris gave me a sympathetic smile. "I bet accepting the coven's invite didn't help."

Ronin shook his head, looking a bit more serious than before. "I can't believe you accepted. That was like signing off your death wish."

Guilt bubbled up again and I forced it down. "I had to. If I didn't, we wouldn't be here right now. I needed a way in. This was it."

"Good point. Where do we explore first?" Ronin ran a finger on the edge of a wainscot panel. "It freaks me out how clean it is in here. It's cleaner than my place."

Iris looped the strap of her bag around her shoulders. "We could check the bedrooms first." She flicked her gaze around the lobby. "I doubt they'd leave any evidence of any spell work lying around for visitors to see."

I nodded, checking my phone. "Good idea. I've already seen the living areas."

Together, the three of us climbed up to the second floor and searched the first bedroom. Just like everything else, it was squeaky clean. So was the second bedroom and the third and every single bedroom, including the ones on the third floor. Nothing. Nada. We checked the attic, and all we found were cobwebs, dust mites, old boxes, and mice poop.

My mood souring, I climbed back down to the main floor, my eyes everywhere at once.

"Maybe you're wrong about them," said Ronin. "Maybe they're just a coven of horny, old spinsters. Some are, you know."

"I'm not wrong." I knew it in my heart, the Sisters of the Circle were responsible for cursing the town and getting in my head. The evidence was here. I could feel it in my witch bones.

"The basement," I blurted, wanting to kick myself in the ass for not thinking about it sooner. "It's gotta be the basement."

Iris looked past me to the hallway. "But where's the entrance? I didn't see a door. Not all the houses in Hollow Cove have basements. Some just have a crawl space."

"This one does." It had to. But if there was a basement, where was the door?

My eyes found the staircase, and I was moving again. I stood facing the wall below the massive wooden staircase that led to the other levels. Usually, the basement stairs coincided with the staircase going up to the other levels. They were stacked together. Head room and all that. But we only saw wainscoting and navy-blue wallpaper above it.

No door.

Yet I felt something. Call it my witchy intuition, or my new badass demon mojo — something was calling to me.

It was almost undetectable. Almost. But I *felt* it — a quiet humming of power.

Acting on instinct, I pressed my hand on the wall, and my heart lurched in my chest. A rush of energy leaked through the wall, gliding over my skin.

"There's definitely something here," I said as I removed my hand.

Iris followed my example and pressed her hand on the wall. "She's right. Wow. I would have missed it if it weren't for you. How did you know it was there?"

I stared at the wall. "My demon mojo." I had no idea how, but I knew I was right.

"That's all very informative," said the half-vampire, his fangs gleaming in the light of the hallway. "But it still doesn't give us a way in. Do we bust down the wall? I don't mind."

Ronin rolled his shoulders, getting ready to use his vamp strength to knock it down.

"Wait," I said, pulling him back. "I don't want them knowing that we know. At least not yet. Not until I have proof."

"Okay," said Iris. "I can make up a molecular potion that will break down our molecules to enable us to move through walls."

"No shit," said Ronin, looking impressed. "You can do that?"

Iris smiled. "I can, but it'll take at least a day or two."

I shook my head. "We can't wait that long. Marcus and the others will be trapped in their beast forms by then. We need to do this now."

"How?" asked Ronin.

I stared at the wall. "Maybe it's not that complicated." I'm not sure how I knew. I just did. I took a breath and said, "Open."

And I shit you not, a door materialized in the wall space I was staring at.

The wall rippled with a quick flickering of color, and when it settled, a door made of what looked like oak stood in its place.

The air thrummed with the same power I felt before, only stronger. Much stronger. And familiar, but I just couldn't put my finger on it.

Ronin whistled. "Damn, Tess. When you're good, you're good. That gave me chills."

I beamed and hitched up my dress. "Thanks."

With my blood pressure spiking, I pulled the newly materialized basement door open and found a flight of stone stairs staring back at me that led down into complete darkness. Yeah, my favorite.

But just as soon as my boot hit the first step, a series of lights illuminated the stairs, bathing everything in a soft yellow.

"Nice," said Ronin, his head just above my left shoulder. "You have to admit that was kind of impressive."

Taking it as a good sign, I climbed down the staircase with Iris and Ronin following closely behind me.

A flicker of something cold and dark rippled in the air. It tugged inside my chest as an icy shudder ran through me.

Sweat beaded on my forehead as I hit the basement floor and looked around. Stone walls surrounded us, and packed earth met our boots. It was unfinished and dark with no visible exits except for the stairs behind us. The ceiling was at least seven feet high, which was an impressive height for a basement in a house of that age. Chairs, tables, and a desk were strewn against the walls as though to make a larger space in the middle of the basement. And then I saw why.

The first thing that hit me was the stench. The air was hot and smelled of mildew and rot, like a few decomposing bodies might be hiding in here. They probably were.

The next thing I noticed was the giant summoning circle, lit with black candles and painted in, you guessed it, blood.

It was by far the largest magical circle I'd ever seen, fifteen by fifteen feet at least, and took up a major part of the basement. Strange runes I'd never seen before were written in fresh blood inside the circle, suggesting more of an angelic script than the common demon summoning.

What's the third thing I noticed? Well, that would be the portal that hovered above the circle.

I blinked at the undulating black hole looming before us, rippling like black water.

"Holy fairy tits," cursed Ronin, his eyes wide as he stared at the shimmering black void. "Is that… is that a…?"

"A Rift," I answered, tension pulling through me. "A doorway into the Netherworld."

CHAPTER
18

The Rift heaved. I could feel the faintest presence of another world there, where energy pulsed and thrummed just beneath the surface of reality, of our world. The air around me suddenly shot down ten degrees cooler.

Rifts were small pockets, crevices in the Veil that enabled demons to cross over to our world. Sometimes they were unintentional, and sometimes they were created.

Just like this one.

And yet Jack, the Soul Collector demon's job required that he traveled to our world, but it was more of a world-jumping, or teleportation. It was a different kind of travel. This was a hole.

Holy fairy tits, Ronin was right.

But I couldn't see through to the other side. I wasn't sure what to expect—a red, burning world with millions of screaming souls? But that didn't sound right. At least, not the way my father described his home world. But the Rift felt solid somehow as though it wasn't fully transformed. Incomplete.

The hum of constant power was similar to the power I'd used only just recently. Demonic power.

"It's a crossroads between worlds," said Iris, eyeing the Rift. "I've never seen one before."

I scanned the circle, feeling the power thumping. "Could this be the cause of what's been happening to the shifters and weres? To Marcus and the others?"

Iris looked at me. "No. Whatever's affecting the paranormal community is a curse. An elaborate one but still a curse. Opening portals have nothing to do with removing the ability to shift. There must be something here." The Dark witch moved to a side table I hadn't noticed. "I hate being right."

"What?" I joined her, my hip bumping against the table. "What is all this?"

The buzzing of flies was enough to make me want to puke. A large bowl with what could only be blood sat on a table surrounded by blobs of melted wax that used to be candles. Next to it were symbols carefully wrought in white chalk.

Blood was everywhere, scattered in droplets and splashed against the wall. Along with pulp, gelatinous masses of flesh that looked like the remains of a heart rested on the table.

The remains of a dead animal, goat I guessed, from the tiny horns lying crumbled in the corner. The upstairs was spotless, but the basement was the complete opposite. I'd seen my share of nasty, but this was utterly disgusting.

Iris picked up a sheet of paper stained with bloody fingerprints. "Here's your proof."

I leaned over. "This is the curse?"

"It is. It's called the Goblet of God," answered the Dark witch, handing me the paper. "It's a transfiguration curse. It's why the shifters and the other paranormals can't change back. I've never heard of any witch or wizard being able to do one. This is top-level magic. Above Merlins. Above everyone."

I stared at the writing, barely visible in the lack of light. "I've never heard of the Goblet of God. Don't think I've even read about it in one of Dolores's books."

"I have," said Iris. "Not only is it the most advanced magic around, but it also takes months of preparation. Five months at least to get it right." She picked up an empty bottle with what looked like a green-like substance dried at the bottom. "Looks like they had it in liquid form."

"We know they've been planning this a long time." A fly buzzed near my head, and I brushed it away with my hand. "How did they get the curse to spread over the town so fast?"

"The water."

Iris and I both turned to look at the half-vampire.

He shrugged and said, "The town's water supply. It's what I would do if I wanted everyone to get cursed at the same time. It's the only way to ensure everyone would get infected. We all use the town's water. We drink it. We use it to wash ourselves. We're covered in it."

Damn. Ronin was right. "It means I drank some too."

"We all did." Iris put the bottle back on the table, her face wrinkled in disgust.

I felt sick to my stomach. If I had ingested the contents of the curse like everyone else in town, I wasn't showing any effects. The only curse I suffered from was Jemma's annoying voice inside my head.

I set the piece of paper back on the table. "The curse was a diversion," I said, realizing I'd just spoken my thoughts out loud as it all started to make sense. The pieces all fell into place.

"For the Rift," agreed Iris.

"To keep me and my aunts busy trying to find a cure while they keep pouring their powers into opening the Rift."

"But why here?" Ronin crossed his arms over his chest. "They could have made a Rift anywhere else. Why in Hollow Cove?"

Good question. Very good question.

But before I could focus on that very question, the sound of metal rattling pulled my attention behind me.

I spun around, a power word on the edge of my lips as I scanned the semidarkness, my heart surging with adrenaline.

A line of metal cages was pressed up against the far wall. At first glance, they appeared empty, but when my eyes found a familiar tiny creature, my heart sank.

"Gigi!"

Horrified, I dashed across the basement. A large chalk-drawn triangle was painted on the wall behind the cages. Within the triangle, runes and symbols spelled out a complex spell I'd used to summon demons. Sketched on the ground around each cage was a chalk-draw triangle, confining the summoned demon.

Whatever demons were in these cages were trapped.

"Oh my God. Gigi. What did they do to you?"

The tiny demon's nose was bleeding, and her brilliant orange fur was dull, almost a tawny color. Her batlike ears hung loosely against her head; her large black eyes were sunken, and she was thin. Too thin. She looked like a starved cat.

"Bad witch," said the demon as more blood poured down from her nose.

Rage came swarming up, and before I could control it, my demon mojo popped in to say hello.

Black tendrils shot from my hands and hit the dirt floor with a blast. Chunks of earth pattered the stone walls as a cloud of dust rose. The earth beneath my feet trembled with my demon power as I tapped into it.

"Take it easy, Tess," warned Ronin. "We don't want you to bring the house down on us."

I clenched my fingers into a fist and took control of my emotions to let some of my anger go. Now I understood the wailing I'd heard when I was getting my magical makeover from the Stepford witches. The coven was channeling these demons' powers and probably using them to build this portal.

With a quick glance at the other cages, I noted three piles in smoking puddles of what must have been demons soiled the bottoms of the crates. The putrid smell of rot made my eyes water.

"She's the only one left alive." Iris was eyeing the other cages. "Judging by the degree of decomposition, they've been here a long time. Gigi was probably the last demon they summoned."

"They won't summon her again." I reached out and grabbed the door on Gigi's cage and yanked it open. The tiny demon stayed where she was.

I turned to Iris to ask her to draw the rune that would break the tie Gigi had to the binding triangle, but the Dark witch was already at work with chalk in hand. With a brush of her other hand, she erased an existing rune and drew a new one.

I felt a whisper of energy as Gigi jumped out of her cage and landed on the floor.

If the demon had been in tiptop shape, she would probably have attacked us, which was in her nature. But she swayed on the spot, barely able to stay upright. If Gigi didn't go back to the Netherworld soon, she would die. She'd look like a smoking puddle of goo like the others.

Gigi's black eyes focused on me. "Home. Me home." The demon pointed to the other triangle on the wall, the one that kept her in our world.

But I needed her to answer some questions first.

I knelt next to the tiny demon. "I promise I'm going to send you home, but I need you to tell me: do you know why the bad witches did this? Do you know why they want to open a Rift?"

The orange demon blinked. "Home. Gigi."

My heart gave a tug. "I'm sorry, Gigi. I will send you home. But first, you have to tell me. Do you know why they created the Rift?" I pointed to the rippling black mass for good measure.

The tiny demon glared at me. And for a second, I thought she wouldn't answer. "Gigi, no no," said the demon, shaking her head. "Bad witch. Hurt. Home."

I let out a breath. I felt bad for the tiny demon. "Okay, Gigi. You're going home."

I stood and walked back to the wall of cages and swiped my hand across the chalk-drawn triangle on the wall. "I release you, Gigi."

And with a pop of displaced air, Gigi vanished.

I turned around and examined the Rift. "What is the only reason to open a Rift?" I asked, though I already knew the answer.

"To let demons out." Iris scanned the circle below the Rift. "These markings. These markings are old. It's Enochian."

"Enochian? Sounds dirty," said Ronin.

Enochian was the language of demons. And I wasn't well-versed in it. Hell, I wasn't versed in it at all.

I looked at the Dark witch. "What are you thinking? You've got those data lines on your forehead again."

"That this isn't just an ordinary Rift," answered Iris. "It's why it's still open and we've been here a while, but nothing came out."

I nodded. "Because it's not finished. That's exactly what I think. Either they're missing a part of their spell, or it still needs work."

"Exactly."

I pressed my hands to my hips. "I remember reading about a Rift that can open indefinitely, in one of Dolores's books. Can't remember which one, and I don't remember what it's called. But it's like a permanent hole in the Veil. A leak."

Ronin cursed. "Are you saying these witches are trying to open the gates from hell, permanently?"

"That's exactly what I'm saying." I looked at my friends. "The only reason they'd do this is to let demons come out through the Veil." I looked over my shoulder to the cages. "These witches borrow their magic from demons, the same way a Dark witch would. But their way is more sinister, twisted. They're able to drain the demon's power to the point of killing them." I looked back to the Rift. "I know these types. They always want more power. And with a Rift, they don't have to summon demons anymore. They'll have a permanent supply. A permanent supply of unimaginable power."

If I was right, Hollow Cove would become hell on Earth. Literally.

Ronin raked his fingers through his hair. "Great. Just freaking great."

"Yeah, but which ones." Iris shared a look with me. "Lesser demons like Gigi are fine, but Greater demons? Mid demons? These witches are fools if they think they can manipulate a Greater demon."

They were fools. Power-hungry fools. It was the most dangerous kind of crazy.

"Now what?" asked Ronin.

"We need to leave." Come to think of it, we'd been down here a long time. I yanked out my phone. My half-hour deadline was over by ten minutes. I snapped a few pictures of the curse and stuffed my phone back in my pocket. "I don't want them to know we were here." If they found out, they might change the curse or do something worse. I needed to keep them thinking we were oblivious."

"How are you going to explain Gigi Houdini's disappearance?" asked Ronin.

"Easy." I grabbed a wooden spoon I'd spotted from the table that was stained with something I'd rather not think about and rushed back to the cages. Holding my breath—because you would have to—I shoved the spoon into one of the demon puddles, scooped some up, and dumped it in Gigi's cage. I closed the cage's door and stepped back.

"There. They'll never know she's gone. They'll think she died like the others." I tossed the spoon back across the table.

"Wait." With chalk in hand, Iris erased her previous rune and traced back the original. Then she moved to the wall and did the same for the triangle I'd erased there. She stepped back. "Now we're good."

I gave her a quick smile. "Thanks. Listen. I'll check with my aunts and maybe my father about how to close a Rift. It's not completed yet, so I'm thinking we still have time. But first, we need to break the Goblet of God curse." I exhaled, trying not to breathe through my nose. The stench of rot was making me dizzy. "We have the curse. We can now focus on a counter-curse. Right? By this time tomorrow, everyone will be normal again. Dolores will see that I've been telling the truth." I doubted things would ever be the same between us, but it was worth a shot.

"Uh… about that." Iris had a strange look on her face. "The thing is… with a curse that complex, it'll take just as long to draw up a counter-curse. And that's if it's even possible."

My tiny happy bubble burst. "You can't be serious?" When she didn't answer, I added, "That's not an option. There *has* to be another way. Iris? You told me yourself. Marcus and the others don't have that long. If we don't help them soon… there's no coming back." A sliver of ice dropped down my spine, making me shiver.

Iris bit her lower lip. "I'll have to think about it. It would really help if your aunts could help. We'd need all brains on board for this one. Can you talk to them?"

"I'll see what I can do."

My heart was heavy with dread and fear as we hurried back up the stone stairs and out of the large Victorian home.

If we couldn't find a counter-curse soon, Marcus would be lost to me forever.

CHAPTER
19

"**A**nd this is a copy of the Goblet of God curse we believe they put in the town's water supply," I said as I placed my phone on the kitchen table so my aunts could see. "It's proof that the Sisters of the Circle did this." I didn't want it to sound like an "I told you so," but what choice did I have. "I think they did this as a diversion so we'd be looking the other way while they worked on their Rift."

I leaned back and crossed my arms over my middle, waiting for their reactions. Silence, thick and uncomfortable, took over, making my voice seem louder. I was glad I had taken a few minutes to rush upstairs and change into my jeans and T-shirt. Looking like one of the Stepford witches while trying to blame them for the curse wouldn't have been very effective.

Ruth reached out and pulled the phone closer so she could get a better look. After a moment, she said, "It's a biggie. Months of work for a curse like this—oh no."

"Oh no… what?" I didn't like the sound of that.

Ruth met my gaze, her eyes compassionate and sad. "It says… the curse will be fulfilled at sunrise on the second day."

Fear rushed me and I nearly fell over. "It's almost three in the morning. We have less than two hours before sunrise." It was much worse than I thought. I thought I'd have another day. Not a couple of hours.

Ruth nodded and passed the phone to Beverly next to her. Beverly stared at my phone but said nothing before she handed the phone over to Dolores. The tall witch ignored her, her face empty of emotion.

"It's true," said Iris, breaking the stunned silence. "We saw it too. The Rift. The spell work. They're not who we thought they were."

"They're kind of who *I* thought they were," commented Ronin, echoing my thoughts exactly as he took a mouthful of his beer.

Beverly took a sip of her red wine and carefully set the glass on the table. "But why come here to open their Rift? Why all the pretenses? They could have just as easily opened a Rift anywhere around the world."

I shook my head. "I don't know why. I haven't figured out that part yet."

Dolores slammed her hand on the table, making me and everyone jerk. "I don't believe a word of it."

And so it begins…

My jaw fell. "Wow. Even with this proof, you still don't believe me?"

Dolores's eyes narrowed dangerously. "I think you're clever enough to make this whole thing up," she said, though she didn't sound so convincing.

Beverly folded her hands on her lap. "Dolores, come on. Iris and Ronin were there too."

"We were," said the half-vampire as he wiped his mouth with his hand. "I saw it. Everything Tess is saying is true. The Stepford witches had a giant demon portal in their basement." A flutter of gratitude went through me that he was using my made-up names.

Dolores glared at me for a long moment. "I'm going out for a walk." And with that, she marched out of the kitchen. A few seconds later, the sound of the front door closing reached us.

I threw up my hands, exasperated. "Argh. She makes me so angry sometimes. Even with proof, she doesn't believe me."

"Oh, she does," said Beverly as she chucked the last of her wine in one gulp. "She's just too stubborn to admit it. She'll be back. Don't worry. And she'll help. You'll see."

Tension left my body. "You're going to help? All of you?"

Ruth looked at me like I had just squashed her favorite spider. "We're Merlins. It's our job to protect our town."

Right.

"What should we focus on first?" asked Iris. "The counter-curse or the Rift?"

My heart thrashed, and I was starting to feel nauseated. "We work on the counter-curse. Ruth said we have until sunrise. That's not a lot of time."

Beverly poured herself another glass of red wine. "But if we don't destroy the Rift before it settles, it's a permanent hole in our world that any vile beast from the Netherworld can step through. We'd have to leave this town. Leave our home. This house. It'll be overrun by demons."

"It's true," agreed Ruth. "Many paranormal communities have been destroyed this way because of witches or wizards or sorcerers who didn't understand the dangers of playing with Rifts. They were careless, and they paid for it with their lives."

Well, that wasn't good. I flicked my gaze to Ruth. "Ruth. Now that you've seen the curse we're up against, how hard would it be to make a counter-curse?"

My gaze moved to Iris, and she gave me a hopeful but nervous look. If Ruth couldn't crack a counter-curse, we were most definitely going up shit creek without a paddle.

Ruth's face wrinkled in thought. "Hard. Yes, very hard. But not impossible."

"Good." I took faith from that. Now the harder part. "And how fast can you make it?"

Ruth bit her bottom lip as she concentrated. She picked up my phone again, her blue eyes intense as they moved over the screen. "A direct counter-curse of the curse in question would take too long. Months, at least."

I flicked my eyes again at Iris. She'd been right about that.

My heart sank to somewhere around the kitchen floor. We were doomed.

"But there are ways around it."

I perked up. "And this is possible?"

Ruth smiled, looking like Mrs. Claus with her pink cheeks and white hair, and I swear her eyes twinkled. "Anything's possible."

"If we're about to do a group hug, I think I'm going to throw up," commented Beverly, though I could see a tiny smile on her perfect lips.

"I'll need at least an hour, two at the most," said Ruth as she glanced over to the potions room just outside the kitchen. "I have everything I need to start right here. I'll need both Beverly's and Dolores's help. It'll go faster with the three of us."

That was cutting it close, but we were out of options.

Ruth picked up my phone. "Can I keep your phone with me?"

"Sure." It wasn't like anyone would be calling me. Marcus couldn't. I didn't even think his big gorilla fingers could text. The thought of the chief had my stomach caving in. I quickly brushed it away. Having a meltdown now was not an option.

"Then it's settled. We'll split into groups," I announced. "I don't have the know-how to conjure up a counter-curse, but I think I might be able to destroy a Rift. With my dad's help." Davenport House was one of the only ways I could see my father. I didn't think he'd want us to lose that.

Beverly smiled at the mention of my father. She stood up, pushed out her chest, moved to the basement door, and cried, "Obiryn! We need you!"

A few moments later, the door to the basement swung open and my father stepped through.

"Something wrong?" He moved swiftly around the kitchen, his dark blue business suit moving with him as he surveyed the room like he was expecting something. His silver eyes gleamed. He carried himself with tension that wasn't there before. Clearly, he knew something was not right.

"There's always something wrong, but we're all good, if that's what you mean," I told him.

The tension in his shoulders eased a bit. "Glad to hear it." After a few beats, his handsome face brightened at the sight of my aunts. "Ruth. Beverly. Hello." He joined us around the kitchen table, his black shoes glinting in the kitchen light. "Ah, Ronin and Iris. Nice to see you again."

"Hi." Iris gave him a finger wave, while Ronin greeted him with an unreadable expression and a slight nod.

"Is Dolores out on a date?" asked my father, looking around the kitchen.

Beverly spat the wine from her mouth and then dabbed it with a napkin. "The last time Dolores was out on a date was when bell-bottoms were in style."

"She went for a walk," I told him.

My father's silver eyes shone as they met mine. "Well then. Am I to assume you haven't invited me to tea?"

"You assume right," I said. "We've got problems."

My father lost his smile. "Tell me everything."

And so I did.

Everything—from how the Stepford witches got me all dolled up to even the part where I let Gigi go and finally Ruth working on a counter-curse.

"So, my question to you is," I was saying, "how do I destroy a Rift? Is it even possible?"

My father stroked his beard. "They're not solid objects that you can destroy. But you can create a disruption that will remove them. It'll be difficult... but not impossible. With your abilities, I don't see why you couldn't."

I didn't care to hide the surprise and relief that probably showed up all over my face. "Tell me. How do I do it?"

"There are two ways to remove a Rift," answered my father. "You can send a blast of kinetic force into it, like setting off a bomb that will ultimately affect the energies required to sustain the Rift, which then cancels the energies that maintain it, canceling it out. Or you can sew it up."

"Sew it up?"

My father nodded. "Stitch the hole in the Veil like you would, say... a pair of pants or underwear."

I wrinkled my brows, yeah, not going there. "That sounds more difficult somehow."

"It is. Your best option is the first."

I exhaled, feeling better that we had a working plan. This was going to work. "Okay. I can do this—"

A scream erupted from outside, followed by a metal sound of something hitting the front door.

The hairs on my body stood up and practically ran away.

And then another scream, and another that was abruptly shut off.

"That sounded really close," said Ronin.

"What the cauldron is going on?" asked Ruth, her blue eyes round.

"Dolores!" shouted Beverly.

Fear and adrenaline sparked through me. Dolores. She was out there.

I acted without thinking and dashed out of the kitchen, sprinting to the front door.

Pulling on the elements around me, I readied a power word and yanked the front door open.

Stardust Drive was teeming with demons.

"Oh… crap."

Okay, so they were the lesser kind, more animal-like, and less intelligent, but that didn't make them any less deadly.

Whatever had hit the door was gone now. Something huge and black and hairy came hurdling across the front lawn. It stopped, seemingly having caught my scent, its three red eyes focused on me. Its massive jaw opened, grazing the snow-covered lawn. It took a decisive step toward me, then its head whipped around, and with a thrust of its powerful legs, pushed off into the night after what I realized, in horror, was an alpaca, more specifically, Maddalena, the owner of Boutique Maddalena.

"There goes the neighborhood."

A tide of demons swept over our little town. Ear-piercing shrieks echoed as they attacked anything that moved, ending with strangled moans.

Dolores was out there on her own. I needed to find her and bring her back.

I stepped off the porch and hurried over to the street. More screams split the night air, not human but more animal. I caught sight of a cougar ripping out the jugular of a bat-like demon before tossing it to the ground, only to be hit again by another one. Things darted from the shadows, barely visible with only the streetlights. Tall, dark slithering shapes glided over the snow like wraiths.

"Great. We've got wraiths."

I knew what this meant. It meant the Rift was finally complete. It meant we were too late.

I heard a muffled scream that seemed to have come from down the next street. I lifted my gaze to see a half-dozen reptile-doglike demons attacking together and swarming over a wolf. The wolf yelped once and then nothing.

My heart felt like it was about launch out of my chest. Marcus was out there somewhere too. I had to find him.

"Tessa."

I turned at the sound of my father's concerned voice. He stood in the middle of the walkway. He was out of Davenport House.

He was *out* of Davenport House?

My father's face was mostly hidden in shadow, but there was no mistaking the shock and concern I saw. "Tessa. I shouldn't be able to do this."

I looked past him toward Iris, Ronin, Ruth, and Beverly standing on the porch, watching my father with the same confusion mixed with fear expressions on their faces.

I stared as my demon father walked down the snow-covered pathway toward me like it was the most natural thing in the world. When I knew it wasn't.

When I'd first made the discovery that my father was Obiryn the demon and not Sean the loser, he'd explained that he'd been stripped of certain privileges when it came to our world because of me and the relationship he'd had with my mother.

Whatever his leaders had done to him kept him from traveling to our world as a normal demon would. Only the ley lines and Davenport House gave him that ability.

And now he was walking toward me.

Panic was a white-hot flare, and my lungs burned. "It's bad. Isn't it?"

My father's eyes fastened calmly on my face. "If I can walk back on this plane, it means the Veil that protects you… is gone."

Well, shit.

CHAPTER

20

My father could not have dropped a bigger bomb on me if he tried. Did I mention this was *not* my night?

"I felt a disruption in the Veil yesterday," said my father. "A disturbance in the Force. A glitch in the Matrix." He smiled.

I would have laughed, but I was so wired tight, I thought my head was about to pop off my neck and roll down the street.

"I wasn't certain before, but the fact that I'm standing here next to you is proof. I shouldn't be able to stand here. Yet, here I am."

"Sonofabitch." I threw my gaze back toward the street, with ribbons of panic pulling through

225

me. "I thought I'd have more time. It's just happening so fast. We're too late. The Rift is complete."

"No. I don't think that's what's happening here."

I stared at my father, my mouth open. "What do you mean?"

"The Rift is what's causing the Veil to collapse around you, yes. The amount of energy pouring into the Rift is catastrophic, like pouring water into a balloon. It's expanding. Sooner or later, it'll pop, but in the meantime, it's creating cracks in the Veil. It's opening small pockets. It's why so many lesser demons are passing through. But once the Rift is removed, the Veil should repair itself."

"You're saying we've still got time to remove the Rift?"

My father nodded. "Yes." He took a ragged breath. "But not for long," he said on the exhale. "You'll need to hurry."

Not only did I still have to fight my way through the sea of demons to reach the Rift and possibly fight Jemma and her coven, there was still the threat of the curse on the paranormals of this town.

Easy peasy, right? But I had to do something. I couldn't let the people of our town die.

"Fuck me sideways, but I'd say we're screwed." Ronin was next to me in a blink of an eye, his vamp speed in full bloom. His black eyes narrowed on a six-legged demon with a red-and-purple-striped body. "I'm a bit out of practice. Nothing like a good demon killing to get my vamp juices flowing—no offense," he added to my father.

My father looked at Ronin. "Non taken. These are mindless, vile creatures bred to kill and feed. We hunt and kill them in my world as well."

"Good to know," said Ronin. He turned toward me. "We doing this?"

I grinned at the half-vampire. "You read my mind, my friend."

"Tessa, you need to know something." My father's voice was pitched with alarm, which had my insides twisting. "If *I* can leave this house… I'm afraid demons can venture inside."

Great. That's all I needed.

A scream of pain filled the air with a nightmarish cacophony, which interrupted my thoughts. I turned around in time to see a howling horde of demons crashing through windows from the houses across the street and sprinting through doorways.

If I wanted to save my community, I needed to act now.

"Dad. Stay here and protect Ruth. She needs to finish her counter-curse. Right now, that's the most important thing." It was to me. "You're the most powerful person I know. I need you here."

227

My father beamed at me and pressed a hand to his chest. "I'll protect her with my life."

Yeah, my father was awesome.

I looked over at the porch. "Iris," I called out. "Can you help Ruth?" With Dolores still missing, Ruth was going to need her help. And although Iris was a Dark witch with some pretty badass skills, she didn't have the type of defensive magic I had with my power words or my newer demon mojo, which still needed refining and training. She'd be better served inside Davenport House with the counter-curse. Not to mention that I'd feel a lot better if she was there helping Ruth.

"Yes, of course," answered Iris. "Don't worry. We've got this." Her smile vanished as her gaze moved to Ronin, and I could see the worry etched all over her pretty face.

I stood there a few seconds, watching my father close Davenport House's front door behind him. Then I gathered my will, sinking into pure focus.

In a blur of talons and fangs, Ronin put on a burst of speed that must have been some kind of vamp record, and with a howl, he threw himself at the nearest demon.

And then I was moving.

I never thought I'd be throwing myself into killing a mass of demons, but here I was. Just goes to show how my life had changed.

A nauseating stench of rotten flesh hit me, and I gagged. Damn, that was nasty. I blinked, my eyes adjusting well enough to the darkness to see them, and part of me wished I hadn't.

I felt eyes on my back. With my heart in my throat, I spun around and found six pairs of gleaming, red eyes staring at me. A blast of cold terror struck me like a sledgehammer.

Lean and muscular, the size of ponies, they had leatherlike skin the color of dry leaves. Massive paws ended with sharp, black talons. White bones showed through gaps of rotten flesh, oozing yellow and white, putrid juices. Maggots and flies poured from the open wounds. Ew. Okay, that was gross.

The light from the streetlamps reflected off their skinless, wolflike, elongated skulls. Deep-sunken, dead eyes fixed on me. Jaws opened, and they let out a collective eerie wail, unnatural and unworldly. Their red eyes gleamed with a promise of pain and eerie intelligence. They were lesser demons, by the looks of them, with slightly higher intelligence than the average Labrador retriever.

"Nice doggies. Very nice doggies." Not really.

The closest demon lunged.

Adrenaline slammed into me. I pulled on my will and the elements and shouted, "Accendo!"

But instead of my awesome fireball, a trickle of black tendrils shot out of my hand. I flinched, surprised, as the thread hit the pavement next to the demon, went *poof*, and disappeared. Yeah, I really needed those lessons with my father.

Whoops. "I missed." I laughed.

The demon dog snarled as it came at me.

Shit.

I threw myself to the side and heard the sound of talons scraping the pavement. Pain tore at my leg, and I staggered as it flared up like I'd stuck it in a fire. That damn thing bit me!

Rage filled me as I flung my hands at the demon and bellowed, "Accendo!"

This time my pretty fireballs shot out of my hands and hit the demon in the chest.

Red-orange flames wreathed the demon. It thrashed, trying to run away from the fire, but there was nowhere to run. The flames took on rims of red and gold as they grew, warming my face. The heat from the fire made me take a step back.

I gagged as the scent of burnt flesh assaulted me. The creature struggled and screamed a terrible high-pitched screech before combusting into a pile of gray ash.

"One down, a couple hundred to go."

Movement caught my eye, and I spotted a glimpse of Ronin spinning like a top, his arms out, as he sliced and diced between demons. Even from a distance, I could see a wicked gleam in his eye, like he was truly enjoying himself. Enjoying killing. That was not the

Ronin I knew, not my easygoing friend. It was as though I was staring at a stranger.

I didn't have the luxury to think this over as another demon came at me.

I blinked. "Oh, goodie. It brought its friends," I mumbled as another came sprinting.

Using those mere seconds, I channeled the energy from the elements, willing them to me and bending them to my will. The air cracked with the sudden inflow of magic.

In a blur of teeth and limbs, the demons charged.

With out-of-this-world speed, the creatures came at me like a pack of famished wolves. I jumped back, my focus lost, just as a head hammered into my side, the force knocking me off my feet. I fell hard. I looked up and saw teeth and eyes above me, yellow liquid oozing from their wounds like water from a tap.

Double ew.

The smell? I couldn't even begin to describe it. It was that bad. Vomit threatening. I scrambled backward, trying to come up with a power word but failing as my concentration was replaced by primal fear. I didn't want to die. I didn't want to be torn apart and eaten by these ugly bastards.

I rolled and pushed to my feet amid a flash of teeth and talons. I slipped on something crunchy yet liquidy and landed headfirst into a snowbank.

Contrary to what you might think, a snowbank is *hard*, compacted snow. And it hurt like a sonofabitch.

I was in a compromised position with my butt in the air like that. Thank God Marcus wasn't here to witness my humiliation. Or anyone, for that matter.

Instincts kicked in. I pulled my head out of the snow, spun around, and kicked out in time to catch one of the demons on the side of the head.

I heard a loud crack, and the demon went down.

"Ha!" I said, proud of my Chuck Norris move, but I wasn't an idiot. I knew it wasn't dead or knocked out. It would be back on its feet in a matter of seconds.

My head throbbing, I blinked the pretty black stars from my eyes as I strained to focus on summoning my magic.

My instincts suddenly screamed, and I flung out my arms, screaming, "Fulgur!"

A bolt of white-purple lightning hit one of the demons.

It exploded like a demon piñata.

It would have been cool if the other demon wasn't already on me.

Red eyes gleaming with hatred and hunger, it snarled and then lunged.

Oh shit.

The demon crashed into me with the force of a moving car. It pinned me to the ground with one paw, cutting off my ability to breathe. Putrid breath assaulted my face as the demon leaned forward, opening its jaw like it was measuring how to get my entire head inside. A strand of yellow drool ran from its jaw and hit my face. I retched. It hovered above me, its body quivering in anticipated delight at devouring me.

Nice. This wasn't going so well. Maybe I should have stuck with Ronin.

I was pissed. First, because a demon had pinned me to the ground in my town, and second because I was certain I'd just swallowed some of its spit.

My lungs burned as I tried and failed to get any air. And when my vision started to go black, I knew I was in serious trouble.

CHAPTER

21

In the midst of life, we are in death, or some crap like that. Me? I was neck-deep in the crapper and sinking fast.

The demon was going to suffocate me to death and then eat me. Not exactly the way I wanted to go. But I didn't make the dying rules. You got what you were dealt.

Searing, white-hot pain exploded in my side as I felt teeth sink into my flesh and back out again. Yikes. That hurt like a bitch.

I tried to focus on a spell, but my head felt like it was full of water. I couldn't think beyond the pain.

Movement flashed in my peripheral vision followed by an ear-splitting roar I knew all too well.

In a flash of black and gray, a massive silverback gorilla knocked the doglike demon off me with a powerful thrust of its body. In a burst of fur and muscles, the gorilla grabbed the demon and lifted it as though it weighed nothing at all before tearing it in half like it was merely a hot dog and tossing it.

Okay. I could work with that.

I sat up. The sudden rush of air in my lungs had my head spinning.

Two more demons threw themselves at the gorilla, one on his back while the other had its jaws sunken into the gorilla's shoulder. The gorilla barely took notice as he exploded into motion.

He swatted the demon-dog on his shoulder like it was an annoying mosquito and took its head between his massive hands, crushing its skull. I heard a pop and the sound of bones crushing, and the creature went limp in his hands.

He tossed that one too.

Marcus the gorilla reached back and pulled the last demon dog from him, hauled it across his back and, you guessed it, tossed it.

Only this time he leaped in the air and came down on the demon's head with the weight of a car on an egg. The head? Well, there was no head, only a thin smear of black liquid and what could be fur and some teeth, maybe an ear.

"Uuuu kaaaeee?"

A gigantic hand dangled before my eyes. Wait? That voice had come from the gorilla. And I understood it.

I watched him for a moment, stunned. Then I wrapped my hand in his, and he yanked me up to my feet. Pain flared from the spot where the demon had bitten me, but apart from some throbbing, it wasn't as bad as I thought.

"I've had better days. But yeah, I'll live." I let go of his hand and stared into his gray eyes. "You speak? Have you been practicing without me?" He'd never spoken to me or even tried before when he was in his beast form.

The gorilla showed me all his teeth. Which, if I were a regular human, I'd have peed myself.

"Ehsss," said the gorilla and then puffed out his chest proudly.

I could *definitely* work with that.

A long cut marred the left side of his face. His right forearm had deep puncture wounds, like something with big teeth had taken a bite. But he didn't look like any of it bothered him. A fierce light backlit his eyes, and his posture became predatory, wild. He looked… he looked dangerous and marvelous, and my pulse thundered with excitement.

"Paaakk." The gorilla gestured behind me.

I turned around and cursed.

A moving wall was behind me. A wall of wolves, bears, cougars, deer, coyotes, foxes, a gorilla, boars, bison, and some black panthers. Too many to count. Oh, and the trees were lined with eagles, hawks, and vultures.

His pack. Well, his pack was the entire freaking town—all the surviving shifters and weres. Goose bumps riddled my skin at the hissing, growling, monstrous shapes. It was a massive, powerful line of defense. A killing one. It was extraordinary.

And they were all waiting for the big silverback gorilla's orders.

Marcus the gorilla's gaze dipped to my leg where a demon had bitten me. Rage and fury and a number of emotions I couldn't read sparkled in those gray eyes.

His posture shifted, and the muscles on his shoulders and neck bulged. His stare became vicious and primal, and cold licked up my spine.

He oozed ferocious power and strength. This was the reason the town had chosen him as their chief. He was also their alpha. Because Marcus was the strongest, the fiercest of them all. He was scary as hell, and it made me all warm and fuzzy inside. I loved it.

Ronin stepped into view. I'd lost sight of him, and I felt a sense of relief when I spotted him. He strolled our way, and he was annoyingly clean, without a single drop of demon blood nor a speck of flesh on his person.

"I spotted about twenty demons going down Shifter Lane," he said, not even a trace of fatigue or strain in his voice after fighting those demons. "They're going after the older shifters who've barricaded themselves in the gazebo."

The new gazebo—I'd accidentally burned the previous one—was just a wooden skeleton without any walls that would give them protection.

Adrenaline still sang along my legs and arms. "We need to go. They'll die if we don't do something." The elderly in our town were anywhere between seventy and ninety years old. Yes, they might have more strength than your average human, but they didn't have the reflexes or the power needed to fight a horde of demons.

The gorilla's eyes narrowed suddenly. "Wwuuaarr."

"War?" I asked.

He nodded, seemingly proud of our excellent communication skills.

Ronin cocked a brow and flung a taloned finger in our general direction. "Is that? Did King Kong just speak?"

"Yeah. He did," I said proudly.

"The chief's a talking monkey," laughed Ronin, but he clamped down his jaw at the snarl twitching on the gorilla's lips.

"Ah… meet you guys there." In a blur of clothes, Ronin shot down the street and was gone.

Behind me, I felt the restless, ravenous rage from the shifters and weres.

I looked at the gorilla. "Go." I tapped into the nearest ley line. "My two legs can't run as fast as you." And with my injured leg, I wasn't running anywhere. Possibly limping.

The gorilla shook his head.

"No?" I eyed him. "Look. I'm not that hurt. I can fight. You're not the boss of me—"

Before I could react, the gorilla grabbed me and hauled me over his back. I found myself straddled up on him like I would a horse.

"Holy crap," I shrieked as I found myself sitting above the colossal gorilla.

"Aann onn," said the gorilla, and I swear I could hear a smile on his face.

"Okay." My heart skipped a few beats. I couldn't help the grin that spread over my own face. I leaned slightly forward and wrapped my arms around his neck as I pressed my knees tightly against his muscular rib cage. His was much bigger than his natural counterpart. He wasn't King Kong, but he wasn't your average silverback gorilla either, possibly twice the normal size.

His thick, coarse, springy hair rubbed against my hands and face, silky and smooth. In fact, he was unbelievably comfortable, like a warm down comforter, and part of me wanted to bury my face in his fur and go to sleep.

But we had demons to kill and people to save. You know, the usual stuff.

The gorilla let out a growl that was pure primal and commanding.

And then we were moving.

I let out a shrill of excitement, and I think this time I actually peed a little. But who cared when you got to ride on the back of a giant gorilla?

Muscles bunched and coiled under me as Marcus the gorilla propelled himself forward in a burst of speed. Houses and buildings blurred past me.

A pure, joyous squeal ripped from my lungs, and I felt the gorilla's throat rumble with deep laughter.

A girl could get used to this ride.

The gorilla leaped over a car—yes, a freaking car—and for a second I nearly lost my grip and tumbled off his back. Not that falling would hurt that much. I was more worried about my ego. But I latched on, my grip on his throat tighter, but not too tight as to choke him.

Wind lashed at my face, my hair tossing into my eyes. I got an occasional glimpse of the whirling masses that were the shifters and weres running side by side while the massive gorilla roared.

A demon, black fur and yellow eyes from what I could see, came at us from the right side with its jaw open. The gorilla didn't stop. He didn't even slow down. He swatted the demon with his right arm, almost in a lazy effort. The demon flew back, its head angled unnaturally as it crumpled to the ground.

Three more demons barreled our way. Like a brutal rhinoceros, the gorilla never stopped as he plowed his way through, trampling over the demons.

We hit Shifter Lane within moments. When the new gazebo bounded into view, I could see the growling, seething masses of demons surrounding it, and the half-dozen wolves, cougars, and goats above it. There were more than twenty demons. More like fifty now.

My eyes scanned the area, and I spotted Ronin, slicing the neck of a humanoid demon using his talons as though they were blades, like a much better-looking version of Freddy Krueger. Just as the demon collapsed, another threw itself at the half-vampire. Ronin spun around and hooked two talons right in the jugular of the demon. And just as that one fell, another came.

Ronin was good, but he was going to need our help if he was going to survive this.

I looked for Dolores, hoping to see her with the paranormals inside the gazebo, but I saw no sign of the tall witch.

The gorilla stopped and lowered his body to the ground. I swung my left leg over the

241

gorilla's back and slid to the ground like a pro. Just as my boots hit the hard snow, my legs buckled, feeling like the bones that used to support them were made of rubber, and then I fell. My arms were swinging as I tried to regain balance but failed.

Not exactly the easy dismount I was going for.

I leaped to my feet, my face flaming. "I'm good. I'm great." Humiliated, but great.

But my shame would have to wait.

"Fiiett," said the gorilla as he pointed at himself and then at the mass of demons circling the gazebo.

"Fight. Let's fight," I agreed and pulled on the elements around me.

With a powerful thrust of his back legs, he hurled himself into the wave of demons, his arms out like he was trying to bat as many as he could in one leap.

I swear the wereape was enjoying this a little bit too much.

He slammed his body against the lesser demons, picking them up and crushing them together. Their skulls snapped like smashed eggs as Marcus leaned steadily in one direction—to kill the threat.

The sounds of battle blared in a combination of cries and shouts, making my ears whistle: the sounds of efficient, brutal violence mixed with the howling of pain and breaking of bones. The air smelled of blood and sweat with animal and sulfur.

The attack was a bloody, brutal, primal, and violent killing. It was an annihilation. It was a kill-all-demons-before-they-do-us-in kind of killing.

I lost sight of Marcus the gorilla under the throng of battle, but I knew he was here somewhere, obliterating the demon threat.

Okay, then. My turn.

Feeling a little crazy, I dashed, more like hopped, into the fight as the power words spilled from my lips. I'd been using them for a while now, so they were practically second nature. As easily as I drew breath, I drew my magic.

A shape slithered my way, carrying the scent of carrion and death.

"Accendo!"

I blasted a fireball at a giant rat, no, a worm, no, a worm-rat, whatever. Flames engulfed it until all I saw were flames.

And then the worst thing that could happen happened.

The worm-rat grew in size—and then exploded.

And you guess it. I was hit. Everywhere.

Vision blurred, I wiped my eyes, trying not to vomit at the stench that was now all over me.

"Word of caution. I wouldn't use fire on those maggots again," said Ronin's smiling face as he appeared next to me. "Don't worry. Ruth has a garden hose. It'll be my pleasure to hose you down, baby." And then he was gone again.

If he didn't have that vamp speed, I would have kicked him in the ass.

Pissed because I smelled like a corpse, or worse, I pulled on the elements again, letting the magic course through me.

And found my mark.

A ghoul.

And he was a big sonofabitch.

CHAPTER
22

I'd never encountered a ghoul before, but it didn't take a genius to recognize it from the images in Dolores's books.

It stood around seven feet tall. Its features were warped disturbingly by the knobs of cancerous masses covering most of its face. Its flesh was red and raw like it was turned inside out, and it was naked and male I guessed from the nasty that dangled between its legs. It was more apelike than humanoid, its talons grazing the earth where it stood, hunched back and waiting for its next meal.

I wrinkled my nose at the stink of sulfur and carrion. From what I remembered in my reading, they were mean, dirty, and equipped with supernatural strength. They were strong sons of bitches. Ghouls weren't the brightest lights in the Netherworld harbor. But what they lacked in intelligence, they made up for with sheer strength.

The ghoul swirled around to face me, its distorted features furious, and strings of flesh hung from its drooling mouth around fishlike teeth. Nice.

"Witch. Kill. Eat," said the ghoul, speaking in low, cruel tones, and I brought my attention back to its putrid face. Its pitch-black eyes shone with fury and a savage hunger.

I gave the ghoul a mock shocked-impressed expression. "I'll give you points for speaking," I told it. "But I'm not the one dying tonight, handsome."

With no warning, it lunged at me, slashing with talons and fangs. Damn. This thing was fast.

I could never outrun this ghoul. I wasn't known for my great sprinting abilities. Thank the cauldron I was a witch.

I shifted on my feet, gave the ghoul a predator's smile, and called on the elements.

"Inspiratione!"

Fractures of red energy blasted out of my outstretched hands and slammed into the ghoul.

It shrieked in pain and staggered back, clutching at its face with its black blood gleaming in the moonlight. It fell to the ground, its wails blending with the sounds of ripping and tearing of flesh. Then I heard the popping noises that could have been bones breaking. The ghoul writhed and thrashed around for a second and then imploded, vanishing and leaving behind nothing but a few strings of glistening slime in its place.

I staggered, feeling the weight of my magic's payment starting to take a toll on my body, my adrenaline no longer hiding it. The pain in my leg and my side were still there, throbbing.

The sound of crackling laughter spun me around.

Another ghoul appeared before me. Its head quested from side to side, assessing me. No doubt my bleeding leg was drawing it to me. The stench of carrion rolled off it in waves.

In a burst of speed, it came at me.

"Great."

With enormous effort, I pulled on the elements around me, pouring my will into my power word.

"Evorto!"

The force of the power word hit the ghoul. It stumbled and froze, its eyes wide with fear.

And then it blew up.

But this time I was prepared.

I threw myself to the side, hitting my hip bone on the hard pavement and avoiding most of the meaty chunks that flew in all directions.

"Okay. Ow." My left wrist seared in pain. I pushed myself to my feet, knowing all too well that lots more ghouls were still out there.

Dizzy, I fought a sudden burst of nausea and took a steadying breath.

The more I pulled on the surrounding magic, the more my body felt it had been in the meat grinder. My insides were assaulted by the pricks of needles, but I fought it. I didn't really have a choice.

I'd lost track of time for a while. I didn't know how long I battled, fighting off lesser demon after lesser demon until it became rather mechanical.

Dodge demon attack. Power word. Rinse. Repeat.

The sound of talons gouging the pavement, and the scent of rot and sulfur rose. I turned my head, searching, and a sickly feeling of dread rolled through me.

More masses surged the streets, hundreds more. The roads were pouring with more lesser demons, like monsters with one controllable mind—to kill. It didn't matter how many killed, for every one we took down, three or four more took their place. The onslaught wouldn't stop. Not until we closed the Rift.

"Damn it," I cursed. There were just too many.

A shape came at me from my peripheral vision.

A giant spider-like demon, the size of a Great Dane, sprang at me.

And I never even heard it.

Instinctively, I drew in my will and pushed out my magic.

"Accendo!"

My pulse throbbed, but I never stopped gathering my magic as a burst of my fire struck the demon spider. It went down in a wailing scream of fire and ash.

A howl of fury pulled my attention toward the gazebo. I knew that howl.

It was hard to see with all the writhing, fighting bodies, but I could spot the silverback gorilla anywhere.

Trouble was, his head was being smashed against the side of the gazebo by a creature twice his size.

I shook my head. I wasn't surprised. Of course he'd go for the biggest, meanest-looking demon.

The beast that had my gorilla in a headlock looked like a twisted version of Bigfoot. It stood at least nine feet high with wicked-looking spikes protruding from its back and covered in matted, gray fur. Oh, did I forget to mention that Bigfoot had four arms? Yeah, it did.

The silverback gorilla pried himself free of Bigfoot's hold, twisted around, grabbed hold of what looked like one of the park benches, and smashed it against the head of the demon.

Bigfoot fell to the side, but he was up in almost the same moment, smashing his four fists at the gorilla's head. The gorilla tumbled to the side.

An ugly grimace skewed the bigfoot demon's face as he advanced on the gorilla.

"Marcus!" Fear quickened my feet as I rushed over, my pain forgotten, as all I could think about was Marcus.

The bigfoot demon hit the gorilla like a freight train hitting a cement wall, and the two fell to the ground in a blur of fists hitting flesh, snarls, hissing, teeth, and dark fur. Each beast pummeled the other with their fists, breaking into a rabid frenzy of blows. The ground beneath my feet shuddered and quaked. Each crushing punch sent bile rising my throat.

Marcus…

Fear bled into me.

A second later, and the gorilla was on Bigfoot's back. A vicious blow to the side of its head and the demon stilled. The gorilla smashed his fist against the base of Bigfoot's skull and drove it right through soft flesh and muscle, causing black blood to ooze. And then he yanked out his hand, taking with it part of the demon's spine.

That was pretty gross.

Bigfoot went limp, teetered, and fell, taking the gorilla with him, and both slammed into the side of the gazebo like a great big tree.

I heard the loud, piercing sound of wood cracking and splintering. I looked up.

"Damn. Not again."

The new gazebo fractured and broke. It fell to the ground, beams sticking out in the snow like the carcass of some dead animal.

Yeah. Gilbert was going to blame me for this one too.

Then sudden silence hit me. Panting, I wiped the sweat from my brow and looked around.

The demon flock stood still. They weren't moving, except for their heads questing from side to side like they were listening to something. They were sensing something for sure, but what?

And then in a burst of speed, they ran in the opposite direction from us.

What the hell?

A grunt came from Marcus the gorilla. I turned to see him pointing to the east, a heavy sadness brimmed in his eyes. The glow of the rising sun painted the back of his head with gold, making it appear on fire.

Real fear hit, the kind that roots you to the spot, the kind that's final.

The curse. The Goblet of God would be fulfilled with the rising of the sun.

It meant the paranormals were stuck in their animal forms. It meant I'd lost Marcus.

It meant this time we were too late.

CHAPTER
23

The sun rose over the horizon, burning gently through the last of the night's cold air, and soft, golden light washed over us, warm and strong. It was lovely, and I never thought seeing the rising sun would fill me with so much hate and despair.

But it did.

All the surviving shifters and weres stirred as their gazes fixed upon that glowing, yellow disk, and my heart shattered at the deep sorrow I saw on their faces.

It was too late. All hope of breaking the curse was lost.

It was over.

I sat next to the gorilla on the curb, my butt numb from the snow and the ice-cold concrete. My body shook from both the spent adrenaline and the fear as I held on to the gorilla's hand, not wanting to let go. I feared if I did, it would be the last time I'd see him or hold him in this way.

The fact that I could feel the gorilla's hand trembling made it a hundred times worse.

"Saarrwee," said the big gorilla, and I turned to see muscles playing along his jaw. His gray eyes bristled with tears as his lips moved, but no words came out. He was struggling, not with trying to formulate words that I could understand but with what he needed to say. I already knew. He was telling me he had to leave.

"Don't." I slid closer into his side and wrapped my arm around him. My head fell onto his chest. "Don't say it," I whispered. Tears pricked, and grief stained my heart. Once the tears started coming, I found that it was impossible to stop them. They just kept on coming and coming until I was a slobbering, snot-teared mess. I wasn't even concerned about it.

This wasn't how I'd imagined my life would go. Losing Marcus to this curse wasn't part of my plan. I'd intended to move in with him later today. I'd been a fool to think I could fix this. That I was strong enough. That my abilities were enough. I had to come to terms with that this was beyond my level of skill. I failed. We'd failed. Ruth, Beverly, Iris, and my father, who I knew worked tirelessly to get a working counter-curse.

But they had failed too.

Just thinking of never seeing Marcus again tore a hole in my soul; it was like I would lose part of me. Part of my life.

I could feel a terrible weight settling across my heart. Damn it. Hadn't I been through enough? Hadn't my life handed me enough pain and misery and grief already? And now I was losing Marcus?

Not to mention that all these shifters and weres had families too, children. They had lives, human lives, and now they'd be forced to give it all up and live like animals. Did they even know how to do that? Where would they go? There weren't many safe places for them, away from prying human eyes. My heart clenched at the thought.

It was a mess—a nightmare come true for me and all of us.

We both sat in silence, staring at the rising sun as the sky painted with streaks of bronze, orange, and blues and a bouncing white cloud.

A bouncing white cloud?

I blinked and slipped away from the gorilla. I stood up slowly as the small, white-haired witch ran across the street with a crazed, wild expression on her face, hauling a bag nearly as large as her behind her.

I squinted. "Is that… Ruth?"

"Eesss," growled the gorilla on his feet next to me. "Esss Ooth."

I looked behind her, half expecting to see my father. But as a full-fledged demon, there was no way he could walk out into the morning light without getting himself killed.

Ruth peeled open the bag and removed what looked like three large blue-and-red fireworks.

I leaned slightly forward, staring. "What the hell is she doing?"

"Looks like Ruth wants to party," said Ronin, looking as defeated as I felt. He had a can of beer in his hand, which I had no idea where it had come from. He took a long sip and smacked his lips. "No shame in that. No shame in celebrating the end."

"But fireworks? Really?" I started forward, my heart lurching to match my hurried steps. "In the morning? In daylight?"

I didn't know of any fireworks that actually worked in daylight. What was the point? Unless…

I started to run.

Because these weren't your average fireworks. This was the counter-curse!

With a mad gleam in her eye, Ruth breathed a few words on each of the fireworks in her hands, and the fuses lit with a yellow flame. On her knees, she settled them on the ground in an upright position, evenly placed, and then scrambled back, her hands over her ears.

Three seconds later, the magical fireworks shot into the sky.

I stopped and stared, shielding my eyes from the sun as the fireworks kept climbing and climbing until they were about the size of a fly among the clouds.

And then... wait for it...

They exploded, with a thunderous, sharp, booming impact.

Shards of glowing blue-and-red dust that looked a lot like fairy dust fell from the sky like glitter.

It fell on everything—me, the snow, the leafless trees, roofs, cars, sidewalks, streets, the smashed gazebo, and the shifters and weres who had survived and had come out to see what the fuss was about.

And then something truly magical happened.

The shifters began to *shift*.

First, it was a black wolf, a big sonofabitch, who shifted back into a muscular black man, buck naked, and wow, was he ever spectacular in his nakedness.

Moving on... moving on...

Next, an eagle jumped down from the old oak near Davenport House. The bird ruffled its feathers, and the next thing I saw was a seventy-year-old, pale, naked woman who stood up proud and stretched, the girls swaying as she started doing some jumping jacks.

Then there were two massive bears. I blinked, and then there were two massive ladies. Hello.

After that, a white-tailed deer, three more wolves, cougars, a black bear, a red-tailed hawk, a bobcat, four coyotes—they all shifted and changed back into their human forms until it looked like the entire town of shifters and weres had turned back.

And all of them naked.

In broad daylight.

Parts bounced and flung in all directions as the shifters settled into their human forms, and I mean *all* parts.

It was like a nudist beach, without the beach, and in the middle of winter.

Hollow Cove was a naked fest.

Great googly moogly.

I couldn't help the smile on my face, really couldn't. It's not every day you see hundreds of naked people, all shapes and sizes, running nude in the streets early in the morning. And I hadn't even had my coffee yet.

Everywhere I looked, someone was naked. A couple of paranormal ladies in their forties stood still in the cold January air, still shocked in the wave of their transformation with hands on their privates, but they really didn't do much to hide anything important.

"Looking good, Giselle." Ronin stood in the middle of the street with a strange, happy smile on his face, clapping at the running naked townspeople like he was encouraging marathon runners. "Susan. Your husband's a lucky fella. Ah, Franky boy. Always keeping it *up*, I see." Ronin clapped enthusiastically. "Mike, the ladies are gonna know that was a sock in your pants." He laughed. I laughed. Damn, this was insane.

"Ruth's the best," said Marcus, his voice silky and smooth and rough.

I spun around.

Yup. My gorilla was a man now. And a naked one.

This was an *excellent* morning.

I rolled my eyes over every inch of him. Apart from a few cuts and bruises that were already healing, his glorious, very fit, golden-brown body was rippling in muscles because there was no room for anything else. I'd seen him naked many times, though I'd never get used to seeing that kind of naked. The *super* kind.

"Looking nice and tight, Marianne, very nice," encouraged Ronin, and I pulled my attention, very unwillingly, over to the half-vampire. He caught me staring and flashed me his teeth. He raised his beer and turned back around. "Careful where you swing that, George. Though it is a mighty sword."

"God, I loved this town," I murmured. This had to be the strangest thing I'd ever witnessed or been part of, and I wouldn't change a thing.

Ruth had her arms crossed over her chest, a smug, satisfied smile on her cute face as she watched the scene. I joined her.

"You did well, Ruth."

She smiled at me. "We all did. All of us."

"Girls!" Beverly came running across the snow-covered street, which was more of a light jog in her ankle heel boots.

Though cute and stylish she was, I didn't like the worried frown on her pretty face or the wideness of her green eyes. The fact that she was waving what looked like a cue card didn't settle well with me. And when I saw Iris hurrying to catch up, her face pale and uncertain, I knew she wasn't coming to watch the naked fest.

Beverly stopped short and pinched her side. "Let me catch my breath," she wheezed, thrashing that card around.

"What's on the card?" I asked.

It was either a job or bad news.

Beverly's face was blotchy and creased with strain, her eyes sunken with fatigue and worry. She handed me the card. "I can't look at it anymore. Take it. It's addressed to you, Tessa. Take it!"

"To me?" I took the card and read it.

Dear Tessa.
I know what you've done.
Come to the house in the next five minutes or your
beloved Aunt Dolores dies. Come alone, or she
dies. Try anything stupid, and she dies.
Sisters of the Circle

The Stepford witches had Dolores.

CHAPTER
24

Just when I thought we were nearly home free of these Stepford witches and their outfits, they'd up and witchnapped Dolores.

Yes, there was still the issue with the Rift, but from what my father had told me, I didn't think closing it would be such a big deal. His faith in my abilities cemented my own. If he thought I could, I felt reassured I could.

With the demons gone for the day, I'd figured I had at least until sundown to get a crew together and get rid of the coven once and for all.

Guess I didn't have the luxury of time anymore.

I was both impressed and glad Ruth had managed to destroy the curse in a few hours. It just went to show that my Aunt Ruth was a much better potions master than these bitches — yeah, I said bitches. Kidnapping my aunt and threatening her life? They were bitches.

So much for some naked celebration with Marcus. But after that bomb about Dolores, everywhere I looked, I saw red — red and the popping of each Stepford witch head off their bodies. It was an awesome visual.

After the long night I'd had, I should have been on the verge of exhaustion. But after a quick drink from Ruth's healing elixir, this one in a chocolate flavor, I could have run a marathon. I was energized, pissed, and eager to battle.

The card had said to come alone, or Dolores died. Yeah, I wasn't really good at following instructions.

Did I go alone? Hell no. I wasn't stupid.

I knew I was walking into a trap, but what choice did I have? I had to go. She wanted me for something. That was obvious. And she was using my Aunt Dolores to get it.

When I reached the tall Victorian funeral home, I paused for only a moment to reel in my emotions, which were paper thin with my erratic pulse, and then I climbed the steps.

A complex lattice of glowing, green-and-purple runes and sigils covered every inch of the door's frame. Energy flowed, pulsed, and swirled over and around the door. My skin pricked with their power. Wards. And they hadn't been here a few hours ago. They were new. Fresh.

"I knew they'd ward it. Why make it easy. Right?" I clenched my jaw, rage making it difficult to concentrate. Warding the door now could only mean one of two things. One, I was the only one who could pass through, and two, once I did, I'd be trapped inside.

I didn't recognize the wards, and I didn't have time to try and figure out how to remove them. I had no idea what they were doing to Dolores. Was she even alive? I shook my head at the thought. Thinking like that would only make things worse, and possibly get me into trouble.

Just when I reached the door handle, a flash of baby blue stepped into my line of sight.

"Let me go in first," said Marcus, his thick, muscular thighs barely contained in the tight baby-blue sweats and top I'd found in Dolores's closet. What? It was the only thing that fit, barely. Yet it molded to every inch of him, and I mean *every* delicious inch.

I watched him, his tight ass, really, as he grabbed the door handle—

"Wait!"

Too late.

Marcus cursed and leaped back, holding the hand that had touched the door handle. "The damn handle burned me," he hissed.

"You big dummy." I took his hand and turned it over. The wards had left a nasty, blistering scorch mark in the palm through several layers of flesh. If he'd been human, he'd be on his way to the hospital with a third-degree burn.

"He's a wereape. He'll heal," commented Ronin as though reading my thoughts. The half-vampire was inspecting the front windows next to the porch. "The same runes are repeated here. On every single window I can see."

"He can't pass. None of us can." Iris moved toward the door, her nose an inch from the doorframe as she inspected the runes and sigils. "This is a complex trespassing ward. We can't get through unless we want to burn to death."

"Nice," muttered the half-vampire. "It reminds me of the time my friend Vaughn fell asleep in one of those tanning beds. Burnt him to a crisp. Poor bastard."

Iris's dark eyes met mine. "But you can. Your name is written in the ward."

I nodded. "I figured as much. So much for bringing backup. They knew I wouldn't listen."

"Apparently." Iris moved away from the door and let out a sigh.

Ronin leaped onto the porch in a single bound. "So, now what?"

I looked to Iris. "Can you break the wards?" I figured I would go in first, but I'd feel a hell of a lot better knowing my friends could come through after. Hopefully.

The Dark witch pressed her lips in a tight line. "I can't make any promises, but I'll try. It might take a while."

"Good enough for me."

"Not for me." A frown knitted Marcus's face, his eyes tight. "I don't like the idea of you going in there alone. If you wait for Iris—"

"I can't wait for Iris," I told him. My adrenaline was pounding and my voice was harsh. I regretted how snappy it was. "Dolores needs me. God knows what they're doing to her… still doing to her." My imagination was running wild. I needed to put it to rest.

Marcus's muscles popped along his shoulders and neck, his jaw clenching. "I know that. Beverly called the White witch council. They'll be here soon."

"And soon Dolores might be dead. I'm going. You can't stop me."

The wereape shifted on his feet, tension visible all over his body as he tried to contain his rage. He looked like he was about to punch a few holes in the door or beast out into his excellent gorilla form. Ronin involuntarily took a step back.

Marcus was programmed to protect those he cared about, to protect me. And not being able to was seriously messing with him.

But this wasn't about me. Well, maybe a little. My Aunt Dolores needed me.

Marcus's steps were silent as he took my elbow possessively, his worried eyes darting to mine. The concern he had for me had my heart ache. A crazy part of me wanted to grab his face and kiss him.

So, I did.

I leaned in, grabbed his sexy face between my hands, and kissed him. It was quick, but it was enough. My lips pressed against his, soft and warm, and then I angled my head and deepened the kiss. Electricity pounded through me, and heat gushed into my core as he let go of my elbow and grabbed my waist, pulling me against his hard chest.

I let go before things got out of control, my body all warm and tingly and energized. "For luck."

Marcus's face twitched, but his muscles relaxed, and I could see he wrestled with a smile. "Be careful."

"I'm always careful." Yeah, who was I kidding?

Still feeling the warm effects of the kiss, I took a deep breath, grabbed the door handle, and pushed open the door.

The energy of the ward spilled over me, humming, and a tingle ran from my fingertips to my middle. But there was no pain, no burning.

Once I stepped through, I turned around. "Still alive," I told a worried Marcus.

He was silent, the worried gleam back in his eyes and his posture holding a repressed fear. No man had ever looked at me like that—like the fear of losing me would undo him. And I looked quickly away before I lost it.

I waved my hand to Iris and Ronin, trying to brush off Marcus's intense gaze. "If I'm not back in ten minutes… and if you're still working on the wards… get Ruth and Beverly. They'll help with them." I turned, leaving the door wide open.

And then I was running.

I made for the basement, or rather that hidden door that would take me to the basement below the staircase. I knew they'd be in the basement. Where the Rift was.

When I reached the staircase, I ran behind it. Surprise, surprise, the once-hidden doorway lay open. It was a silent invitation to enter.

I obliged.

The thought that perhaps Jemma and her coven had done something to my magic, like stripped it or something, came to me. A smart witch would disable her opponent before they entered her house. But when I reached out and pulled on the elements, a torrent of magic answered.

Weird. If it were me, I would have stripped their magic as they had entered my home. Why did they leave me with mine? Didn't they know I could hurt them? Kill them? Maybe they were just arrogant. Or maybe they thought my magic wouldn't make a difference. I didn't like that. It meant that whatever they had was stronger.

Ignoring my thoughts, I ran down the stone steps, my boots echoing loudly but barely audible over the white noise pounding in my ears. I didn't care how loud I was being. They knew I was coming.

I reached the bottom and stepped into the basement. The Stepford witches, all six of them, circled the heaving black hole looming in the center of the basement, the Rift. They were their usual 1950s' full-skirted, tea-length, swing dresses, but this time they were identical. All red dresses with matching red shoes and, you guessed it, red lips. The sea of red disgusted me.

But that's not what had my pulse rocketing and tears filling my eyes.

In the corner, suspended in the air by invisible chains and strung up with her arms out like on a crucifix, her face pale and bloodied and bruised was my Aunt Dolores.

Her head lolled to the side, and her eyes were closed. Her long, gray hair was matted, and strands stuck to her face in clumps of wet blood. I couldn't tell if she was still alive or dead.

Anger slid through me, shaking me to my core.

"Welcome, Tessa." Jemma met my glare and flashed me a smile. "Glad you could make it."

CHAPTER
25

Fury and desperation finding their release, I tapped into my will to the elements around me. Finding the power word I needed, I opened my mouth—

"Ah, ah, ah…." cautioned Jemma, and something about the warning in her voice jiggled my bones and stopped me dead.

That wicked smile never faltered on her face as she flung a red, manicured fingernail in Dolores's direction. "See that ward below her? The big, glowing, green one?"

My eyes settled on the gleaming, green circle with a series of runes sketched inside it. "You try anything, any magic to set her free"—she snapped her fingers—"and her neck will snap like a twig. You don't want to be responsible for her death. Do you? Your precious Aunt Dolores. She tried so hard to be one of us. Now she is. We all have a part to play. This is hers."

At that, a chorus of laughter erupted from the other Stepford witches.

I imagined their heads blowing off, one at a time.

Glowering, I swallowed hard, hating the glee in Jemma's voice at the expense of my aunt. "No. I don't want any more harm to come to her. Please. Don't hurt her anymore. I'm here now." I took some comfort in knowing that Dolores was still alive. Or maybe she wasn't, and Jemma was just playing with me.

Fine, I'd play along until I figured out a way to get Dolores back safely.

The Rift swelled and settled again. I could still feel the presence of another world just beyond that black mass, but so far, no uglies were coming out. They wouldn't. Not until the sun went down.

First, rescue Dolores. Second, kill all the Stepford witches, and then I'd deal with the Rift.

Yay, look at me. I was making plans.

"What do you want from me, Jemma?" I said her name like it was poison on my lips. I hated the bitch, so why bother hiding it. I looked up at Dolores, but still, her eyes were closed.

Jemma was silent as though she was waiting to get my full attention. That, or she wasn't very bright. She pressed her red lips together and said, "You have the biggest part to play, Tessa."

"Which is?"

"You are the only one who can set our mistress free."

I cocked a brow. "Your *mistress*? Am I missing something here?" I threw my gaze over the other witches, recognizing only now the delighted, excited energy and the nervousness in their postures. They were jumpy about this mistress. This Greater demon, no doubt.

My eyes settled back on Jemma. "Let me guess. If I say no, you'll kill Dolores?"

Jemma's eyes glittered brightly. Her smile was serpentine. "I knew you were a bright witch. You take after your Aunt Dolores."

My gaze flicked back to Dolores and my breath caught. Her dark brown eyes were fixed on me. She was alive, very much alive if the frown on her face was an indication. And she was pissed. Even better.

Hiding my relief, I kept my face blank. "Where is your mistress? And why does she need rescuing?" I didn't want to venture too far in case they changed their minds and offed my aunt while I was gone. But right now, I wasn't the one in charge. Not yet.

Jemma's face turned serious. "She's in the Netherworld, silly. Where else would our mistress of darkness be?"

I blinked. "The Netherworld? Then why didn't she cross over with the other demons." I pointed at the Rift. "There're holes in the Veil because of your Rift here. It's like Swiss cheese at the moment. Free pass for all bottom-feeders."

Jemma's eyes radiated anger with dangerous intensity. "It's not that simple. Not for her."

I let out a breath. "And you need me to set her free? How?" My heart gave a jolt. "You can't ask me to go through there," I said, pointing at the rippling Rift. "I won't survive in the Netherworld." I wasn't entirely sure that was true, but I wasn't ready to find out. Not today. Even if I was part demon, it didn't mean that place wouldn't be toxic to me.

Something occurred to me. If they believed I could cross over, did that mean these witches knew who my real father was?

"Our mistress has been imprisoned for over a millennium," Jemma was saying.

"She's been wrongfully accused and banished," commented Gretchen, her face grim under her perfect makeup. "Banished from those who love and adore her. She's captive, trapped in a horrible place. And only you, your *unique* heritage, can set her free."

Aha. Well, crap. There was my answer. But who told them?

Tension tightened my muscles. Now everything started to make sense. "This whole time, it was never about using the Rift to draw more powers from demons for your sick purposes. It was about this mistress of yours. Wasn't it? You're trying to break her out of some Netherworld jail?"

"No, *you* are," answered Jemma, an amused, dangerous smile on her face.

I had no doubt in my mind that they'd tried to free her, many, many times, but couldn't. The fact that this demon mistress was in a Netherworld jail with some serious demon magic security didn't bode well with me. "Do I dare ask her name?"

"Lilith," chorused the witches, which was truly creepy, in a robotic sort of way.

I stifled a shiver, trying to disguise it by shifting my weight. "No, way? Lilith? As in Satan's bride or something like that? The queen of hell?" From what I knew about Lilith, what I'd read, there wasn't a cell on her body that wasn't evil. "I thought she was a myth?"

Jemma threw back her head and laughed, the sound resembling a hyena's. "How absurd. She is very much alive and real. Lilith is a goddess, silly Tessa. Our mistress of the night. We pray to her, worship her."

"And you want to set her free because…"

Jemma's smile turned chilly. "For one thing, no goddess should be kept locked up. It is cruel and wrong. Our mistress has promised us great power."

Of course. Here we went with the crazy.

I had a decision to make. Either free this Lilith or let Dolores die. It wasn't a hard decision.

My eyes found Dolores again, seeing her bound up like that and bleeding had my anger sore again, but I pushed it down. It wouldn't profit me or Dolores if I lost control. She was staring at me, her eyes wider than normal. I knew she didn't want me to agree to this, but I didn't have a choice.

My heart pounded madly in my chest. What was I doing? Was I actually considering going through with this? Releasing an evil goddess from some Netherworld prison? Helping the same coven who'd cursed our town and now kidnapped my Aunt Dolores?

My breath slipped from me in a wisp of sound. "And if I agree to this, you'll let Dolores go?" I asked, my eyes narrowing suspiciously. I didn't, for one moment, trust that these witches would keep their word, but I was out of options.

Light flashed in Jemma's eyes that looked a lot like greed. "Of course. You have my word."

Liar. "Fine. I'll do it." I knew she was lying. I could practically smell it on her, but I couldn't risk her hurting or killing Dolores. Even if I managed to release Lilith, it was a stupid thing to do. I'd deal with the consequences later. If someone had imprisoned her before, I had to believe it was possible to do it again.

The Stepford witches all clapped happily and then hugged—actually hugged each other over this, like they'd just won the Socialite of the Year award. Yeah. Bunch of sickos.

Sweat dripped down my back and temples. I looked over at Dolores, and her face was pale, frightened. Her lips twitched like she was struggling to tell me something. Too late to turn back down. I didn't see any other way to save her.

If Iris had managed a way to break through the ward, they would have been here by now.

I was on my own.

Tense, I cast my gaze around the witches. "I'm assuming you know what I'm supposed to do. Right?" I didn't want to make it that easy for them.

A wicked gleam lit Jemma's eyes, and she gave me a lazy smile. "A spell." I had time to see behind her eyes, the greed and anticipation that motivated every move she made, every step she took.

I narrowed my eyes. "Just a spell?"

"A spell to unlock the cell and set free our mistress."

A spell to unlock the monster from its cage. "Right. Where's the spell?" I looked toward the other side of the basement where I'd seen the

277

scrap of paper they'd used to write the Goblet of God curse.

From inside her skirt pocket, Jemma retrieved a piece of paper. She handed it to me and said, "Clear, well-articulated words, please. You do know how to read Latin?" she said, her voice mocking.

I snatched the paper. "I try."

Fear coursed through me, quickly followed by anger. Yes, what I was doing was stupid. I knew there was a chance Jemma or even this Lilith would end me after I set her free—*if* I set her free. But I was betting on the arrogance and hope that they'd let us live since we weren't a threat, not really. It wasn't much. But it was all I had.

And then… and then I was going to kill them all.

I stared at the spell. The words were complicated, though a few I recognized. I knew the stakes were high, disastrous if I didn't read it right or if I messed up on my pronunciation. One of these possible scenarios would be messing up the spell in a way that would have the opposite effect. That *I* would be sent through the Rift.

Yeah, I was going to take my sweet time.

"Here." Yasmine pushed a small, athame blade at me. "You'll need this too."

I took the blade, black and encrusted with rubies on the handle. "You need me to bleed too?"

Jemma moved to the edge of the blood circle that enveloped the Rift. "You need to put a drop of your blood on the circle. Then you say the spell. It's time. Our mistress awaits."

My heart thrashed in my chest. My legs didn't seem to want to move.

Jemma eyed me like I'd just told her I used up all her hair spray. "A drop of blood. Then the spell. Do it. Do it now."

Resolute because, well, I had to be crazy to agree to do this. I moved to the edge of the circle and faced the Rift.

I could feel Jemma's eyes on me, but I kept my focus on the circle. Afraid of the hold she had on my mind, she would see right through me. See my plan.

My plan was simple. Kill Jemma, and then jump a ley line with Dolores.

The only way I could free my Aunt Dolores was to kill Jemma. It was the only way to break her spell, her ward. And I'd have to do it quickly. My window of opportunity would be slim, seconds.

But I had the ley lines. They didn't. I was going to grab Dolores and ley line our asses out.

Then we'd come up with another plan.

My pulse quickened at the thought that the goddess might kill me upon her arrival. I mean,

I'd be pissed, too, if I were locked up in jail for that long. Hopefully she wouldn't.

Grimacing, I sliced the base of my left thumb with the knife. Too late to back down now. Then I leaned over and squeezed my thumb until a drop of blood fell on the circle.

The circle's magic snapped up immediately. The air grew tight and heavy with a kind of energy I didn't recognize. Power rushed through me. A visible shimmer of orange and yellow rushed around the circle like sparks from a fire. The cold energy screamed and surged through me, burning the inside of my body as it seemed to come from everywhere.

My eyes widened as I tracked the energy's path along the circle, burning as it flowed around it like liquid fire.

Damn, a drop of my blood could do that?

And then something weird happened.

The Rift, the black sheet of rippling energy, thinned somewhat, enough so I could see through it to the other side.

At first, I saw the shadow of a city, huge and not unlike one of our big cities such as New York or even London. Yet different. It was dark, really dark. And I couldn't see stars in the sky or even a moon or clouds, for that matter. And then it hit me. There was no light in the Netherworld. No sun or moon. Just a plain, endless dark sky.

And then the images shifted, moving fast like I was in a ley line. Buildings blurred until I couldn't make any sense of what I was staring at. The Rift wavered and shifted, and then I was staring at what looked like a cage suspended from the roof of a massive cavern lit by flaming torches. There was enough light to see a shape standing in the middle of the cage, but the image was blurred, and I couldn't make out the face.

"It's working!" cried Candice excitedly.

"Our mistress will be free!" shrieked Holly, and the two witches embraced each other like giddy high school girls.

"She's the one," I heard Joan say, and when I looked over, tears fell freely down her cheeks.

The other witches all moved about excitedly, but I was too busy staring at the spell to give a damn. I tossed the knife on the floor.

Here goes nothing.

I stared at the spell in my trembling hand, and with a labored breath, I read it.

"Sanguinem istum do, veneficae et daemonis, ut Lamia liberet. Voco ad te deam Lamia. Sanguis ad sanguinem reditus ad me."

Translation. They needed the blood of a half-witch and half-demon to set Lilith free. My unique blood.

I tossed the paper with the spell on the ground. I didn't want to touch it anymore.

The air shifted, and I felt the dark energy around me crowd inward, trapped within the confines of the circle. The hairs on the nape of my neck prickled and stood on end. I felt a wave of energy cascade over me, cold and unfamiliar. I shook as the energy sifted through me like a surge of adrenaline through my veins, my soul. It moved through me, alien and cold like a faint ache, orienting itself like iron to a magnet.

I fell to my knees as the pressure inside me throbbed and ached. Fear struck hard as I felt the painful sensation of stabs over and inside my body like I was about to be torn apart from the inside.

I heard someone yell. I recognized that voice. I looked up to find Dolores's wide eyes pinned to me. Her face said it all.

What the hell did I just do?

The Stepford witches' eyes glowed like deer eyes in the glare of headlights.

"Lilith, mistress of the shadows, goddess of the night," chanted Jemma while the others followed her lead and held hands. The energy gained momentum into a feral, raging current as they chanted.

A red, six-inch heel appeared through the Rift followed by a red leather pant leg, owned by a long leg. Next came a fitted, red leather jacket and the rest of the body. A red floppy hat hid most of her hair, but the loose strands I could see were red. Her skin was the color of new snow, smooth as the finest marble, with ruby-red lips that matched her outfit. She wasn't old. She wasn't young. She was an ageless being of indeterminate years, like my father. And stunning.

She was tall, a little over six feet without the heels. With them, she was truly impressive to look at. Who knew the queen of hell had some serious style?

Her red eyes flashed as they settled on mine. They blazed with a cold, ageless, righteous rage. Yikes. Her gaze held me, and I was rooted to the spot with my nerves jangling. I'd never looked at a goddess before or been in the presence of one. Should I kneel? Bow?

The fact that I was already technically on my knees probably saved me.

Her red eyes shone with a dangerous light as she moved past me. Fear slithered through me, but I pushed it down at the starkness of her expression. If she saw, smelled, or even just sensed my fear, I was a goner. Or so I thought.

I caught the scent of her perfume, something rich and spicy, with no traces of sulfur or anything that would indicate she'd just stepped out of a Netherworld jail.

"Mistress!" howled Jemma. She threw herself at Lilith's feet, the other witches all doing the same, pulling at her pants and slobbering all over them.

I wanted to puke.

Lilith pulled her eyes from me for a moment, and I took that time to take a breath.

I looked up and found Dolores still suspended by Jemma's magic. I met my aunt's gaze and gave a nod of my head. *Hang on* I told her with my eyes, hoping she'd get the message.

I was either going to succeed or get my ass killed in the process.

Hey. A witch's gotta do what a witch's gotta do. At the moment, it was saving my aunt.

Lilith looked down upon her subjects, and something like a grimace flashed on her face.

It was now or never.

With adrenaline still pumping in my veins, I pulled on the elements, my demon mojo, the ley lines, everything, and bent them to my will. I held them there, the magic, and then—

Lilith flicked her hand in a slashing gesture.

My concentration staggered for a second as the six witches froze, and I saw a strange expression flash on Jemma's face. Her eyes suddenly widened in fear as she fell back, convulsing, thrashing, scratching at her throat as though she couldn't get enough air into her lungs.

Next, Gretchen started thrashing around too. Then Holly and Candice until all six witches were flopping around the ground like fish on the beach. Unnerving, wailing cries erupted from their throats as they all convulsed with sudden spasmic seizures.

The scent of burnt hair assaulted my nose. I couldn't stop staring as their bodies tightened helplessly, muscles shuddering like they were being electrocuted.

Their skin turned bright red, like burning coal, and then they all burst into flames. Tall, yellow, and orange flames licked up the thrashing witches. They burned for a few beats in a burst of sizzling smoke until all that remained were ashes.

And the Stepford witches were no more.

CHAPTER
26

It was over pretty quickly. I must have been in a state of shock because I just couldn't stop staring at the six piles of gray ash that had once been those horrid witches.

Damn. Had that really happened?

A nervous laugh threatened to come out despite the seriousness of the situation, not to mention that I might be next.

I coughed at the smell of burnt bodies, my stomach rolling. Yup. It did happen.

One minute the Stepford witches were a coven of gossipy, snobby, fake women, and the next—incinerated into piles of ashes.

And not a single cell in my body felt sorry for them.

I felt a thump of impact, of something heavy hitting the ground, and then the sound of Dolores's moan as she rolled on the basement floor. That shook me out of my shocked stupor.

Without thinking, I rushed over to her side. "Dolores! Oh God, I'm so sorry they did this to you." Guilt gnawed on my insides. The only reason they tortured her was because of me. None of this would have happened if it weren't for me, for my unique blood. I searched her pale face, my gut twisting at the bruises and dried blood.

Dolores blinked up at me, and I saw clumps of blood in her nose. "I'm the one who's sorry. Can you ever forgive me?" Her voice was stronger than I had anticipated, and I felt some relief wash over me. Her eyes were defiant and brimming with tears, but I could see the regret in them as well.

My eyes burned, and I blinked fast, trying to hold it together. I needed to be strong. "Forgive what? See? It's already forgotten," I said with a forced laugh, my voice filled with emotion. I cleared my throat. "Can you stand?" If I could get her home, Ruth could fix her in a jiffy.

"I think so. Yes." Dolores nodded. I held her, and she didn't say anything as I hauled her to her feet. "Wretched witches," spat Dolores. "I was a fool. Such a fool."

I opened my mouth to tell her to forget about it for now, but the sound of heels scratching the dirt-packed floor brought my attention back to the queen of hell.

Damn. How could I have forgotten about her?

Lilith dusted off her red leather pantsuit. "Urgh. I couldn't stand these blabbering idiots. Irritating as hell. They were giving me a migraine. I could never get them to shut up." She glanced at the floor. "Well. Guess I finally came to my senses." She let out a laugh and her gaze slid to me.

I froze. So did Dolores.

"Tessa Davenport," purred the queen of darkness, her voice silky and venomous like a snake's and… strangely familiar.

Familiar!

"You," I said to her, forgetting for a moment that I was addressing a goddess as I let go of Dolores and slowly took a step closer to this being from the Netherworld. "You're the voice in my head." The realization hit me like a sledgehammer to the gut.

It had never been Jemma's voice. It had been Lilith's.

Holy shit snitch.

Lilith wiggled her black manicured fingernail at me. "Right you are, little demon witch. And thank you very much. You have no idea how long it's been since I've been out. That cell was positively dreadful." She pumped a fist in the air, red eyes blazing with some hellish fire. "See? I knew you could do it. Women empowerment, and all that. Go, team."

Cauldron help me. What have I done?

"Why didn't you tell me?" I asked her, a little pissed that I'd been taken for a fool. "This whole time, I thought Jemma was playing with my mind. You could have said something."

Lilith adjusted her hat. It was truly fabulous. "First, that drone of a witch doesn't have the power to control her mind, let alone anyone else's. And, would you have helped me if I did? Would you have let the *evil* queen of darkness out of her cage? No. You wouldn't. You would have put your family and friends first, the safety of the world, and all that crap. You have a bit of a goody-two-shoes streak. It's really annoying. You need to be bad. Bad is good."

"Why were you locked up in the first place? What did you do?" I heard Dolores's intake of breath at my question, but too late, I was a pro when it came to word vomit when I was nervous.

Lilith tsked. "A girl must keep some secrets."

Wow. Okay. Still, the fact that she needed the blood of a half-witch, half-demon, spoke volumes. Someone had put her in there for a reason, and I was going to find out by who and why.

I pressed my hands to my hips. I wasn't finished. "You killed your groupies. Don't you need them or something? Moral support?" Not that I wanted them back, but still.

Lilith rolled her eyes dramatically. "The Stepford witches? Yes, I know what you called them. I was in your head. Remember?"

"I remember."

Lilith pursed her lips. "I don't need them anymore. They were a means to an end. I needed them to get to you. And now that's done. Besides, aren't you glad they're dead? Look what they did to your aunt? To Marcus? They cursed your town. They were going to kill you both, you know. So, I kind of did you both a favor." She wiggled a finger at us and I tensed. "You owe me."

I wasn't sure, but owing favors to a goddess seemed to be on the "not so good" list.

Lilith looked around the basement and screwed up her face. "This is just as dreadful as my jail. No. It's worse. Where are we, exactly?"

"Hollow Cove," said Dolores, surprising me. "A small town in Maine."

"Ah, yes," answered Lilith. "I know where Maine is. It's where Stephen King lives. Love him."

I stared at her, intrigued. I couldn't help it. "How is it that you speak in a modern way like that?"

"When you've been locked up for as long as I have, trust me, you find ways to entertain yourself. Learning the modern lingo is a hobby of mine. Helps pass the time. So was torturing mortals. I was very good at it." She waved her hand dismissively. "But that's for another time."

"Won't they know you've escaped?" I had no idea who the *they* were, but I was certain my father knew. And I wanted to know as well.

Fury, cold and terrible, flashed in Lilith's eyes. She smiled a feline smile with her red lips. A cold feeling rolled down my throat and spread into my chest, making it hard to breathe.

"I'm counting on it," she answered, her voice velvet ice, which sent another shiver through me.

Not the answer I was going for. I took a deep breath and tried to get my hammering heart under control.

Lilith stared at me for a beat longer than was necessary. "I see the fashions have changed again. How marvelous." She made a gesture with her hand, like a witch would when performing a complex spell.

The air shifted with energy and the smell of spices rose.

And with a shimmering mist, Lilith's red leather outfit vanished. In fact, her entire physical appearance disappeared.

Instead of a red-leathered, hat-wearing goddess, stood a voluptuous blonde in a low-cut top and fashionable tights with black ankle boots. She reminded me of Allison.

New Lilith's body shimmered again, and next stood a beautiful, dark-skinned woman in a pale-gray skirt suit. Then a young woman in her twenties appeared with locks of black hair and jeans that were way too tight. I blinked, and I was staring at an Indian woman in a gold, pink, and white sari.

Lilith was changing her appearance like she was flipping through TV channels.

Jesus. Now, that was giving me a migraine.

After a few more moments, a thirtysomething woman with waves of glorious red hair down her back, wearing a pair of jeans, black ankle boots, and a short red leather jacket to die for, stood in the dingy basement. And when her appearance didn't change for another few moments, it seemed Lilith had finally decided on her appearance. Guess being a goddess had its perks.

"Impressive," I blurted. It was. It totally was. Maybe I was a little envious too.

Lilith's red eyes gleamed, a smile on her full mouth as she cocked a brow. "I know."

Dolores snorted, and I unconsciously stepped to the side, shielding her with my body as Lilith's eyebrows rose.

"So," I began, my heart still pounding hard in my chest. "Now what?" *Please don't kill us*, I thought as I stared at the six piles of ash. That was not how I wanted to go. I'd rather die fighting than being obliterated into dust. But it's not like I had a fighting chance against a goddess. I wasn't an idiot.

Lilith let out a sigh and said, "I need to get out."

My lips parted. "Wait? What?" I stared at her. "Where are you going to go?"

A small quirk touched Lilith's lips. "I need sex. Lots of sex. Centuries' worth of sex. I'm going to find myself a strong, virile male specimen—no, make that *three* virile male specimens—and have lots and lots of sex."

"She sounds just like Beverly," muttered Dolores. She had a point.

Lilith whipped her attention to Dolores, and my blood turned to ice. "Is she fabulous?"

I nodded and breathed a mental sigh of relief. "She kinda is."

Lilith beamed and tossed a long, red lock of her hair from her face with her hand. "How wonderful. I must meet her."

Oh boy.

"But it's *daylight*," I told her, looking around for the basement windows and realizing there weren't any. "You can't go anywhere. You'll die or burn or something." *Very articulate, Tessa.*

Lilith winked at me. "You're so cute. I'm a goddess, Tessa, darling. Not a demon. I can walk anywhere I want. Day or night. Don't worry. Nothing can harm me."

Crap. I didn't think that was a good thing.

With a soft pop of displaced air, the fire that burned over the blood circle went out. And then the blood dried and cracked and flaked to a dark brown until it was barely visible anymore.

Weird.

The Rift rippled, and the images from the other side blurred, replaced by a black sheet again, closing off the doorway to Lilith's prison.

The air shifted, and I felt a slight tug, like a suction. I stared as a piece of paper, the spell I had uttered that had released Lilith scattered over the basement floor, like a leaf in a breeze. The paper sailed in the air and then disappeared through the Rift, inhaling it like a vacuum.

My hair and clothes whipped around me as the suction from the Rift intensified. The ground shook as dust and debris fell from the basement ceiling, and a sound like a clap of thunder boomed.

I jerked at another blast as the walls shook, splitting to the ceiling. A thunderous rumble echoed up through our feet, making my teeth chatter. A soft pattering of dust sifted down, and I met Dolores's wide eyes.

"What's happening?" I yelled over the howling winds, wiping my eyes.

Her face tensed. "The whole house is coming down!" she yelled back.

A wave of dusty debris rolled over us, clogging my lungs, and making my eyes tear.

"Look out!" cried Dolores as she pulled me toward her, just as one of the metal cages Gigi had been trapped in soared across the basement, missing me by an inch, and was swallowed by the Rift.

And then all the remaining cages flew across the basement and disappeared inside the Rift. Next came books, an old wooden chair, candles, a ceramic bowl, that carcass in the corner that could have been a goat, everything and anything was picked up and sucked into the black, ripping mass.

A wailing, whirling torrent of wind whipped around me. I staggered, dragged by the currents of magic, the Rift pulling me toward it like the giant mouth of a hungry beast. I fought against it, but it was hard, like swimming up the current of a raging river.

"A black hole," I heard Dolores shout.

"Yes. I can see that."

She shook her head, annoyed, her long, gray hair whipping back and forth in the wind. "The connection, the magic from the witches that bound this spell, well, it's gone. It left when they were incinerated. It's creating a vortex."

I looked toward where I'd last seen their ashes. They were long gone, sucked into the

Rift. And that would be our fate as well if we didn't find a way to close it soon.

I raised my voice. "So what does that mean for us?"

Dolores fixed her eyes on the Rift. "It'll draw in energy to replace the power. It's creating a vacuum where all that power used to be. The vacuum will rip away the life energy of every living thing within five miles."

Fear rolled a knot in my guts. "That's the entire town."

"Precisely." Dolores's expression flickered with alarm, her lips compressing into a thin line, and I could see her visibly shaking. Her eyes were more sunken than usual, her long face gaunt. Whatever the Stepford witches had done to her was taking its toll. She looked tired, but she still had that determined spark in her eye that I knew all too well, the defiance I'd inherited. She still had a bit of fight in her.

Squinting, I caught a glimpse of Lilith crossing the basement as she made her way to the stairs.

"Lilith!" I shouted over the roaring winds. "What about the Rift? Can you help us close it?" I pointed to the rippling, black mass. I wasn't in tip-top form with all the power words I'd used in my battle with the demons and the sudden influx of magic that was used to break out the queen of hell from her prison. Dolores was in no shape to do any kind of magic. She needed rest.

Besides, Lilith was a goddess. She could deal with a little vortex, right?

Lilith turned around, her long, red hair loose against her back, which was strangely not affected by the winds from the Rift. "Sorry. Not my problem. Do whatever you want with it. What do I care?"

If I wasn't so pissed off, I might even like her.

And just like that, the queen of hell climbed up the stone stairs and was gone.

CHAPTER
27

The queen of hell had abandoned us in our hour of need to go have sex. Why was I not surprised?

I turned my attention back to the Rift. Energy from it came whipping down around us, wild, undirected, and spewing everywhere with a hurricane force. The air hummed with energy as objects flew everywhere, sending them rolling and bumping across the basement floor to finally tumble into the mouth of the Rift. It was getting worse, stronger.

When I stepped closer, a cold feeling shot through me, leaving me dizzy and a little weak as though the Rift was sucking the life out of me and draining my life force.

Uh-oh.

The Rift was both pulling me physically and trying to suck in my spirit, my soul.

Fear sending big waves of adrenaline, giving me a nice boost of strength, I staggered and braced myself against the nearest beam for support. Power raged around me, charging the air with wild, dangerous magic, surging about like a massive funnel.

"Tessa, get back! Don't get too close to it," yelled Dolores over the howling winds. She clung to an iron drainage pipe against the wall to my left, her face hidden by shoots of her long, gray hair as her clothes whipped around her.

"It's getting worse!" I shouted over another burst of wind, feeling weaker and weaker every second. A cold sweat trickled down my back.

"Tessa!"

I turned to the sound of someone shouting my name and saw Iris, Ronin, and Marcus hurrying down the basement stairs.

"Stop!" I shouted. "Don't come down here!"

Iris hit the bottom first, her eyes wide as she took in the scene.

"Ahhhh!" She slid toward the Rift as though she was wearing a pair of ice skates, as the supernatural black hole sucked her in.

In a blur, Ronin snatched her up, and then both were next to me, Iris clutching on to the same beam. Her arms and legs wrapped around it as her dark eyes widened with fear.

"Where are the witches?" cried Iris over the gushing and howling winds.

"Dead," I yelled back. In a flash of baby blue, I turned my head in time to see Marcus holding on to what looked like a large sewage pipe while his other hand clutched Dolores.

"Are those my clothes?" I heard Dolores ask.

Marcus shrugged. "Do you want them back?" He caught me staring and flashed me the kind of smile that had my belly doing the tango. He was so damn hot in those sweats. If we weren't in the middle of an end-of-the-world kind of situation, I might have thrown myself on him and ripped off those clothes to expose his glorious nakedness.

"Tess." Ronin pointed back at the entrance to the basement. "Who was the hot redhead?"

"Lilith," I shouted back. "The queen of hell. Long story."

"Tessa, what's happening to the Rift?" Iris's face paled, and I could see her starting to shake from exertion. "Why do I feel sick?"

I heard a metallic, ratcheting sound behind me and spun in time to see the hot water tank fly across the basement and vanish into the mouth of the Rift.

"At least they'll have some hot water," commented Ronin.

My eyes fell on Iris. "The spell to open the Rift and free Lilith backfired. Too much power without the magic that bound the spell in the first place. It's creating a vacuum that'll draw in energy to replace the power. It'll rip away the life energy of every living thing within five miles."

The half-vampire put his lips together in a whistle, but I didn't hear it. "Damn, Tess. We leave you alone for ten minutes and the whole world goes to shit."

He had a point.

"The longer we stay here, the more our life energies will be drained," said Dolores. "We'll be lifeless sacks. Bags of blood and bones. Nothing else."

"Then we have to stop it somehow," said Marcus, the muscles on his shoulders and neck tight. "Can you shut it down?"

I nodded, my grip slipping on the beam. "My father said we could destroy it with some magic bomb," I informed him.

"That won't work." Dolores's frown reached the bridge of her nose. "A normal Rift, yes, that might have worked. But this is now a vortex. Anything you throw in there will only be pulled through and detonate in the Netherworld."

Great. "The last thing we need is some pissed off Greater demons. Can we stitch it up? Close it?" When she didn't answer, I pressed, my throat beginning to ache from all the yelling.

"Dolores? Can we close it? My father seemed to think I could." I didn't like the fact that she wasn't answering.

Dolores kept staring at the Rift. "Your magic won't be enough."

"Why don't I like the sound of that?" I heard Ronin ask. And I kind of felt the same way.

"What do you mean?" Panic crawled around my insides. My heart pounded so hard that it was making me nauseated. If we didn't find a way to close it quickly, we were all dead. Us, and the entire town.

After a long moment, Dolores said, "With enough power… we might."

Ronin's eyes lit up. "That's good. Right? So, where do we get this power? Are we talking about power lines? Portable batteries? What?"

My aunt looked at Ronin and shook her head. "Not that kind of power."

"How, then?" I yelled, my arms burning with the effort to hang on. If we didn't do something fast, I wouldn't have the strength to hang on much longer.

Dolores looked over at all of us. "There should be enough magic between all of us."

Ronin pointed at himself, looking surprised and pleased. "Me too?"

"Yes, you too," snapped Dolores, and I was glad to see her like her old self again. "Shifters. Weres. Vampires. All have their own magic. It's what enables them to shift, and what gives vampires their super strength."

"Super looks," said Ronin, which won him a smack on the arm from Iris.

"You all have magic. It's inside you." Dolores took a breath and added, "We need to tap into it. And we'll bind our magic together. Together as one. With it… our collective power should be enough."

She didn't sound convinced, but at that point, I didn't really care. It was something. We had to do something. And I had faith in my aunt. If any witch knew how to close this vortex, it was my Aunt Dolores.

"Well, whatever you need to do, you better do it quick," called Marcus, the strain showing on his face, as he was still holding Dolores.

Dolores closed her eyes for a moment.

"Is she taking a nap?" Ronin looked horrified.

"I'm not, you idiot," shot my aunt. "I'm concentrating. I need to focus if you don't want to end up in tiny vampire pieces."

Ronin grabbed his crotch as though those were his precious pieces. "Yes, ma'am."

Dolores's eyes flicked open after a moment. "We'll need to bind our magic. To do that we must hold hands and form a circle. Weave our magic together. Our energies will spill into each other to form a single mass energy. Two spells. One to bind our energies and the other to seal the Rift." She looked over at Marcus and then

Ronin. "Don't worry. It's not hard. All you'll need to do is repeat the words. Okay?"

"Sounds easy enough," agreed Marcus. He wrapped his leg around the same sewage pipe, tested it with a tug, and then stopped, seemingly satisfied it wouldn't give. He then grabbed Dolores's hand and reached out to me with the other. "Tessa, give me your hand."

I smiled. "I love it when you order me around." Following his example, I wrapped my leg around the beam I was holding, reached out with my right hand, and clasped on to his. I met his eyes and saw that fierce protectiveness there. His grip was tight, and I knew no matter what, he'd *never* let go.

Next, I turned my body slightly and waited for Iris to let go of her hold on the beam with her arms to give me her hand. When she was ready, I reached out, and I took her hand in mine.

And then Ronin grabbed Iris's hand and reached out to take Dolores's until we formed a circle and were all connected physically, closing the circle.

It was kinda cool. Normally, magic circles were formed by witches. Ours was a paranormal one. Instead of just witches, we were witches, a half-vampire, and a wereape.

Now, this was a badass coven.

Dolores's face was twisted in concentration, her hair still whipping around her made her look a little crazy, wild.

"Tessa. Iris," called Dolores, her voice booming over the wailing gusts. "I'm going to need you both to tap into your powers. And Tessa. That means your elemental magic, your ley lines, *and* your demon magic. All of it."

I nodded. "Okay." I'd tried to do just that before being interrupted by the deaths of the Sisters of the Circle. We'd see what happened.

"What about us?" cried Ronin.

"Your life energies will be sufficient," answered my aunt.

Marcus's grip on my hand tightened, his gray eyes filled with alarm and regret. We both knew if this didn't work, it would be the end of us. Of everything.

Dolores glanced around us, her face grim. "I'll say the first spell, and then we must say it all together. Ready?"

"Ready," we all said collectively.

Dolores narrowed her eyes. "Please take your time. No mistakes. The fate of this town depends on it."

"Yeah, no pressure," yelled Ronin.

"Whatever happens," continued my aunt. "Whatever you feel…" Her eyes pinned us in turn. "Don't. Let. Go. You hear me? Not until we finish sealing the Rift."

I frowned, searching her face. "It's going to hurt. Isn't it?"

My aunt didn't answer as she drew in a breath and closed her eyes again.

Yeah, it was going to hurt. A lot.

Iris squeezed my hand firmer, and I could feel it shaking.

I squeezed it back. "It's going to be fine. We've got this." Yeah, I had no idea.

I took a calming breath as a tiny thrill of excitement rushed in, knowing we were about to pool our life forces together. It was pretty amazing.

I drew the energy from the elements around me, the ley lines, and my newest addition—my demon mojo. I wasn't sure exactly *how* to channel it, so I kind of just channeled my chi, my core. My demon magic was in my blood, so it was the only thing that made sense.

Within me, the first hints of cold energy spilled from my core, and I knew I was right. My demon mojo was saying hello.

"In this darkest hour," recited Dolores, "we call upon the goddess and her sacred power. Join our powers and see them rise, a force unseen across the skies." She paused and added, "Together now," commanded Dolores, her voice rising above the howling wind, with authority.

"In this darkest hour," we chanted in unison, "we call upon the goddess and her sacred power. Join our powers and see them rise, a force unseen across the skies."

I sucked in a breath at the sudden outpour of our combined magic creeping up my hands and arms.

Our energies, our life forces, twined together, making new energy beat inside us. It seeped into me, forcing it into a new pattern and shape.

My heart thrashed as I felt a surge of cold, familiar power cascade over me. Iris's Dark magic. Then a warm wash came spilling down my sides—Dolores's magic.

I struggled to keep my breathing even as something cold and unfamiliar seeped inside me. Dark, like Iris's magic, but different. It was wild, and the scent of blood filled me. I tilted my head to hide my unease as this new energy pooled into me, my fingers cramping.

And then something odd happened.

I felt the barest brush of someone else's mind. Thoughts of cars, beer, and a naked Iris rose inside my mind's eye—images I could *never* unsee now. It pulled my attention to Ronin.

Holy crap.

He was glowing—and not the twilight version. I'm talking a golden glow with streaks of red that coiled and shimmered in and out of his body like a mist. This was his life force, his vamp mojo, his aura. And I could see it. It was cold, dark, and beautiful.

The feeling subsided, replaced by another unfamiliar feeling, though this one was also wild, like the spirit of a wolf that couldn't be tamed, which was both exciting and alluring. It was warm, like sunshine on my face.

I didn't have to look at Marcus to know I was feeling his aura. And when my eyes looked at him, just like Ronin, Marcus's body was coated in a shimmering layer. Only his was streaked with silver, gold, and orange. It was beautiful.

Wild magic whispered through my mind with a desperate need to protect: Marcus's magic. It was such a rush to feel that, to be inside his soul like that. Part of me never wanted it to end.

I felt drawn to it. My chi seemed to hum with his aura. My skin tingled where his aura touched mine, raking over my skin like silk. His aura was like a liquid sensation, racing through my body and setting it alight with heat.

I could feel the heat from Marcus's skin rising, just like mine. I felt his aura slip into mine and I gave in to it freely, our auras blending into one.

I had no idea if this was normal, but I felt as though I had opened something between us. Like a door that was locked and now was open.

I met his gaze and saw a wild glint in his eyes, but I also saw a fragile vulnerability that one day I would be lost to him.

It made me want him even more. And it also made me realize something. We were a unit.

I wanted to stay there, surrounded by his beautiful life force, but then we still had a Rift to close.

I stared, amazed as energy rushed through me and the others, circling within the confines of our linked hands with a visible shimmer of orange, yellow, and red.

I could feel Iris's and Dolores's energies just as I could feel Ronin's and Marcus's, each different, each uniquely them.

So far there wasn't any pain, but we all knew that didn't mean there wouldn't be any.

"Hear us, Goddess, in this place and in this hour," chanted Dolores. "Close this door through time and space. Let it go back to the other."

"Hear us, Goddess, in this place and in this hour," we recited together. "Close this door through time and space. Let it go back to the other."

Nothing happened at first.

Then with a soft trail of electrical current, our combined energies hummed: stored, and waiting.

The power of the spell exploded out of us like five beams of blinding lights, of combined energies, of auras, of life forces, and magic.

The beams merged into one.

And it hit the Rift.

With a flash of light and a thunderous boom, the two energies met and warred.

The Rift started to spin on itself, slewing back and forth in a gushing spout of unearthly flames.

I hissed as searing pain screamed through my body, power overflowing and hitting every cell like cold daggers. A seeping cold reached my core, icing the edges. My world spun, and the control on my magic began to falter.

Marcus's hands squeezed harder on mine, telling me to hold on.

Because it hurt like a sonofabitch.

Fire exploded in me at his touch, and I gasped, my body jerking.

But I never let go. None of us did.

The drums of our power thundered and wound high in us, through our minds, our connection, our bond. I strained, trying to keep control of my magic, but the effort was draining me, and I felt nauseated.

And then the pain and energy faded and lifted.

I blinked and stared out into the basement in time to see a small black dot the size of an apple fold in on itself, again and again, until it disappeared.

The Rift was gone.

I felt Iris's hold on my hand let go but Marcus didn't. Instead, he pulled me into his big, strong arms, crushing me on his chest. I sagged into him, letting the warmth of his body soak into me. His rough hands sent tiny thrills all over my skin. The urge to tear off his clothes rushed me, and I took a breath, fighting off a wave of lust and libido.

Regrettably, I pulled out of his embrace before it got me into trouble.

"Dolores," said Ronin, as he came around and touched her shoulder. "That was ballsy. I don't care how old you are. You're a real badass."

My aunt's face flushed, and she shrugged away from his touch. "Watch yourself, Vampire. That mouth of yours will get you into some serious trouble someday," she scolded, but I could see the smile quirking her mouth as she stretched to her full height of five ten.

What could I say? Ronin was right. Dolores was a badass. Without her quick thinking and her spell know-how, we'd have been goners.

I cast my gaze around our group, marveling at how powerful we'd been together and seeing happy but tired faces all around.

I could feel every bone in my body ache, every muscle throb, and my head was thumping with the beginning of the migraine of the century.

I grinned. Yeah. It was going to hurt like a bitch tomorrow.

But it'd been worth it.

CHAPTER
28

What do Davenport witches do after saving the town from imminent death?

They throw a party, of course.

Ella Fitzgerald's voice blared from the old record player as she sang, *It don't mean a thing, if it ain't got that swing.* The walls shook at the booming of the orchestra, and the floors vibrated with the bass loudly enough to shake the snow off the roof. It sounded like an actual orchestra was playing in the living room, no doubt with a little help from House.

Everywhere I looked, I spotted a new face. The living room was wall to wall with people I'd never seen before. I'd never seen Davenport this crowded, ever. It was as though the *entire* town was squeezed in. But that was impossible. Unless… unless House had quadrupled its size to let everyone in, like he'd done with my room up in the attic.

The air smelled of cigarette smoke, booze, and the must of mortal bodies sandwiched together. It reminded me of what a nightclub would be like, back in the '40s and '50s. I thought it was awesome.

And who was the star of this glorious celebration you ask? Me? Nope. It was my Aunt Beverly, of course.

She'd made sure there was space enough for a dance floor. *Her* dance floor.

She wore an emerald-green swing dress from the 1940s, which matched her eyes, with a low neckline and short sleeves. Her full skirt lifted as she twirled beneath the arm of a handsome man in his fifties.

She looked amazing, as usual. Her blonde hair was pulled into a messy bun, which accentuated her cheekbones and perfect makeup. Her face was flushed, adding to her beauty as she and her partner glided across the dance floor.

A man came forward and tapped Beverly's dance partner on the shoulder, clearly wanting to cut in. The newcomer was shorter than her partner but thicker in the chest and shoulders. He was younger, too, and very handsome. I pegged him for a were of some kind, possibly a werewolf.

Beverly's partner glared at the younger male; his eyes blazed, and when he blinked, I saw his eyes change from round mortal orbs to vertical pupils, like those of a cat. Wow. This guy was probably one of the werecats, maybe one of the cougars I'd seen. Not surprisingly, it seemed as though all weres had inherited the possessive gene. This guy continued to stare down the new male, clearly not wanting to surrender his dance partner, like she was his property.

The muscles on the younger male's neck popped, and his jaw clenched, and I felt my eyes widen in excitement. They were going to fight. Now that was entertainment.

Beverly caught on quickly and sidled over to the younger male, her hands on his chest. "Gentlemen. There's no need for this. You don't have to fight over me." She giggled, but by the huge smile on her face, she was loving the fact that they were. "There's lots of me to go around." She laughed again, pulling the newcomer with her, and then the two of them disappeared in the crowd of dancers, leaving the taller male looking frustrated.

"Beverly, you're such a tease," I mumbled, shaking my head.

Smiling, I made my way toward the dining room, careful not to spill the contents of my wineglass. Ruth had arranged a display of yummy canapés and every finger food you could imagine. As if on cue, my stomach growled like a beast crawling around the inside of my belly, trying to get out and get some food in there. I couldn't just ignore my stomach. After the night I'd had, I was ravenous. And when a witch is hungry, she eats. Never deny a witch's stomach.

As I moved toward one of the buffet tables, my eyes on Ruth's famous cheese balls—which were excellent with red wine by the way—I caught part of the conversation Gilbert was having with my Aunt Dolores.

"It pains me to do this," he was saying, which was doubtful coming from him, "but you give me no other choice. *I* am the mayor of this town." He adjusted his plaid bow tie under his brown corduroy jacket. "And I'm very exacting in my duties, such as they are." Gilbert's face twisted into a smile, which had happened twice since I'd been here, and he handed her a white envelope. "Here. This is for you."

"What's this?" Dolores grabbed the envelope and tore it open. Her eyes nearly disappeared into her scowl. She grimaced and shook her head. "You're billing *us* for the gazebo? After we've just finished paying for the new one?"

The little shit.

Gilbert looked positively happy, which was never a good thing. "I am. This was all *your* niece's fault. And yours. If you hadn't entertained these witches, none of this would have happened. We practically lost all our humanity because of you Davenport witches. You're just as foolish and reckless as your niece."

Dolores's expression turned hard. "Let me remind you that you entertained them as well, Gilbert, as you well know. I remember you cozying up to Joan, though you never had a chance. She preferred her men to be at least taller than her breasts."

Gilbert's face turned beet red. "Why you miserable old—"

"Careful, now," warned my aunt, who, let's be honest, could roast the little owl. "You don't want to lose any more inches. Do you?" Her gaze moved to his groin, her brows up expectantly.

Gilbert's expression turned sour, but he clamped his mouth shut. The muscles on his face twitched, and I knew he was thinking of a comeback, another insult.

Part of me wanted to go over there and stuff his bow tie down his throat. I started for him, but the flick of my aunt's hand rooted me to the spot.

Dolores gave me a warning scowl, so naturally, I moved on to the buffet table, though strangling the shifter owl would have been the icing on the cake, the grand finale to a horrible few days. One could still hope.

Iris bumped her hip against mine as she joined me by the buffet table, a glass of red wine in her hands.

"Any luck with the locator spell?" I asked and stuffed my mouth with a cheese ball, trying to resist from moaning but failing.

Iris's pretty face scrunched into a pout. "No," answered the Dark witch, her voice filled with frustration. "I tried again right before we came here, and nothing. Not even a spark. Sorry, Tessa. But even with a strand of her hair, I have no idea where Lilith is. She could be anywhere by now. She could be in Paris. Iceland. Or a jungle in Madagascar."

I snorted and nearly spat out my cheeseball. "I don't really see this goddess trudging through the Madagascar jungle. I got more of an urban feel from her. Besides, she was locked up for a very long time. All she wants is to party. And have lots of sex. My guess is she's in a city somewhere she can get her hands on all these males she wants to bump uglies with."

Iris laughed. "She sounds kind of fun, for the queen of hell, I mean. That's not how I pictured her at all."

"Yeah. And that's a problem." Not having a clear idea of who she was, wasn't going to help me figure out where she could be. She could be anywhere and anyone, now that I knew she could change her appearance in the blink of an eye.

But I still needed to find her.

After we'd left STIFFS' FUNERAL HOME, I had learned that Iris had snatched a hair from the goddess's head as she'd strolled past them through the exit. With the Sisters of the Circle dead, the wards on the door had vanished, enabling my friends to get through.

Iris took a sip of her wine. "Maybe we can just pretend you never let her out. I mean, what harm can she do, really?"

"A crap load of harm, I'm sure. And I bet she'll enjoy it too." Which was a scary thought, but I knew I was right. The goddess of hell had a mischievous streak in her.

"Well, maybe you should just let her go and forget about it. Think of the future." Iris raised her brows, her dark eyes on something across the room.

I followed her gaze to the sexy, manly male who was chatting with Dolores. His gray eyes and scrumptious physique were enough to send any red-blooded female into sexual convulsions.

"I'm sure Marcus would like to have some quality time with you," said Iris, her gaze back on me.

Heat pooled in my middle as Marcus turned at the mention of his name. Damn that wereape hearing. He angled his body in a way that suggested he was listening to our conversation while having his own with my Aunt Dolores.

I let out a breath. "Me too. But I can't just pretend I didn't release Lilith from some Netherworld jail. She's going to do something. I know she will. It'll be big, and it'll be because of me."

"Don't say that. You're not in control of her actions. She's a goddess. She does what she wants."

"Exactly. And if she goes on some merciless killing spree... say... she kills all redheads because she wants to be the *only* redhead in the world, I'll be responsible. I let her out. She's my problem."

Iris popped a kalamata olive into her mouth. "Maybe she's a blonde now."

"Maybe." Images of Lilith's shape changing flashed in my mind. "I want to know who put her in there and why. I'll see if my father knows anything. Knowing him, he probably does." I had wanted to ask him earlier today, but I had fallen asleep as soon as I had entered my bedroom. There was a reason Lilith was locked up and why she needed the help of my blood to let her out. Whoever did it had kept her from using her power, which was undoubtedly unmeasurable.

Having spent a millennium locked away in some cage would do things to a person. It would drive them mad, even a goddess, I would imagine. She was horny, I got that, but probably pissed at those who'd locked her up. I would be if I were her. The other thing I knew for sure was she'd want revenge. 'Cause that's what I would want as well.

Maybe those who'd put her away in the first place would save me the trouble and lock her up again. Doubtful. I wasn't that lucky. Especially not these days.

Worse, if the "they" figured out I was the one who let her out… A sick weight settled in the pit of my stomach. Another complication to be added to my list of growing problems.

"Well, she did get rid of the Stepford witches, so she can't be all that bad, considering what they did."

"Just a tad."

"They tried to kill Dolores."

My eyes shot to my aunt. She looked great tonight. And you could never tell that just a few hours ago, she'd come close to dying. Beverly had done a fantastic job of spelling the bruises and cuts on her sister's face, and I suspected the extra plumpness to her cheeks that wasn't there before. She looked younger.

The image of Dolores suspended in the air, nearly lifeless and beaten, sent a shock of fury coursing in me.

A shoot of black tendrils blasted from my fingertips.

A sudden storm of flying bits of deviled eggs, fruit and cheese kabobs, asparagus bruschetta, and canapés engulfed both me and Iris as the table of goodies exploded.

Whoops. I really needed to get my demon mojo under control.

"See! See!" cried Gilbert. "I told you! She has no regard for the property of others. Still undisciplined and blatant. You have no business holding a Merlin license."

I lowered my brow, my demon mojo coursing through my veins, itching to get out and roast me an owl.

Dolores gave me a bulldog look, which sobered me right up.

Iris plucked out the cheese curd that fell into her wineglass and popped it into her mouth. "Wow. Dolores looks really angry."

I smiled, letting out a breath. "Yeah. I'm so glad to have her back to normal again, looking like her old self."

"Coming through! Coming through!" Ruth barreled into the dining room like an avalanche, Hildo riding her shoulder like a pirate's parrot.

Her pink apron had flashing fluorescent words that read, THIS WITCH RUNS ON WINE.

Ruth stood still for a moment, arms outstretched before the fallen and very broken buffet table. She narrowed her eyes in concentration, her lips moving in a silent spell.

The black cat's yellow eyes shone, and I could see they were sharing their magic, witch and familiar. I felt a tiny pang in my chest. They were perfect together.

The scent of marigolds, lavender, and pine rose in the air. Then with a clap of her hands, the broken table legs and top rose along with the white tablecloth. They hovered for a moment, and then they came together like pieces of a puzzle, snapping into place until they looked as though they'd never been mashed by my demon mojo. I was impressed.

The table slowly drifted to the floor, followed by the white tablecloth, which was spotless, with no evidence of any spillage. The food that splattered the floor peeled itself up and dropped into the black garbage bag that had suddenly appeared. Then it zoomed out and disappeared into the kitchen.

Ruth smiled and tugged on her apron. "There." Her face scrunched up in thought as she scratched her head. "Something's missing."

"That'll be the food," answered the cat.

"Oh!" Ruth shot a finger in the air, spun around, and then she, too, disappeared into the kitchen, the cat's rear end swaying on her shoulder.

"You need to control your temper," said Iris, though a smile reached her face. "Find a way to release all that tension."

"I can help with that."

I turned to a handsome face that belonged to a broad-shouldered male with tousled, dark hair. His nondescript, long-sleeved, black shirt did nothing to hide the muscles that were barely contained.

Iris cleared her throat. "I think my vampire's looking for me," she said, pointing to Ronin, who was in a conversation with that muscular, black were-male I'd seen earlier this morning. Iris gave me a knowing wink and then moved away.

Marcus took my hand and pulled me closer. "I have a surprise for you," he purred, hauling me toward the kitchen.

"You're going to cook for me?" I would much prefer him to cook for me back at his place.

Ruth was busy pulling a tray out and setting it on the counter. Hildo sat next to it, a saltshaker tied to the end of his tail as the cat sprinkled some salt over her canapés.

Marcus smiled and picked up the white bathrobe that was hanging from the wooden peg rack by the back door and handed it to me. "Here. Put this on."

I grabbed the bathrobe and immediately recognized it as my own. "I need to be naked for his surprise?" Yay me. Yay me. Yay me.

His gray eyes pinned me, burning with domination and desire. "You do. I'll wait here while you change."

I was no fool. I rushed to the potions room, which was just off the kitchen, and forty seconds later, I wiggled my toes in front of the kitchen's back door.

"You don't need a bathrobe?" I asked him. A pair of slippers waited for me on the doormat. I slid my feet into the cold slippers, anticipation making my stomach tight.

The wereape smiled. "I can tolerate cold better than you."

Very true. And it piqued my curiosity to a higher level.

We stepped out the back door onto the wooden porch that had been shoveled recently. The cold brushed against my warm cheeks, but I barely noticed, my excitement making my blood boil and my skin feel hot.

"Come." The wereape took my hand and led me down a snow-cleared path that cut through three feet of snow. My heart quickened with every step as I followed his big, manly shoulders. Tall, flaming tiki torches lit the path as we crossed the backyard.

"You cleared all this snow?"

"I did."

"Where are we going?"

"You'll know when we get there."

Curiouser and curiouser.

But we didn't have to go far.

There in the middle of the backyard, hidden cleverly by a row of tall cedars and lit with a string of white Christmas lights, was the biggest cauldron I'd ever seen. It was large enough to fit three people comfortably, two with an amplitude of room to do lots and lots of things.

Steam rose in white coils, though no fire was beneath the iron base. Magic, or he'd been busy hauling hot water from the kitchen.

When I looked back at Marcus, he was buck naked.

Was it Christmas again? Yes, yes it was.

My eyes trailed down his muscular chest to his thin waist and on to his... um... lengthy manhood. What? You would have too. Trust me.

The sight of him made my skin flush despite the cold, and my hormones took off like rockets. Hell, I was so hot right now, I feared I might spontaneously combust.

His clothes hung haphazardly on the cedars like he'd tossed them. He probably had.

I looked at the chief. "How?"

"Ruth helped me," he said, looking smug. "It's spelled to stay at the perfect temperature for as long as we want. You deserve a nice break. I wanted to do something special, just for you. I thought you might like this."

I thought I might have purred. Or moaned. I think I did both.

With a stupid smile on my face, I ripped off my robe, tossed it to join Marcus's clothes on the cedars, kicked off my slippers, and grabbed the edge of the cauldron. I was aware of the chief's eyes on me. Hell, I could *feel* them, seeing all my folds as I bent over the cauldron.

I looked down at myself. I had three stomachs! Crap. How the hell did this happen?

Granted, bending over something while naked was not the most attractive position, and my breasts looked like eggplants. But one look in the chief's direction, seeing that unmistaken desire for all my stomachs and folds, I forgot all about them.

The hot water assaulted my skin as I slipped my first leg in and then the other. I let out a moan as I settled down into the cauldron, my butt resting on the warm iron bottom.

"Wow. This feels amazing." I rested my arms on the sides of the cauldron. "I never thought a boiling cauldron could be this comfy. Don't know why I never tried this before." I let my head fall back and looked up into the night sky. The moon was a silver splendor, strewn with pale clouds and brilliant stars. No wind. It was a perfect night for a skinny dip in a cauldron.

The sound of water splashing reached me, and I looked down in time to see Marcus lowering himself across from me.

We stared at each other for a while in comfortable silence until the chief spoke.

"Have you thought about my offer? You moving in with me?"

I wanted nothing in the world more than to wake up next to this sexy man every single day for the rest of my life. If I should be so lucky, but the time wasn't right.

"I want to move in. I really do." I raised my right foot and slid my toes along his chest, teasing. "But not yet…"

Marcus grabbed my foot and placed it firmly on his chest, desire heady in his gaze. "I get it. You need your aunts." I shivered as he traced his thumb around my ankle, reveling at how his touch made me feel like my skin was on fire. My breath caught at the rush of feeling, the burning traces of need settling deep and low.

I blinked, trying to keep my eyes from rolling back into my head. "No. It's more like *they* need *me*." At least, that's what I told myself. But it rang true. I knew if I left now, they'd be devastated. They didn't deserve that. It wasn't the right time.

I lifted my left foot and dropped it on the chief's right bicep, my big toe tracing around his nipple and enjoying seeing it harden. "They need me, but it won't be forever."

For the first time in a long time, I knew exactly who I was and where I was going. And right now, I was going to stay here, in Hollow Cove, in Davenport House with my three eccentric aunts, and fight whatever came at us next.

Because we all knew something always would.

Not to mention, I still had Lilith to find. I couldn't just let her be. I was going to find her. But not tonight. Tonight, it was me time. And that meant lots of gorilla love. Just for me.

I stared at my sexy male—and yes—*my* sexy male. Because he was *all* mine.

He must have seen something on my face because, the next thing I knew, he grabbed my left foot while still holding my right one, spread my legs—and pulled me toward him until I straddled him, feeling *all* of him.

I squealed as his big, rough hands slid over my back and pinned my waist, holding me there. Yeah, like I was going to go somewhere.

"Tessa," he growled as he dropped his mouth on mine and then shifted with a trail of kisses along my jaw, down my neck. Yup. I was definitely going to spontaneously combust.

Good times.

Don't miss the next book in The Witches of
Hollow Cove series!

ABOUT THE AUTHOR

Kim Richardson is a USA Today bestselling and award-winning author of urban fantasy, fantasy, and young adult books. She lives in the eastern part of Canada with her husband, two dogs and a very old cat. Kim's books are available in print editions, and translations are available in over 7 languages.

To learn more about the author, please visit:

www.kimrichardsonbooks.com

Printed in Great Britain
by Amazon